Dangerous Descent

by

Evie Jacobs

A Dangerous Skies Adventure

Copyright Notice
This is a work of fiction. Names, characters, places, and incidents are either the product of the author's imagination or are used fictitiously, and any resemblance to actual persons living or dead, business establishments, events, or locales, is entirely coincidental.

Dangerous Descent

COPYRIGHT © 2024 by Evie Jacobs

All rights reserved. No part of this book may be used or reproduced in any manner whatsoever without written permission of the author or The Wild Rose Press, Inc. except in the case of brief quotations embodied in critical articles or reviews.
Contact Information: info@thewildrosepress.com

Cover Art by *Lisa Dawn MacDonald*

The Wild Rose Press, Inc.
PO Box 708
Adams Basin, NY 14410-0708
Visit us at www.thewildrosepress.com

Publishing History
First Edition, 2024
Trade Paperback ISBN 978-1-5092-5699-0
Digital ISBN 978-1-5092-5700-3

A Dangerous Skies Adventure
Published in the United States of America

Chapter One

Anyone who thought an FBI job glamorous never sat in a cold car on an unlit side street in the middle of the night.

Since joining the Bureau eight years ago, Eric Erickson had never been in a car chase—or a gunfight. Sure, there'd been some tense moments, but undercover assignments were all about the mundane—blending in and acting like a regular Joe. Or in his case, a regular Eric. Today, if things went as planned, that was all about to change. A wave of anticipation rippled through his chest. He pulled on a black stocking cap before glancing in the rearview mirror.

For three weeks he'd put on his pilot's uniform, eaten lunch in the airline break room and met up with coworkers for drinks after work. Today, the stakes would change. Today, he'd get a new route, a new copilot, and gangsters for passengers.

Reaching beneath the steering wheel, he brushed the grip of the tiny handgun in his ankle holster. Man, he wished he had his service weapon, but the Glock 27 would have to do. His cell dinged from the passenger seat. Time to go. He took a deep breath.

Fidelity. Bravery. Integrity. The FBI motto. Words he lived by.

As he exited the car, a cool October breeze nipped at his nose and ears and rushed up the sleeves of his jacket. He tugged on the hood, slid his hands into leather gloves, and jogged across the dark street.

He trotted down a short embankment, crouching through the shadows until he spotted the gas station near the main road. Using the darkness for cover, he found the single-track mountain bike trail he'd scouted earlier and began the uphill trek.

Despite his pace, his body wouldn't warm. Denver was beautiful, but he was beginning to see why a coworker declared Colorado "the land of boogers and chapped lips."

Approaching the split in the trail, he slowed. A familiar face emerged from the shadows.

"It's cold as balls up here." Grant Morgan's refined British accent made the crude comment sound like a melody. He held up a plastic bag with the bug and transmitter.

Eric grabbed the baggie and shoved it into his coat pocket. "No kidding. Let's get this over."

"Hold up, mate. We have some things to talk about."

That was the other thing about Grant's accent—everything sounded like a lecture.

"Okay, talk. Quick."

A dark curl escaped Grant's knit hat and stuck to his forehead. "I know this assignment means a lot to you." *He has no idea.* "But if you see anything that looks like trouble, get yourself out of there."

Eric grunted his affirmative. "Don't take unnecessary risks. Yes, Dad."

"Good." Grant slapped him on the shoulder. "Let's go."

By the time they arrived at an eight-foot-tall chain-link fence, the muscles in Eric's back and shoulders had pulled into knots. He did a few neck rolls, shook out his upper body, and gripped the galvanized steel.

The other agent's stare bore into him. "Stay in contact. I'm here if things go sideways."

Eric nodded, then pushed the tip of his shoe into a link and climbed. At the top rail, he swung a leg over and dropped to the ground. He stepped quietly, sticking to the perimeter and, after several minutes, arrived at the tarmac. Staying in the shadows, he prowled among the planes until he found the King Air owned by Rocky Mountain Charters.

The owner had a sketchy history, but it was his newfound relationship with a notorious crime family that had landed him on the Bureau's radar. Eric's mission was twofold: ferret out the relationship and record incriminating conversations.

His other target was Vincenzo Alario, a man so vicious and unforgiving, he'd once choked a man with a wad of dollar bills for cheating at a game of cards. But that was only one transgression in a lifetime littered with them, each more heinous than the last.

Eric's pulse roared like an F-15 throttling for takeoff. More than anything, he wanted to see justice served. He'd endured a lot in his life, but treating Alario like a regular man would test him like nothing he'd done before.

He reached into his pocket and pulled out the cabin door key. Palming it had been easy. He'd manipulated the security guard into conversation, distracting him with a newly-discovered secret weapon—the Broncos. Once the guard had exhausted his predictions for the upcoming Dolphins game, he left to start his rounds and forgot to secure the lockbox.

Eric popped the hatch, unfolded the stairs, and climbed into the dark plane, sweeping the narrow beam from his small flashlight across the cabin. The bug in his pocket differed from the one he'd hidden in the owner's office a couple of weeks ago. The plane didn't allow for a live surveillance feed. To compensate, he had an internal storage transmitter to hide as well.

The light rail that ran the length of the cabin above the windows seemed a suitable location. He placed the bug dead center between the two groups of seats, then walked to the cockpit. The transmitter would be safest here. He wedged it into a nook above the rudder and clicked the button on the mic clipped to his lapel to update Grant. "It's done. Heading back."

"Copy that."

Eric made his way to the door at the back of the aircraft and smiled grimly. For more than twenty years, he'd thought of this moment. Hell, he'd even dreamed about it. Now that it was here, he wouldn't let anything stand in his way.

Chapter Two

A sharp pain shot from Elise Hughes' knee to her hip, forcing her to slow to a walk. The usual run around her neighborhood had been a mistake, but she always felt better for having done it. Scratch that. *Almost* always. Not even those magical runner's endorphins could soothe her today.

Last night, she'd slept like shit. But a call from her brother would do that.

The conversation had started cordially enough, and she'd been glad to hear Jack's voice, but once they caught up on the mundane day-to-day goings on, he launched into a sermon about their brother Nate. "You know how he is. He's sorry, but he'll never say it. Someone has to make the first move. It needs to be you."

"That's not going to happen." After nearly six months of not speaking, she couldn't believe Jack's first phone call was to tell her she should apologize to their oldest sibling. "Or did you forget the things he said to me?"

"Elly, can we give it a rest?"

"No. He called me spoiled and ungrateful. Said I didn't appreciate the family's sacrifices. He's been harping on this holier-than-thou routine for as long as I can remember. This time, he needs to ask *me* to forgive *him*."

To be fair, she'd left Florida for Denver without

saying goodbye, but her entire life had been one directive after another, with Nate hovering, telling her what she could and couldn't do. Or at least that was what she told her brothers. The truth was there were too many memories. Everywhere she looked, she saw reminders that the one person she'd trusted the most wasn't who she thought he was.

A fact Jack decided needed stirring. "Dad's dead, Elly. Fighting with Nate isn't going to change that. It's time you accept it and get your butt home."

Why did her brothers insist on acting as if their father's lies hadn't changed everything?

"Oh, yeah?" Disappointment and bitterness leeched into her voice. "And you two need to accept that our father was a criminal and it got him killed."

She'd hung up and it felt good. For about thirty seconds. Until she stopped to wonder how many months they'd go without speaking this time.

Hugging her arms to her body, she navigated the neighborhood, walking past a liquor store and ice-cream parlor. The brisk Denver air enveloped her. Though not quite fall, the mornings had turned cool, and on most days, she savored the crisp contrast against her exercise-heated skin.

But not today. Today, only one thing could make her forget the infuriating conversation with her brother. Getting airborne. Never did she feel more at peace than the moment the wheels lifted off the ground.

Rounding the last corner of her route, her building came into view and a feeling of calm washed over her. The tiny one-bedroom apartment still didn't feel like home, and that was okay. She preferred to think of it as a sanctuary, her place to escape reality. A place where nothing had gone wrong.

She stepped onto the porch of her first-floor unit and slid her key into the lock. It wouldn't turn. She jiggled it, then twisted the knob. With a huff of frustration, she wrenched the key to the left one more time.

Snap.

She stared at the useless top half of her key, then bent, closing one eye to peer into the now-jammed keyhole. Fan-fucking-tastic. She kicked the door with the toe of her shoe. What were the chances she could get help at this hour of the morning? Yanking her cell from the zipper pocket in her running pants, she dialed the building's twenty-four-hour service number and was told someone would be by in a few minutes.

More than an hour later, one of the maintenance guys showed up. Red-eyed, hair mussed, and a scowl fixed on his face.

Elise glanced at his nametag. "Morning, Justin. I was about to throw a rock through the window."

He grunted, then produced a piece of jagged wire from his toolbox and crammed it into the keyhole. When he slid it out, the broken key came with it.

"That's it?" Elise stepped past him and over the threshold of her now-open apartment. She couldn't believe it had been a ten-second fix.

Justin handed her a new key and was trudging back to the office before she had a chance to thank him. She stepped farther into the apartment, closed the door, then took a moment to appreciate her surroundings. Thrift-store furnishings, brightly patterned homemade throw pillows, an aerial photo of Denver metro. Best of all? The space contained zero mementos. Nothing at all to remind her of home.

She glanced at the wall clock mounted over her kitchen table, then ticked off tasks on her fingers. Grab a clean uniform. Shower and dress. Eat breakfast. Get her ass to work.

All doable—if she hurried. She moved to the hallway closet and popped open the door on the top half of the stackable appliance. Empty.

Not possible. She'd been certain she'd put her uniforms in the dryer last night. With a mounting sense of dread, she lifted the lid and peered into the washing machine. Four wet shirts and four wet pants, stretched and twisted around the agitator.

Maybe if Justin hadn't taken his sweet-ass time, she wouldn't be staring at a pile of wet clothes with no hope of getting them dry. She let out a defeated sigh, tossed the garments in the dryer, slammed the door and pressed start. Who was she kidding? She had no one to blame but herself. And it wasn't the end of the world. She could always get another uniform in the airline office. She'd go over in her workout clothes, then shower and change in the small locker room off the pilots' lounge.

Decision made, she hustled to the kitchen and plucked the remnants of a half-gallon of milk from the fridge and shook the carton. The tightness in her muscles eased. If a bowl of cocoa-flavored cereal with obscene amounts of sugar didn't make her feel better, nothing could. She reached for the box . . . that she'd finished yesterday. Biting down on her lip, she growled. Could this day get any worse? She snatched up her keys, ignoring the scrape of metal against the linoleum countertop and headed to her car.

With a commute of fewer than three miles, she spent more time sitting at a stoplight than actually driving.

Dangerous Descent

Once she crested the top of the hill and saw the chain-link fence surrounding the airport, her anxiety ebbed. Any day she got to fly was a good day. She drove around the back of the business offices and held her employee badge against the scanner to open the gate.

The lot was small, but there was one parking space she could always count on. Meant as more of an extra-wide spot for motorcycles than a car, it was a place where no one else ever parked. Luckily, she had an old beater and didn't care if it got dinged. The arm lifted, and she drove in.

Just in time to see a black crossover squeeze into her spot.

She let her forehead drop against the steering wheel. One thing. At this point, that's all she wanted. For one thing to go right today. She took a deep breath and lifted her head. The genius had parked right up against the curb and couldn't open his door without hitting a tree. A tall, lean form unfolded from the car. He shut the door and turned.

The new guy.

The morning sun cast his face in shadow that highlighted chiseled cheekbones. His dirty-blond hair, short on the sides and longer on top, was styled up and to the right. Part Norse god, part underwear model.

She shook her head, hoping to banish the image of him in boxer briefs posing from beneath a film of cellophane on a men's underwear package. He'd been here a few weeks and was impossible not to notice. This morning, a light coating of stubble colored his jaw and chin. He looked a bit like someone who'd pulled an all-nighter.

It was odd to see him here now. As far as she knew,

they had completely different schedules. Good thing, too. A man who looked like that would be a constant reminder of her neglected libido.

He caught her stare, and his mouth quirked into the crooked smile of someone used to things going their way.

She raised her fingers in greeting, then mashed her foot into the gas. *Overflow parking, here I come.*

****

Need. Coffee.

Eric felt a little like one of the zombies in that new dystopian TV show everyone was talking about—stiff, unkempt, red-eyed. After his middle-of-the-night outing, he'd gone back to his hotel planning on a few hours of sleep, but it hadn't happened. He'd been too keyed up to relax and was paying for it now.

Nothing a hot, dark cup of caffeine wouldn't cure. He entered the small kitchen adjacent to the pilot's lounge and spotted an almost-empty carafe sitting on the coffee-maker hot plate. At the counter, he took a mug from the drying rack, and managed to get it about three-quarters of the way filled.

He slid the glass pitcher back into place and considered it for a moment. Should he start another? Nah, it could wait. At least until he'd finished his first cup.

Closing his eyes, he savored the feel of the coffee sliding down his throat and heating his insides. Whatever ancient person had the brilliant idea to pick seeds off a tree and grind them into a powder was a friggin' visionary. If ever a man deserved Sainthood…

The sound of sneakers squeaking on the linoleum tile pierced his solitude, and Eric jolted, splashing hot coffee on his thumb. He shook it off and set his mug on the counter. His copilot stood in the doorway, glaring at him.

High cheekbones. Squarish jaw and eyes the color of amber. She had full, red lips and wore her dark hair secured into a neat ponytail.

And that body? Jesus. He didn't want to appear obvious but couldn't help a quick perusal. Running tights emphasized the hard angles of her quads and a perfectly round little ass. A pink running jacket was unzipped, revealing a cropped tank and a sliver of tawny skin. He rubbed a hand against his jaw.

Of course, it wasn't like this was the first time he'd seen her. Nope. He'd noticed her the day he interviewed and many times since, almost as though she were a beacon and he was the radar tracking her signal. Somehow, each sighting left him wanting more. A fact more than a little unsettling.

Regaining some composure, he managed what he hoped was a non-lecherous smile. "Happy Friday."

Her face twisted into a sour little ball. She glanced at his cup, then the empty coffee pot. "Didn't think anyone else might want some?"

He opened his mouth to respond. "I—"

"Don't think about anyone other than yourself? Yeah, I get it." She shoved past him to the counter, tossed the wet coffee filter in the garbage and put in a clean one.

"I just got here." Why did he think he owed this woman an explanation? "I was going to do that." He sounded defensive. Good grief, what had gotten into him?

She scowled, started the coffee maker, and wiped up the counter. Her movements were short and jerky. Was she always like this or was something wrong?

His heart sped up a beat. Whatever the case, he needed to fix it. He had to get on her good side. As soon as he figured out how to find it.

Standing around staring at her wasn't going to help. *Think.*

Food. He needed calories to function properly, and other than a croissant he'd grabbed in the hotel lobby, he'd not had breakfast. He eyed the pastry box on the table. A single donut remained. His gaze bounced from the donut to his soon-to-be partner. Should he offer it to her? She didn't look like someone who ate junk food. He stared at the donut. Maple frosted. There was a reason this was the only one left. He picked it up and popped it in his mouth.

"Are you kidding me?"

Crap. He paused, mid-bite, then removed the donut—and hopefully his foot. "Want me to cut it in half?"

"After you slobbered on it?" She wrinkled her nose and held up her hand. "I think I'm good."

"It's maple. No one likes maple."

She responded with a hard glare. "You didn't ask."

He crammed the rest of the donut in his mouth and chewed. Their first meeting—an introduction in the hallway during his new-employee tour of the airport had been brief. Nothing more than a quick handshake, but there'd been a moment where they'd both frozen, staring at one another as though recognizing an old lover.

Lust at first sight? Definitely for him, and judging by the way her pupils had flared, he'd thought for her as well. But just as quickly, mission-preservation had kicked in, reminding him it wasn't the time or the place.

Regardless, self-centered ass was not the impression he'd planned to make this morning. He needed to course correct before it was too late.

She grabbed a bottle of water from the fridge and closed the door with a bang. The muscles in her throat bobbed up and down as she took a long gulp. "Why are you here? Don't you usually work the afternoon shift?"

So, she didn't know they'd be working together. He wasn't going to be the one to tell her, not based on her current mood. "Starting a new route today."

The coffee maker had trickled to a slow drip. Elise avoided eye contact and focused on the four stripes affixed to his shoulder. "Okay, hotshot, how'd you become a captain?"

Hot shot? "Six years flying F-16s for the Air Force."

"And you know we deliver passengers, not bombs?"

The retort rolled off his tongue. "Yeah. This is a heck of a lot easier."

She snorted, and the corner of her mouth kicked into an almost-smile. "I look forward to seeing you in action, Maverick."

"That was the Navy." He had to hand it to her. She had no shortage of comebacks. "You sure you want to be Goose?"

This time she smiled for real. "Considering he *dies* and had a reckless jackass for a partner, no I don't want that at all."

He laughed. The woman who'd walked in here had the warmth of a snowman. This one had fire. Perhaps partnering with her wouldn't be so bad after all.

When the coffee pot beeped, she turned to fill a mug and glanced at him over her shoulder. "Do you want a refill?"

He slid his cup onto the counter. "That would be great."

"Did you notice what I did there? It's called being polite." That smirk of hers was darn-near adorable. Seriously, if he wasn't on the job, he'd be tempted to pursue the attraction.

"I'm sorry about the donut. Can I treat you to something from the vending machine?"

"Yes, thank you. And I apologize for being such a grouch. It's not been the best morning."

"Sorry to hear that." He dug into his pocket for change. "No donuts, but they have cherry fruit pies."

"That works." She moved to the table and dropped into one of the chairs. "I'm Elise. Not sure if you remember. You meet a lot of people on the first day."

"Eric." The pastry plopped into the reservoir. He handed her the wax-paper wrapped pie, then leaned against the cabinet, crossing one leg over the other.

"I know. Eric Erickson." She opened the package, broke off a corner and shot it into her mouth. "What's your real name?"

"Eric." Thank God he'd not had to worry about answering to a fake name. Back at the agency, they'd discussed creating a new identity, but decided the paperwork involved in getting a bogus pilot's license would take too long.

"Shut up. It is not."

"Why would I lie?"

She snorted and held out her hand. "Let's see the driver's license."

"You'll just have to trust me."

Her smile wavered, but she recovered quickly, crossing her arms and leaning back in her chair.

"Okay, fine. Eric is a nickname, but it's what everyone calls me, even my mom."

She narrowed her eyes.

"My given name starts with the letter *A*."

"Andrew? Alex?"

"You'll never get it.

"Albert?"

"Uh, no."

"I'm going to figure it out."

"If you say so." He gazed out the window, admiring the way the pink morning sky cast a purple glow on the mountain peaks. On a nearby runway, a pilot practiced a touch-and-go landing. A prickle of awareness alerted him to her presence at his side. What was it about this woman?

"Looks like the wind is out of the north today." Her eyes followed the Cessna as it touched down, bounced, and lifted back into the air.

No longer staring at the runway or its scenic backdrop, his gaze fixed on Elise. What did he really know about his first officer? Not much beyond the standard background check, but he definitely looked forward to getting to know her better. "How'd you get into flying?"

"Grew up around my dad's charter business and flight school. I've been around planes, in planes, and flying planes as long as I can remember. My brothers, too."

"Decided to strike out on your own?"

"Something like that." She averted her gaze, but then her phone pinged. She fished it from her pocket and stared. "Shoot. I gotta go."

She disappeared into the lounge, leaving him alone

and unsteady, his emotions a chaotic mess. He shook his head. And here he thought turbulence only applied to aircraft.

Chapter Three

A few minutes later, Elise strode across the parking lot to the business offices. What could the airline owner want to talk to her about? And what exactly just happened in the break room? She'd been in a rotten mood, and then ... she wasn't. Eric Erickson had somehow managed to completely change her outlook on the day.

She climbed the stairs to the second-floor offices of Rocky Mountain Charters and inhaled the scent of a cinnamon apple candle when she entered the small suite. Mary Beth Jefferson's pink hair, stiff and sculpted into something resembling a muffin top, bobbed when she looked up.

A smile spread across the older woman's face. "It's good to see you, dear. What can I help you with?" Elise had never met her grandparents but liked to think they would have been something like Mary Beth.

"I got a text from Peter that he wants to see me."

"Oh, that's right. Give me a minute. Last I checked, he was on a conference call." She disappeared down the short hallway.

Elise zipped up her jacket, wishing she'd worn something other than her running clothes.

The cotton candy head reappeared. Mary Beth waved her forward. "He's off the call. Come on in."

Behind a heavy desk too large for the tiny room,

Peter Michelson sat staring at his computer. As always, he wore his dark, wavy hair slicked back from his face and the buttons of his company polo undone.

Elise hadn't quite figured Peter out. He wasn't an aviation nerd like many others in the industry, and she'd seen no indication he even had his pilot's certificate. As long as his clients were happy and paid their bills, he seemed content to let the business run itself. Much different from how she and her brothers ran their tiny airline.

"Have a seat." His gaze remained fixed on the monitor.

She pushed her shoulders back, eager to learn what was going on. "Why did you want to talk to me?"

He took off his reading glasses and stared. "Lenny quit."

"Excuse me?"

"Said the time had come to enjoy retirement. He's pulling up stakes and moving to be near his daughter and grandkids."

"When?" And why hadn't he said anything?

"Told me three days ago."

She digested the news. Lenny had been her partner since she started at Rocky Mountain Charters. They weren't the best of friends, but she couldn't believe he'd leave without saying goodbye. "We have a flight today."

"That's why you're here. I'm assigning Erickson to your routes."

"The new guy?" Her heart beat faster. Could she work with that man and stay professional?

Peter studied her. "Is there a problem?"

She recalled the flush of heat that had mushroomed across her skin when she shook Eric's hand that first day.

The way he soothed her bad temper in the break room just now. The endearing quirk of his mouth when he was about to be a smart ass. Surely whatever attraction she was feeling would wear off. But did she want to risk it? "I don't know that it's a good fit."

"Why not? Did he do something?"

She shook her head, not wanting Peter to think Eric had been inappropriate. "No, nothing like that. It's just a feeling."

"You're the preferred pilot for several of our most important clients. They are all happy with the current level of service. I see no reason to tinker with a good thing."

Elise chewed on her lip. There had to be a way out of this. "Can't you give Eric to someone else? I could team up with another pilot."

"No dice. This guy's got impressive credentials. Big customers get the best. End of story."

"What if I said I'd take all the Vegas flights?" Babysitting rich boozehounds was as bad as it got.

"Sounds like this guy got under your skin." Peter's gaze softened. "Sorry, Elise. I need you where you are."

Dismissed, she stopped to get a new uniform from Mary Beth, then carried herself back to the private terminal. When she entered the building, she hurried to the locker room.

Warm, soapy water ran down her back as she rinsed her hair, but it did nothing to ease her frustration. More than six months she'd given to this company without a single complaint. She didn't say anything when they paired her up with Lazy Lenny. Or about working back-to-back shifts. Not even when sleazy, entitled clients made lewd comments.

Peter could have at least pretended to give it some consideration. And Vegas? Christ. What had gotten into her?

She wrapped a towel around her body and headed for the bench where she'd left her new uniform. Drying herself off, her mind wandered back to the break room and Eric's crooked smile and the twinkle of mischief in his eyes. Sure, he was handsome and funny, but that was no reason not to work with the guy.

She tucked her shirt into her pants, put on her shoes and headed to the pilots' lounge. Time to find what's-his-name and make nice.

He was sitting on a sofa drinking a soda and eating a small bag of spicy habanero potato chips. A clipboard and paperwork rested on his leg.

She took a few uncertain steps in his direction. "More caffeine? You're living on the edge."

The bag crinkled. He winked and extracted another chip. "Nothing says danger like soda and junk food."

Experiencing no unusual heart palpitations, she settled beside him on the worn leather couch. "I hear we're going to be working together."

He tilted his head back and tapped the bag, emptying potato chip crumbs into his mouth. "Sorry I didn't say anything earlier. I wasn't sure if you knew."

"I didn't, but it's okay. I understand."

He held up the clipboard and offered a sheepish smile. "I started the flight planning. Didn't get very far."

She released a heavy sigh. Did she have to do everything? "Have you seen the plane?"

He shook his head.

"Give it to me." She grabbed the clipboard and began adding the aircraft information. 'It's a turboprop.

Almost brand new. Eight passenger seats and a fancy glass cockpit."

Her pen scraped across the paper while he flipped through the pages of a travel book. Calculating the fuel and factoring weather and weight took only a few minutes.

"Who do we have today?"

"Mrs. Richards and Ziggy. One-day trip we do about once a month. Ziggy sees a specialist in Dallas."

"Do you do a lot of these one-day trips?"

She shrugged. Every day and every client were different. "It varies. There's one client who books two round trips every time he flies. He pays us to fly to Jersey to get him and bring him to Denver. Then we fly him back a few days later and he pays for our return flight too."

"He pays for an empty leg every time he flies with you?" He let out a disbelieving snort. "That's insane."

"If I've learned anything flying private charters, it's that people with money will pay almost anything to avoid inconvenience."

"You've been flying charters long?"

"Nearly all my life."

His steady attention penetrated the defenses she kept firmly in place, and she felt the intensity of his stare deep in her gut. Her insides started to tingle, and for a moment, she froze, transfixed and returning his stare.

She wrenched her gaze away and stood, holding up the flight plan. "Let's run this over to the flight service station. Then I'll show you the plane."

****

Twenty minutes later, Eric climbed into the cockpit and slipped into the captain's chair. Elise stood outside the aircraft talking to a pilot from another company. This might be his only chance to turn on the transmitter. He hated to waste battery on an empty plane but didn't know when he'd get another opportunity and today was an important test-run of the equipment.

Later, once they were back in Denver, he'd extract the little hard drive and meet Grant at some off-the-beaten-path location. Grant would then pass it onto the techies to check battery life and sound quality. If all went according to plan, the bug would be ready to record when Vincenzo Alario stepped onto the plane in a few days' time.

Grasping under the instrument panel, he knocked the device from its hiding spot, but then something drew his attention to the window. The guy talking to Elise gave her shoulder a playful nudge. The other pilot tugged on his tie and leaned toward her. Eric's gaze bounced from the dork to Elise. She didn't pull away, but she didn't return his lean, either. Polite tolerance.

Good.

He stilled, somewhat—but not entirely—surprised his mind went there. Since his very first day at the airline, she'd stood out, drawing his attention like a magnet. And it wasn't because she flew the Alario route.

Hell, he couldn't blame the guy on the tarmac. There was something about Elise. Her boldness. Her quick wit. The way she carried herself—straight, tall, and proud. Ready to take on the world.

Even the uniform, drab and shapeless on most pilots, clung to her curves as if cut just for her. She wore no tie, and the top-two buttons of the plain white shirt were undone, teasing a glimpse of smooth bronze skin.

And then there were those lips with a natural pout

that took his brain to places it shouldn't go.

But all that was irrelevant. This mission was too damned important to get distracted.

He rubbed circles against his temples, hoping to massage away the stress. In all the years he'd prepared for this opportunity, he'd never considered how it would feel when the day finally arrived. Anger and uncertainty bubbled in his veins. Would he be able to control himself with Vincenzo Alario within arm's reach? God, he hoped so. Because if not, his possible connection to the gangster could jeopardize the entire investigation.

Maybe he should have confessed to Grant that his obsession began when he was a teenager. But with no official link to his dad, it was nothing more than a theory.

The unproven theory of a grieving kid.

The hot, stagnant air of the cockpit settled on him as unwelcome as a blanket on a summer night. He turned back to the window. Elise and her friend were gone. Time to get that transmitter turned on. Reaching between his legs, he flicked the switch on the small rectangle and shoved it back into its cubbyhole. A pressure on the back of his chair alerted him she'd returned.

She stepped over the console and settled into her seat. "What are you doing?"

"Shoelace came untied."

"I hate that." She picked up the clipboard with the maintenance log. "What do you think of the plane?"

"I see they went with the cheap model." He kept his voice light. There was nothing inexpensive about this bird.

"I know, right? I can't believe they purchased new. My dad only bought used planes."

Bought. Past tense. Her father was deceased. He'd

read that in the file. "So, your brothers run the business now?"

The way her eyebrows squeezed together made him wonder if she would answer. "We each own a third."

He leaned forward, intending to ask why she worked for another charter company if she owned her own, but forgot everything. That fragrance. He inhaled. Lavender? The dish soap of his childhood kitchen. The scent of comfort and love.

"You okay? You look a little weird."

He wiped his brow. "It's hot in here."

"Seems normal to me."

"You were telling me about your planes. How many do you have?"

She answered with a loud sigh. "When my dad ran the business, we had five. My brothers have bought two more—one's a jet."

"Seven? That's a nice sized fleet."

She bit her lip and dropped her gaze. He sensed she wasn't sure how much to share. "Technically six at the moment. There was an accident. We're waiting for insurance."

A million other questions came to mind and not just what happened to their plane. He wanted to know everything—what her brothers were like, why she relocated to Colorado, how she filled her time when she wasn't flying.

His phone pinged. Grant.

—*Need to talk. Now.*—

Eric racked his brain for an excuse to slip away. "Peter wants to see me."

Beside him, Elise stiffened and sucked in a breath. Interesting. Something about him talking to Peter concerned her.

He lifted himself from his seat and stepped over the center console. "I'll try to keep this quick."

Crouching, he made his way down the aisle to the door at the back of the plane but stopped short and turned. "When will the clients—"

Bam. Elise bumped into him. His body stilled. The smell of lavender drifted over him, and the urge to steady her, to touch her smooth skin nearly overpowered him. Rather than give in, he channeled the impulse into a death grip on the passenger seat.

"I didn't know you were there." His words were low and gravelly, his voice unrecognizable to his own ears.

Unable to stop himself, he stared at her mouth and its perfect little *O* of surprise.

****

Elise's entire body reacted to the collision. Shortness of breath. Dizziness. Cognitive impairment. Either she had a virus or something about this man sent her emergency alert system into overdrive.

Eric made a strangled noise and stepped back. Alarm flashed across his face. "I'd better see what Peter wants."

He whirled, then hurried down the stairs two at a time.

A sinkhole opened in her stomach. Nothing like watching a man flee to boost a girl's ego.

She gave herself a shake. All she'd wanted was to ask if he knew the reason for Peter's summons. It wasn't her fault he bumped into her. Hell, he was the one who made it awkward by running away.

Partners needed to be able to anticipate one another's thoughts and needs. Clearly, they were missing that particular coworker dynamic. This was exactly what she'd tried to tell Peter. She and Eric were not compatible. They were oil and water. Toothpaste and orange juice. Two negatively charged ions. They didn't mesh. Never would. The sooner Peter realized that, the sooner they could put an end to this nonsense.

Her shoulders collapsed on a heavy exhale. Who was she kidding? It wasn't their incompatibility that concerned her, but quite the opposite. After months of zero sexual desire, she would have to pick the most inconvenient time to take an interest in a man. And a coworker at that.

She shook her head, bewildered by her response to this person she'd only just met. What was she even considering? A one-night stand? And what if it was no good? Though she couldn't believe that would be a problem. Still, climbing into the cockpit and having to spend hours sitting next to the guy after a meaningless tumble in the sheets sounded like an experience she could do without.

Whatever attraction she felt and however much fun she found his banter, she didn't need a fling, and she certainly wasn't interested in a relationship. No, the last thing she needed was another person in her life who'd eventually leave.

Besides, if she was looking to get involved, it wouldn't be with a pilot. Pilots did nothing for her. Probably something about growing up in a house filled with them.

Though she had to admit, Eric didn't look completely ridiculous in the standard commercial airline uniform. The white, short-sleeved shirt stretched across his broad chest, the flex of his biceps beneath the sleeves, the tight polyester pants wrapping around his ass.

Warm tingles spread up her neck and face. She fanned her shirt. Maybe he was right about the temperature.

Thankful no one was around to hear, she let out a loud, dejected sigh. No amount of delusional self-talk could erase the prick of rejection, and the expression on his face wouldn't leave her alone. First, the sound of his voice. Thick. Deep. And what might have been a glint of desire in his eyes. But then, pure panic. He couldn't get away from her fast enough. An annoyed prickle traveled up her spine.

There was no reason for alarm. She could work with this man. All she had to do now was pretend she hadn't gotten close enough to see the tiny flecks of gold in his emerald-green eyes.

Chapter Four

Dammit. Eric rubbed the back of his neck. What was he thinking? The moment he was within inches of that woman, his resolve disappeared like a magician's coin. But, like sleight of hand, it was an illusion, a misdirection conjured by his brain to avoid facing the hard reality of his current assignment.

He shook his head, hoping to clear away any lingering memories of the encounter in the plane and what it might have meant. Something would need to be done about his attraction to Elise. But later. Right now, Grant was waiting for his call.

He shoved through the doors to the charter offices in case she was watching and went straight out the back. The rear of the building reminded him of a Tetris piece. Clutching his phone, he followed the perimeter until he arrived at a door that said HVAC. Satisfied he was alone, he pushed it open and stepped inside the small, dank room and called the case agent.

Grant didn't bother with hello. "We've been monitoring the bug in Michelson's office."

"Yeah?" Prickles of unease ran up Eric's neck.

"Your first officer was in there a while ago asking to have you reassigned."

Shit. That would explain her reaction to his talking to Peter.

"Did something happen I should know about?"

"No, nothing."

"No idea why she doesn't want to work with you?"

Eric's stomach rolled. "Nope."

"Well, whatever's going on, you need to fix it. The last thing we want is for them to decide to put another pilot on this route."

"I get it."

"Do whatever you have to do to get on her good side."

His mouth went dry, knowing full well he and Grant were on totally different wavelengths about what that might entail. "I'll take care of it."

Eric disconnected the call, stepped back into the sunshine, and leaned against the brick wall.

She'd actually asked for another partner. They hardly knew each other. So why should he care?

The obvious answer was the case. If she got him tossed from the route, it would impact his ability to collect intel. Everything he'd done here—weeks spent learning the company and earning Michelson's trust—would be for nothing.

First things first. Dealing with his partner's reluctance to work with him. He needed to decide which hand to play. Pretend Peter told him of their conversation or say they met about something else? The idea Peter might share her request had worried her. A part of him wanted to call her on it, make her squirm, but sparing her embarrassment seemed the best way to keep her happy.

He pushed off the wall, marched through the building and crossed the parking lot to the tarmac and plane.

Her body went rigid as he settled beside her, but she didn't look up, instead aiming her attention at the maintenance log as if it contained the most interesting information in the world. "What did Peter want?"

He stared at her tense features before speaking. "Signatures. I missed a couple of papers in the new employee packet."

She relaxed, offered a smile, and handed him the clipboard. "Speaking of signatures, you need to sign this."

The document revealed a well-maintained aircraft. At least Michelson didn't skimp on safety. "Looks good."

"I'm about to start the internal check."

"Excellent. I need to familiarize myself with the flight deck."

She handed him the printed checklist and started flipping buttons and levers, a task she'd probably done a hundred times. Finished, she raised out of her seat. "Mrs. Richards should be here. I'll see if she's ready to leave."

"I'll come with you. Might as well get a feel for the relationship with our customers."

He followed her down the aisle at a safe distance to avoid a repeat of their earlier collision. Heat raced to his face at the memory. He couldn't be thinking these things. Or putting himself in situations that might compel him to do something he'd regret. He didn't trust himself to not go full-stupid the next time around.

Crisp air greeted him when he emerged from the plane. A man in a dark suit with a short, cropped hair cut, and a woman in a cream-colored pants suit and wide-brimmed hat stood on the patio, waving at Elise. A small, orange ball of fluff wrapped its leash around the woman's ankles.

They approached their customers. Elise's tone was

amiable. "Mrs. Richards, welcome back. It's nice to see you again."

The woman nodded, but her face showed no emotion and it was impossible to read her eyes which were hidden behind a pair of big, square movie-star glasses.

"Allow me to introduce Captain Erickson." Elise gestured to Eric. "He's a new addition to our team."

Elise squatted in front of the cantaloupe-colored canine and held her hand in front of its pointy little snout. The dog sniffed, then took two prissy steps forward, apparently a carbon copy of its owner. Elise scratched it around the ears.

Eric stuck out his hand. "It's a pleasure to meet you."

The woman's gaze slithered from Eric's face to his feet and back up again in a way that managed to be both appraising and condescending. She didn't move to shake his hand, so he redirected it to the man in the suit standing slightly behind her and who had not yet been introduced. "Captain Erickson." The man's grasp was strong and firm. "You must be Ziggy."

Elise's hand stilled on the dog's head. Mrs. Richards' brows disappeared behind her giant glasses, and the corner of the man's mouth curled into something resembling a smirk. "Do I look like a Ziggy?"

Eric froze, unsure how to avoid making it worse. Mrs. Richards was a regular customer. He couldn't afford to piss her off.

The woman bent down, picked up the dog and shoved it in Eric's face. "*This* is Ziggy."

****

Elise waited. Everyone knew Mrs. Richards treated

her dog like a son and her security detail like a piece of furniture. Elise was curious to see how Eric would respond to the woman's displeasure.

A beat passed. No one said a word.

Finally, he stretched out his hand for the little dog to sniff. "Hey there, Ziggy."

The dog let out a low growl, followed by two sharp barks. Eric snatched his hand back.

"As you can see, Ziggy is a wonderful judge of character." Mrs. Richards stepped past Eric and looked to Elise. "I assume the plane is ready?"

"It is. We can leave whenever you want."

"Now works." She stuck her nose in the air in a way only the truly entitled could manage and shot a side-eyed glare at Eric. "Come along, *Bradley*."

The man followed Mrs. Richards to the plane but slowed long enough to give Eric a sympathetic pat on the shoulder.

Once the trio were out of earshot, Eric spun to face her, a meme-worthy look of annoyance on his face. "You might have told me Ziggy was a dog."

She barked out a laugh. "I didn't know I'd need to."

"Tens of thousands of dollars every month for a one-day trip to fly her dog to see a specialist?" He snorted, as though he'd never heard anything so ridiculous.

Mrs. Richards was difficult and demanding, but Elise couldn't fault her for wanting the best for her little companion. "Ziggy has Cushing's Disease. He gets a monthly treatment at one of the leading clinics in the world."

"Again, information that would have been helpful before I embarrassed myself."

"Stop pouting. It'll be fine." She gave him a playful

push in the chest, letting her fingers linger. It was a solid chest. A hard chest. A very, very firm chest.

His gaze lowered, and for an awkward moment, they both stared at her hand resting atop the breast pocket of his shirt. Then, the realization of what she was doing zapped her like an electric shock. She snatched her hand away, shoved it in her pocket, and spun on her heel.

His long strides easily caught up to her. "How much penance am I going to have to do to get back into Mrs. Richards's good graces?"

"I don't think anyone is actually in her—" She curled her fingers into air quotes as she spoke the words *good graces*. "But you certainly put your foot in your mouth."

There was a part of her that wanted to continue teasing him, but he seemed ready to move on. "So, it'll be about three hours in the air. How long will Ziggy's appointment take?"

"Also a few hours. We're usually home about dinner time."

He nodded, and she had the strangest inclination to ask what he was doing after work. She thrust the notion aside and climbed into the plane.

After checking that the passengers were settled, Elise took her seat in the cockpit beside Eric, and they taxied to the runway. Once clear, they began the ground roll, gaining speed until the plane lifted into the air.

"Denver Departure, King Air November six-six-two-eight Charlie," Eric radioed, verifying radar information for air traffic control while he visually monitored the other aircraft. She increased airspeed and continued to climb.

While he busied himself listening to the aeronautical

broadcast, she inspected her new colleague. Light stubble colored his jaw and accentuated the hard lines of his face, and when he turned his head at just the right angle, she could see the smallest hint of a cleft in his chin.

Several minutes passed before his voice sounded in her headset. "So, this is a one-day trip. How do the overnighters work?"

"More or less the same, except we spend a night in a hotel. There's also a forty-dollar stipend for food and on the return flight, we can wear khakis and the company polo rather than this polyester monstrosity." She tugged on the collar of her shirt.

His expression became pensive, like he was trying to figure something out. "Have you ever worked for an airline?" she asked.

"No. My most recent job was flying cargo. Before that, I was an insurance adjuster."

"For real?" She couldn't help the involuntary scrunch of her nose. "You went from the Air Force to insurance adjuster?"

His expression took on a panicked edge. "Yeah, why?"

Because he looked more like a stunt man than someone who'd work in a boring insurance job. But she wasn't going to tell him that. "I love to fly. It's hard for me to imagine flying a plane, then leaving to do something else."

"That was part of the problem with the insurance gig. At the freight company, I got a lot of time in the air and it paid well, but it was also kind of lonely."

"Do you have a place near the airport?"

"Not yet. Still living in a hotel."

"You're not local?"

"Just moved from Philly." He must've seen the questions forming on her lips because he continued before she could ask her next question. "Came out here with my dad when I was a kid and always wanted to come back." He gave a why-the-hell-not shrug. "What about you? Where do you live?"

"I've got a place down the street from the airport."

He gave a contemplative nod. "I still need to figure out where I want to be."

Talking to Eric was easy, and before she had a chance to reconsider, her mouth was moving and words were coming out. "There's nothing on the schedule for tomorrow. I could show you around."

His responding smile was slow and sincere and annoyingly sexy. "I'd like that."

Shit. What was she thinking?

She wasn't. And that was the problem.

Chapter Five

The trailhead parking lot was empty. Eric scanned for Elise's car, one of those beat-up all-wheel-drive wagons half of Denver seemed to be driving. But, based on the fact his was the only car in the lot, he could safely say she wasn't here. Great. Maybe she'd overslept. Or stood him up. The thought produced a weird little flutter in his stomach.

No, she didn't seem like the type to make plans and then flake. And it wasn't like he'd been the one to suggest they meet at the crack of dawn. That was her idea. She must be running a few minutes late.

He settled into his seat and closed his eyes. Last night had been another night of not enough sleep. After they'd returned from Dallas, he'd hoped to get a moment alone so he could remove the transmitter from its hiding place. Elise chatted while wiping down the windshield, and though he enjoyed her conversation, he needed to get rid of her. Hence agreeing to meet her for an early morning run. The sun wasn't even up yet, for God's sake.

In his haste to have a moment alone, he'd also agreed to take care of the other post-flight tasks, which included cleaning up Ziggy's "accidental" piddle. Or at least Mrs. Richards claimed it had been an accident. Eric wouldn't put it past the woman to train her dog to go whenever and wherever, knowing it would become someone else's problem.

He'd gone straight from the airport to the little dive bar where he met Grant to hand over the transmitter. They'd had a beer, and he'd not gotten back to his room until well after midnight.

Now, here he was, waiting to do an early morning run, followed by apartment hunting. He wasn't truly in the market for a new place—his condo back in Philly was just fine, but she didn't know that, and these activities provided an opportunity to learn a bit more about Alario and his mysterious trips.

A rap on his window startled him, and when he opened his eyes, he was nearly blinded by a bright light aimed directly at him. He raised a hand to shield himself from the illumination. "What the—"

The rap came again. "Come on, Erickson. Let's go."

Eric stepped out of the car to find Elise jogging in place, a runner's headlamp strapped across her forehead. He glanced around the parking lot. Still no other cars. "Where did you come from?"

"I ran here."

He gaped at her, then asked the completely stupid question, "In the dark?"

"It's fine." She waved a dismissive hand. "It was only a few miles and the sun is already coming up."

Only a few miles? He considered himself fit, but it had been a while since he'd done any sort of jogging. "I'm not exactly in running shape. I hope you'll take it easy on me."

"Sure. I thought we'd warm up for about twenty minutes and then do some hill repeats."

Hill repeats? Words he'd not heard since he enlisted. He gulped down his reservations and schooled his face into what he hoped conveyed confidence and composure and not the least bit of concern. "After you."

She responded with a hypnotic smile, and for a moment, he felt suspended in time and place, unable to comprehend the world beyond Elise. He shook himself free of the trance. This wasn't why he was here, and it certainly wasn't why he'd gotten out of bed before daybreak to embark on an hour of his least favorite exercise.

They were silent for a few moments as they travelled along the gravel path that meandered through trees and alongside a creek.

"How was yesterday?" Elise's steps looked effortless as she glided along the trail. Eric was pretty sure he looked like some cartoon monster lumbering beside her.

"Okay." He could already feel his breaths getting shorter but hoped she wouldn't notice. "It was a long day. I'm not sure how you do that back-to-back."

"Sometimes it's tough, but Peter is pretty good about keeping the schedule fair. We rarely work more than two or three days in a row without getting a day off."

Unsure if he'd be able to get more than one word out a time, he nodded.

"Take tomorrow for example. We're flying the client to Chicago, then it'll be a quick flight to Milwaukee where we pick up another regular. The day after that, we fly to Jersey. That's a longer trip, so we'll stay in a hotel and fly back the next morning. It ends up being like two and a half days of work, but then we get two days off."

Jersey. That meant Alario. This was his chance to get some information. "Who's" –*gasp*— "on" –*gasp*— "the" –*gasp*— "Jersey flight?"

Good God, he was out of shape. And she considered this the warm up?

"You want to walk for a bit?" Her eyebrows drew together and she searched his face as though looking for signs of distress.

He held up his hand and lied. "Nah. I'm good."

She nodded in an amused way that said she wasn't buying it but was willing to let him cling to his male pride for a bit longer.

"So…Jersey?"

"A man named Alario, his son, and two of his son's friends."

Eric knew from the intel that Alario was flying with his son Rocco. He wasn't sure who the other two men were but was pretty certain they were something other than friends.

"You know them well?"

"Not really, but you get to be friendly with some of the regular customers."

He nodded, unwilling to try to speak given his labored breathing. They crossed a wooden bridge and the path split in two.

Elise veered to the left and picked up her pace. "The hill is this way."

Eric jogged behind her for a few minutes, but then the path emerged from the trees, and he came to a halt. Elise crossed the street to where the trail cut its path across the hillside. Switchbacks? No one had said anything about switchbacks.

He admired the graceful ease with which she coasted up the incline. As far as information gathering went, this had been a bit of a bust, but he couldn't regret dragging himself from bed. Not when it meant spending his morning with her.

He lurched back into a jog and yelled, "See you at the top."

****

God, he was adorable.

First, he'd struggled to keep pace with her on the run this morning, and despite an obvious lack of cardiovascular fitness, never complained. Now, he was attempting to be a good sport by drinking a snakebite, something he'd never tasted and clearly didn't like.

Elise tried to hide her amusement. "What do you think?"

"Smooth." He joked, making his voice sound strained and raspy.

She laughed and patted him on the back. "We're in an English pub. What could be more British than Guinness and a bit of Strongbow?"

"Either of those two things by themselves." He grinned back and focused his attention on the menu. "What are you having?"

"Shepherd's pie."

He set his menu down and let his gaze wander the room. "Sounds good. I'll do the same."

She watched, wondering what he saw. There was the obvious, of course. Crimson-colored wallpaper. Polished, wood bar with matching furniture. A low ceiling.

The real question was, did he get it?

"You could almost forget you're not in England when you're in here." He shook his head in awe. "To think, there's a busy highway half a mile down the road."

Huh. That was exactly why she loved this place. And he'd gotten it within the first fifteen minutes. She studied his handsome face and felt her fingers itching to touch him. Instead, she spun her pint glass through the condensation ring on the table.

"Did you like any of the apartments we saw?"

He wrinkled his nose, took another sip of his drink, and shrugged. "They're all kind of the same, right? I probably need to focus on location."

"I like being close to work." She cringed, realizing what the statement said about her lack of any sort of life.

"So, what brought you to Denver?"

She leaned back and gave her standard response. "What brings anyone here? The mountains, of course."

He pursed his lips, clearly not buying the disingenuous answer. She should've known he wasn't going to let her get away with the usual evasive bullshit. She started again. "I had some trouble dealing with things we learned after my dad died, so I took a friend up on an offer to deadhead to Denver."

Why was she telling him this? And why did she feel compelled to keep going? "Other than a backpack with my laptop, I didn't pack any luggage. I got an apartment down the hill from the airport and bought a cheap car and some clothes. A few days later, I had a job at Rocky Mountain Charters."

His brows rose, and he stared as if waiting to see what else she might divulge. She felt exposed. That was more than she'd meant to share—more than she'd ever shared before. She laughed uncomfortably. "I guess sometimes I forget normal people don't hitch rides in airplanes."

"How long ago was that?"

"A little over six months."

He tilted his chin and gazed at her, his stare seducing

her to keep going. "Where is home?"

"We lease space at an airport in the Keys." For some reason, she couldn't think about home without thinking of the family business. Separated by more than two thousand miles, she could still picture her siblings behind the counter in the tiny terminal.

"What about when you're not at the airport?" His tone carried a note of amusement. "Or do you live there?"

"I have a house." Pride threaded her voice. God, she loved the small ranch on a quiet side street in Key Largo. "Started saving right after high school. Bought it a few years ago." Happiness pulsed through her veins whenever she thought of her forty-year-old stucco home with its barrel-tile roof. Though in desperate need of a facelift, she adored every inch of dated décor, from the parquet floor to the laminate kitchen cabinets. For one simple reason. It was hers.

She shoved the thoughts away. She didn't want to think about home or the memories she'd left there. "What about you? Where did you grow up?"

"New York."

"In the city? I was born there."

"Brooklyn. No brothers or sisters. Just me and my mom." There was a sadness in his voice and judging by the slump in his shoulders, it wasn't a topic she should pursue. The last thing she'd ever do was force someone to talk about something painful. Stuffing down feelings was a tactic she knew all too well.

The food arrived, and they ate for a few moments without speaking.

"So, who are your favorite clients?" He took another bite of potato and lamb. "Besides, Mrs. Richards and

Ziggy, of course."

She chewed and swallowed a fry doused in malt vinegar. "It's hard to say. Most of our passengers don't engage with us beyond what is required. A lot of them treat us like we're the help."

"Does that bother you?"

"Should it?"

He bobbed his head back and forth. "You spend a lot of time with some of these people. Many of them have requested that you be their pilot. That suggests some sort of a relationship."

There really weren't a lot of customers who stood out. "I guess I look forward to seeing Mr. Alario. He's one of the few clients who talks to me like I'm a real person."

Eric's eyes flamed briefly, but it was gone so fast she must have imagined it.

"They fly between Colorado and Jersey often?" The pitch of his voice lowered. His gaze was intense, unblinking.

She fidgeted with her cutlery. "Every few weeks, I guess. He usually books a week or so in advance and then we fly to Jersey to pick him up."

"Why does he do that? Have you come to him?"

"Never thought about it."

"Wouldn't it make more sense to hire a plane in Jersey? Why use a company based here instead of there?"

Why did she suddenly feel like she was being interrogated? "I don't know, officer. Does it matter?"

He flinched at her words.

God, she was the worst. "I'm sorry. That was rude."

"My fault. I shouldn't ask stupid questions. I'm just

amazed by how people choose to spend their money."

Surely, he'd figured out there weren't a lot of cash-strapped customers flying around on private charters. "I don't know. I don't pay the bills."

"Of course not." He tossed his napkin on the table beside his empty plate. "Maybe we should get the check."

Way to go, mood killer. She'd had a good time today. This wasn't how she'd wanted it to end. In fact, she wasn't ready for it to be over at all. "Want to come back to my place?" The words gushed from her mouth before she had a chance to think better of them.

He stilled, and she guessed he was trying to figure out her meaning.

"I've got a laptop. We can try to figure out where you want to live and make a list of apartments to visit."

"Yeah, sure." A slow smile crept onto his face. "That sounds great."

****

"How about a glass of wine?" Elise popped up and moved to the kitchen while a mounting sense of dread filled Eric's insides.

"Sure, but only one."

Coming here had been a mistake. Of all the stupid things he'd ever done, deluding himself into thinking he could end the evening without a major case of blue balls had to be one of the dumbest.

"Vino de Budget." Elise returned to the couch and handed him a glass of rosé. "Also known as Chateau d'Box."

"Thanks." He accepted the glass and lifted it to his lips.

She looked aggrieved. "Hang on."

What had he done wrong now?

"Aren't you going to check the nose?"

"Pardon?"

"And here I thought you were a connoisseur. Watch." She held the glass up to the light of the window and gave the glass an aggressive swirl. "Now, your turn."

He stared at her for a moment. She was teasing—obviously, but he felt more than a little ridiculous pretending box wine was fancy. Then he saw the look on her face, a mixture of encouragement and delight, and knew he had one option. He lifted the glass and gave it three quick rotations.

"I see you're a safe swirler. That's okay. You're a beginner." She laid her hand on his forearm, her touch simultaneously soothing his discomfort and provoking his desire. "Try again. Really let the oxygen in."

He let out a surprised laugh at her enthusiasm. "Looks like you've had a lot of practice."

"Are you calling me a lush?" She raised her glass for a second demonstration.

If she could make an experience out of drinking box wine, he could only imagine what else she could do. "How's this?" Wine sloshed up the edges of his glass.

She offered an exaggerated nod of approval. "I'm impressed."

God help him, her pretend praise hit him like a ray of sunlight, and his chest swelled with the irrational desire to soak up every compliment she'd offer.

"Okay, step two." She gave him a serious look. "Watch carefully." She stuck her nose in the glass and took a deep breath. "Hints of orange and cherry." She sniffed again. "Burnt toast."

He stuck his nose in his glass and inhaled. "Smells

like wine."

"You can do better than that. Try again."

Might as well go for broke. He sniffed, then made up the first three things that came to mind. "Pepperoni pizza. Fresh cut grass. Vanilla ice cream."

She shoved her hand into his shoulder with a laugh, took a sip and waited for him to do the same. He took a mouthful of the blush-colored wine, and knowing she was watching, swished it around his mouth. He swallowed. "A superb vintage."

She rewarded him with a smile. And God, what a smile it was.

"Okay, let's get down to business." She set her glass on the coffee table and stretched forward to retrieve her laptop. She positioned the open computer on her crossed legs, and as she wiggled herself into position, her knee made contact with his thigh and rested there. He sucked in a deep breath and rubbed the rough stubble of his jaw.

Information. Information. Information.

The mantra he'd been telling himself all day. Why he was here. The *only* reason he was here.

"I know some people like to live where there are things to do. So, what are some of your hobbies?"

He mulled the question, unsure how to respond. He couldn't very well tell her he spent most of his spare time at a gun club working on pistol shooting drills without explaining why. He'd done some competitive shooting events. That might work but would likely also provoke questions he didn't want to answer.

"Mountain biking?"

"Oh, there are tons of bike trails. We can easily find you an apartment within riding distance of some singletrack." She pulled up a Denver Metro bike map.

"What else?"

"Boxing. That's something I've done since I was a kid. Haven't found a gym here yet."

"Huh. Interesting." She stared at him for a long moment, though what she was looking for, he had no idea. Then, her gaze was off him and back on her computer screen, before he realized how much he missed being the center of her focus.

"Why's that?"

Her attention was back, but this time, her fingers grazed his cheekbones. "This pretty face, of course." Her tone started out teasing, but ended as a low murmur, her fingertips now tracing the curve of his jaw.

He didn't move or breathe.

"Don't you worry about getting hurt?"

A moan rose in his throat, but he concealed it with a good-old-fashioned throat clearing.

She snatched her hand away, but not before a look of mortification flittered across her face.

Shit. He'd not meant to make her feel uncomfortable, but honestly, it was for the best.

She brought up another website, this one for a rental company, but still hadn't looked at him. "This is how I found my place. They offer discounts if you sign a lease through one of their agents."

Eric took another sip of his wine. One way or another, he needed to steer the conversation toward Alario. He'd spent an entire day with Elise and still knew nothing new about his target.

Grant had been adamant Eric keep an eye on her. Alario's trips started not long after Elise began working at Rocky Mountain Charters. "They're up to something," he'd said, but Eric didn't see it. He couldn't imagine

Elise mixed up with a scumbag like Alario.

Still, he needed to keep his wits, stay vigilant.

He watched Elise clicking away on her computer, sipping her wine, and licking her lips in a way that made his brain sputter and stall. With his mind stuck in neutral, his body sped through second and third gear. Christ, not now. He sat up straighter and shifted himself a couple of inches away from her, trying to think of anything to keep his arousal in check.

Stick to the mission, you idiot.

"You really think living near the airport is the way to go? You like working there enough to live just down the street."

She shrugged. "It's convenient."

A pang of regret poked him in the heart. If only they'd met under different circumstances.

He tried to relax. Maybe he could still manage to get out of here without looking like a horny teenager. "So tomorrow we go to Chicago and Milwaukee, then the next day is Jersey?"

"Yep."

"And Jersey is the guy we're dropping off and flying back with no passengers?"

She nodded, still scrolling through apartment pictures.

"Do you know what he does when he comes here?"

"He has a daughter who attends one of the local colleges. He comes out to see her. I think he owns a house near the university."

Eric stilled. They knew Vincenzo had property near Boulder, but his only daughter had died more than two decades ago. "What do you know about her?"

"Not much. Her name is Sophia."

He held his tongue. Using his dead daughter as a cover? Even for Alario, that was low. Not to mention, out of character. As far as Eric knew, in Alario's organization, Sophia was revered to near mythical levels.

Vincenzo would never drop her name lightly.

It had to mean something.

He sat beside Elise on her couch, half present as she made a list of apartments for them to visit. Finally, when he could take it no longer, he stood. "It's getting late. I should be going."

For the briefest of moments, she had the look of someone who'd just burned a batch of cookies. She recovered quickly and stood. "I understand."

"Thanks for helping with the apartment."

"I had fun. Besides, you can't stay in a hotel forever."

"Nor would I want to."

She walked him to the door. A current of awareness crackled between them. What was happening to him, and why didn't he want to leave? He hesitated, unsure whether to hug her, shake her hand, or…something else. Since something else was out of the question, he chose none of the above. He waved, then turned toward the street where he'd parked.

Once he was in his car, he pulled out his phone and sent a text to Grant.

—Can you meet? Learned something interesting.—

Chapter Six

Eric was sitting at a back-corner table in the dark brewery sipping on a pint of stout when Grant walked through the door. He didn't bother waving. The other agent would find him.

The chair scraped against the concrete floor as Grant dragged it out and sat. He flagged a waitress and ordered a Newcastle. As usual, he didn't bother with small talk. "What have you got?"

"According to Elise, Alario's excuse for flying to Colorado is to visit his daughter *Sophia*. Says she attends college here."

"That's. . . unexpected." Though his words were slow, Eric could tell by the look on Grant's face he was running through the potential significance.

"That's what I thought. Any idea what he might be up to?"

"Not really."

"It has to mean something, right? Sophia's death started the feud with Aleksander Koslov. But that was years ago."

Grant didn't speak for a long moment, then shook his head. "No idea, but I'll get it to the task force and see if they have any thoughts."

The pint of brown ale arrived. Grant took a long, slow taste. "How are things going with Elise Hughes? Any sense if she has a connection to Alario?"

"If she does, she's a fantastic actress." Eric remembered how easy he'd felt in her company. He gulped his beer. "We spent the day together, and I gotta say, I just don't see it."

"I thought you had the day off?"

"I did. She's helping me look for an apartment."

"Good. Keep her close."

Eric grunted. Grant had no idea how badly he wanted to do just that.

"Speaking of your first officer, the deep background finally came through, and it doesn't look good."

"How so?"

"Seems her father was a smuggler, moving drugs from the islands to South Florida. Died when his plane crashed into the Caribbean. There's an open DEA investigation."

That was what Elise had meant when she said one of her family's planes was out of commission. "Any evidence she was involved with the smuggling?"

Grant shook his head. "She might have known about it, though."

"What about Alario? Was her dad involved with him?"

"No evidence of that, either, but it seems like too much of a coincidence, doesn't it? Her dad's smuggling drugs. The Alario family runs one of the biggest drug operations on the East Coast. Now Vincenzo Alario is a passenger on her plane." He shook his head in a way that said there was more to it than chance. "No way there's not a connection."

Eric's body swayed slightly, and the entire room went out of focus. Elise couldn't be involved with the mob. No. He didn't believe it. And yet, like Grant said, the pieces fit.

"At any rate," Grant said. "It's something to keep an eye on."

He nodded numbly. Was he so taken with Elise he couldn't see her for what she really was?

Grant reached into his pocket and slid a small plastic case across the table. "Everything checked out. The bug worked perfectly. The sound is clear, and the battery lasted the entire day. You're good to go for the trip with Alario."

The excitement Eric expected to flood his extremities didn't come. He'd waited for this moment since he'd been a pimple-faced teenager. But for some reason, the anticipation—the thrill of knowing he was going after his father's killer didn't appear.

Instead, his insides filled with an ocean of dread. Elise wasn't involved.

She couldn't be.

****

Yesterday had been wonderful. Elise couldn't remember the last time she'd felt so at ease with another person. Or had wanted to spend an entire day with someone like she did with Eric. They'd spent hours together and she'd not tired of his company at all.

And then something changed.

His distress hadn't been as overt as the moment they nearly collided in the plane, but he'd disengaged. She'd felt the moment it happened. Sure, he'd hung around for a while longer, chatting and joking, but it hadn't surprised her at all when he stood, saying he needed sleep.

She glanced at the man in the cockpit beside her. He looked the same, had more or less acted the same. But something was different. All day long, there'd been a barrier between them, a newly installed privacy fence with a giant no trespassing sign. The easy familiarity she'd marveled at was all but gone.

Sure, it was for the best, but she wanted to know what she'd done. "Is everything okay with you?"

He startled. The sudden sound of her voice in his headset must have been jarring. "Yeah, why?"

Go for it. "I wondered if I did something. I had a good time yesterday, and I thought you did too, but then out of nowhere—"

"I know."

She blinked away her surprise at his admission. "What?"

"I know I was acting weird." He paused, his eyebrows dipping in a way that told her he was choosing his words. "My situation is complicated. . . ."

Oh God, oh God, oh God. "Are you married?"

He looked legitimately stunned by her question. "No. That's not what I was going to say."

"Girlfriend?" The word erupted from her mouth like Mount Vesuvius.

What was wrong with her? She sounded like a jealous lover. If she'd had any notion to keep her feelings to herself, it was too late now. Any doubt he may have had regarding whether she harbored romantic feelings had been obliterated in three seconds flat.

"I'm not seeing anyone, and I had a good time yesterday, but for reasons I can't explain, I don't think it's a good time to get involved."

If she had a parachute, she'd throw herself from the plane, never to be seen or heard from again. She checked the airspeed indicator and then the navigation panel.

Forty-five minutes. Then they'd be on the ground, and she could get herself as far away from Eric as possible.

"Did I do something to make you want to leave?"

His gaze bounced off her and back to the instrument panel. "I felt really comfortable, and I realized if I stayed, it would become harder to go."

She regarded him for a long moment, waiting for her bullshit radar to ping. It didn't. His words were soft and sincere. Had she made a fool of herself for no reason? Probably.

Now that it was out in the open, maybe she could move on. She'd heard of people banging out the physical tension. Maybe this was the same thing, but instead of sex, it was utter and abject embarrassment. No point in lying about it now. She was attracted to the big oaf. She'd thought the feelings were mutual, but she'd been wrong. It wasn't like this was the first time she'd deluded herself into believing something that wasn't true. Or that someone wasn't who she wanted them to be.

"Friends?" What choice did she have? She couldn't avoid him. Not when they'd be wedged together in the cockpit for several hours every week.

"I'd like to think so." His smile was sad and a bit regretful, and it tugged at those old insecurities of never being enough.

"Want to get dinner after we finish up tonight? Bangers and mash this time?"

He seemed to inhale her words, only to exhale another brush off. He stared at his hands gripping the yoke. "I can't. I'll see you tomorrow."

Chapter Seven

Today was the day.

The moment Eric had dreamed of, waited for, and dreaded was finally here.

He followed Elise from the plane after helping her complete the pre-flight checklist.

And then he saw him. Vincenzo Alario. Standing outside the terminal.

Eric's chest tightened, squeezing at his lungs and making it hard to breathe.

Elise's reaction was quite the opposite. Delight lit up her face when she spotted the man on the walkway. Panic flooded Eric's veins. He wanted to hold her back, keep her from having contact with the monster in old man's clothing.

But he couldn't. That would draw unwanted attention, from both Elise and Alario.

She didn't know the truth—that Vincenzo Alario was a cold-blooded killer. How could she? Because despite what Grant thought, Eric just couldn't find it in him to believe she was involved with the mob.

On first glance, the gangster looked like any typical old man. He was short, with wispy, white hair, and carried his weight around his belly. He wore black slacks and a white button-down shirt, making him virtually indistinguishable from any other wealthy passenger.

Despite the aviator sunglasses, Alario shielded his

eyes as Elise approached. Eric needed to get over there. He hurried through the gate just in time to see Elise shake the mobster's hand, and Vincenzo kiss her on the cheek. Eric cringed but took another step.

The gangster held Elise's chin between his fingers in a familiar gesture. His hoarse voice cracked. "You are such a beauty."

Indignation and disgust swirled in Eric's stomach, but he couldn't give in to base instincts. He had a job to do.

Elise waved away Vincenzo's compliment.

"How is my favorite pilot?" The mobster's voice was warm, but there was a flicker of something else in his gaze.

"Can't complain." Elise glanced about until she found Eric.

Vincenzo followed her gaze, and for the first time, Eric locked eyes with his nemesis.

The old man gave Elise a quizzical look. "A new pilot?"

"Lenny retired." With a sweep of her arm, she motioned Eric over.

The thought of touching the lowlife for anything other than an arrest made Eric's flesh crawl, but somehow, he unclenched his fists and offered his hand.

"I'm pleased to make your acquaintance, Captain—"

"Erickson." Eric took a deep breath and steadied himself to grasp Vincenzo's hand. Cancer had made the man's voice gruff and raspy, but his grip was strong.

"Welcome to the team." The mob boss unwrapped a cough drop and popped it into his mouth. The pungent sting of menthol tickled Eric's nostrils and made him wince.

And then it hit him. This man who'd changed the trajectory of Eric's entire life didn't even know who he was. Eric's muscles tightened. He turned to Elise. "I'll grab the passenger lunches. Maybe a snack. Do you want anything?"

"I'm good."

Without looking back, he crossed the patio keeping his steps as steady as possible. The automatic glass doors opened, and he entered the lounge. They closed with a soft thud. He slumped against the wall, closed his eyes, and pinched the bridge of his nose.

He'd earned this assignment. His expertise on the Alario crime family and his flight experience made him perfect for the job. Of course, he wouldn't be here if the Bureau knew the truth. For now, he needed to stow his personal feelings and focus on figuring out what Vincenzo was doing in Colorado.

Smuggling made the most sense, but the story about Vincenzo visiting his daughter threw Eric for a loop. He saw no incentive for the man to get involved in the vending of marijuana, a legal business in Colorado. Illegal drugs didn't fit, either.

He'd waited a lifetime for this opportunity, for the chance to slip handcuffs on the gangster's fat wrists. He'd imagined the scene so many times, he could see the hair on the old man's arms and feel the sweat of his palms.

After collecting the passenger lunches, Eric grabbed another soda and more snacks for himself and Elise. She'd said no, but she might want something later. He took a seat at one of the café tables near the snack bar.

Luggage thumping over the tile floor drew his

attention. He looked up to see Rocco Alario with two massive men in tow. Christopher Maldonado and Nicky de Luca.

Eric sat straighter. There was definitely more to this than drugs. Why else would Vincenzo bring two of his highest-ranking soldiers? He popped a chip into his mouth and studied the imposing trio.

"Is that the only thing you eat?"

Eric hadn't seen Elise approach. Nor had he realized how many bags of chips he'd gone through. He glanced from her to the small pile of empty packages in the middle of the table.

"Want one?" He tilted the bag in her direction.

She didn't reply, and instead picked up the crumpled vending machine chip packages one at a time. "How many of these did you have?"

"Enough."

"Like a dozen?"

"Maybe." He lifted a shoulder, then leaned back in his chair and folded his arms across his chest. "What do you have against vegetables?"

A look of confusion flashed over her face.

Using exaggerated gestures, he pointed to the bags. "These are made of corn, and these are made of potatoes. Both of which are vegetables."

"I don't see any vegetables, but I do see a pig."

"Oink. Oink."

She shook her head and groaned, the struggle to conceal her amusement given away by a twitch in her cheek. At least she didn't seem angry about the dinner invitation he'd refused last night. He'd said no for two reasons. First, he'd thought it best to spend the night alone, mentally preparing himself to see Vincenzo, though looking back he didn't think any amount of preparation would have lessened the shock of seeing the gangster in the flesh. Second, he couldn't afford to do anything stupid, and being alone with Elise made him want to do lots of stupid things.

Speaking of which, he was staring at her lips.

Embarrassed, he dragged his gaze to her eyes, but it didn't matter. She'd pinned her focus on the brutes at the other end of the lounge. All enjoyment fled at the image of Elise alone in a plane with these men.

"Have you met Rocco?" She waved the man over.

Eric stood and waited. The mobsters ambled their way, and Elise made the introductions. Little did she know names weren't needed. Eric would be hard-pressed to identify three men with more ruthless reputations.

He suppressed a cringe as he shook each man's hand. "Did you enjoy your visit to Denver?"

They grunted and shrugged.

"Are you here on business? You couldn't ask for a more beautiful backdrop."

More grunts.

Rocco directed his attention to Elise. "We're ready to go."

"Get yourselves settled. We'll be there soon."

"Let me help you with that." Eric bent to take Rocco's bag, but the big man wrenched it out of reach.

Elise put a hand on his forearm. "They prefer to take care of their own luggage."

Of course they did.

The goons exited the lounge and crossed the tarmac to the plane. Elise watched them for a moment, the smile never leaving her face. The expression appeared genuine. Affectionate, even. Could she not see them for what they were? Or was there another reason for her friendliness?

"Do you need another serving of veggies before we go?"

"No, I'm good." Eric grabbed the stack of lunches and tilted his chin at the men further ahead. "What do you think of these guys?"

She responded with a not-my-problem shrug. "Most of our customers are good people. Maybe not all of them, but it's not my business." Her voice hitched, and he suspected she wasn't just talking about the Alarios. "I grew up in South Florida, flying passengers to and from the Caribbean and South America. As long as they paid, treated us well, and didn't ask us to do anything illegal, I learned not to ask questions."

He didn't necessarily agree but understood her logic. "Okay, let's get this bird in the air."

Once they got clearance from air traffic control, they were on their way. Approaching critical airspeed, he was hit by the absurdity of the situation. Here he was, locked in an aircraft with the most attractive pilot he'd ever met and four mobsters, one of whom may have killed his father.

Chapter Eight

Keeping the yoke tilted left and the rudder right, Elise eased the nose of the plane off the ground. As they ascended, she welcomed the need to concentrate on something other than the confusing man to her left. Talk about mixed signals. He'd said he couldn't get involved but wouldn't tell her why. Then, just a little while ago, she'd caught him staring at her lips like they were a popsicle on a hot summer day. Regardless, she needed to figure out a way to deal with him and the unwanted—but possibly not unrequited—feelings of desire.

A tiny prickle spread across her skin, and she itched to touch him, to run her fingers along his jaw and through his hair. But none of that was going to happen and she shouldn't waste her time thinking about it.

Maybe she just needed to get to know him. If she'd learned anything, it was that given the chance, people were sure to disappoint. "Do you see your family often?"

"It's just me and my mom, but no, I don't see her as much as I should."

"You're an only child?"

He nodded but seemed distracted. "How many siblings do you have?"

"Just the two."

"How did they handle your leaving?"

"They were ticked. Still are. Especially Nate. Because he's the oldest, he tries to control everything.

He's been that way as long as I can remember. Jack says it started when our mom left."

Funny, but she'd never considered the irony. Years of therapy spent coming to grips with her own abandonment issues, and then what does she do? Walk out on her brothers. She shook off the unpleasant insight. The last thing she wanted was to be anything like her mom.

"Jack is another brother?"

"He's in the middle. Four years older than me. Also protective, but easier to deal with than Nate." Last week's conversation with her brother came back to her. One of these days she was going to need to make things right.

They reached cruising altitude. Eric checked the fuel and noted it on the flight plan. "What are they like? Your brothers?"

She considered how to answer and decided to take the easy way out. "Nate's into poker. Jack's mostly interested in the opposite sex."

Eric's expression turned pensive. "Did running away help?"

Talk about a loaded question. She'd already been more honest with this man than she was with herself. Might as well give a real answer. "It helped in the moment, but I've realized being away has changed none of the truths about my dad."

He frowned but appeared to be considering what to say next.

"It's all good," she blurted, gripped by an overwhelming need to assure him—and herself—she was fine. "I've made friends. I can run or ride my bike to work. It doesn't hurt knowing I can go home anytime I want."

Home. For the first time in months, she missed it. Whether it was this conversation with Eric or the phone call with Jack, she didn't know, but she'd let the bad feelings fester for too long.

Tears built behind her eyelids. She blinked them away. This was not going as planned. She'd set out to get to know him, but somehow, he'd ended up quizzing her and she'd not even realized it. "Maybe we should check on our customers."

Eric slid the curtain separating the passenger area from the cockpit and called over his shoulder. "How's the temperature back there?"

Elise's gaze shifted from Eric to Mr. Alario. The man gave a thumbs up, which seemed to satisfy her colleague. He spun back to the instrument panel without closing the curtain.

She glanced at her client, hoping he didn't take offense. It had become a habit to sit and chat for a few minutes on every flight, but she sensed Eric wouldn't approve. His opinion shouldn't matter, but something about his behavior around Mr. Alario made her uneasy.

Ever since the DEA agent had come poking around their business during the week after they found her dad's plane, everyone and everything was suspect. Leaving town should have put the experience in the rearview mirror, but it didn't. If anything, it loomed larger than ever.

"I also come from a one-parent household. My dad raised us on his own. After my mom left, we moved to Florida."

Creases appeared on his forehead. "My father was a police officer. Shot in the line of duty when I was nine."

A burning sensation filled her throat and chest as she imagined the little boy he must've been. She wanted to know more. The exact opposite of what she'd hoped to accomplish when she started this conversation.

He stared at the instrument panel, his jaw clenching. She resisted the impulse to lay her hand on his and instead studied his guarded expression.

Here was a man who wouldn't give up his secrets easily. The real mystery was why she cared. And how she would feel once she learned more.

****

Eric couldn't understand the compulsion to blurt out his life story. "It happened a long time ago. I had a great childhood. I couldn't ask for a better mom."

Despite his attempt to change the mood, she gave him a sad smile.

He gripped the control wheel so tight the whites of his knuckles flickered. That night. The doorbell. Sneaking out of bed and peering from the hallway into the living room where his mother collapsed into another officer's arms.

He'd run back to his room and hid in the closet but couldn't block the voices or footsteps coming and going throughout the night.

The next morning, they'd waited for the bus, his mother's eyes puffy and filled with tears, a fake smile plastered on her face. Even though she'd not said the words, he'd known his dad was gone.

Eric glanced around the cockpit and swallowed the hard lump rising in his throat.

That night, Mom sat him on the couch after dinner—one of the many casseroles left by friends and colleagues—and explained Dad had been hurt at work and wasn't coming home.

Never once did he cry.

To this day, that dull feeling remained. His whole life, he'd avoided close relationships, instead moving through life like a ghost—always hovering on the outside, an invisible barrier separating him from others.

Elise's stare bore into him. Rather than share any more, he examined the instruments, hoping the conversation would end.

His life had changed in an instant, and all because of the man sitting in the back of the plane. *Don't get worked up. Not now.*

The dam broke and heat flooded his body, but then a calm realization settled on him.

These men were at his mercy.

He could reroute the plane. Go somewhere off the grid. Interrogate them, and finally get the answers he deserved.

It would be so easy.

He glanced at Elise. But unfair to her.

Besides, he'd taken an oath, and that meant something. Giving into impulse was never the solution. If he did that, he wouldn't be any better than the men he hated.

Beep. The fuel sensor glowed red. "The tank got filled before we left, right?"

She pressed her lips into a thin slash. "I took care of it. Why?"

He pointed to the gauge, now showing almost empty. "Have there been problems with it on other trips?"

She drew her eyebrows together, looking more perplexed than concerned.

"Leaks?"

"I did a walk-around. Everything looked fine."

He'd also inspected the aircraft and found nothing amiss. "It looked good to me too."

For weeks, he'd prepped for many scenarios, an emergency landing being one of them. This could be good. An opportunity to get close to Vincenzo.

Her brow furrowed as she worked out the issue. "Well, something's not right."

"Instrument malfunction?" Sensors went bad all the time.

She shrugged, rightfully unwilling to make a diagnosis. "We need a mechanic."

Her demeanor and experience impressed him. A lesser pilot might panic, but she remained composed. The fuel gauge failure was abnormal, but not an emergency.

"Agreed. We're going to have to land." Looking to the GPS chart, he located the nearest runway. "We've got a non-towered airport with a maintenance facility about twenty miles to the northeast."

Elise reduced power to the engines and began the descent.

He needed to get on the radio to announce their approach but wanted to inform the passengers of the situation. They had plenty of enemies, and until he saw their reaction for himself, he wasn't ruling out sabotage.

Eric twisted in his seat. Christopher and Nicky appeared to be asleep. Rocco and Vincenzo spoke in quiet voices, probably plotting whose life to ruin next.

"Hey folks," Eric said. "We need to make an unscheduled stop. A little problem with the fuel. Nothing to worry about, but it's best to make sure."

Rocco gripped the arms of his seat. His face paled. Fear. Real fear showed on his features. The big man's pupils were wide, his body alert. "How fast are we going down?"

Eric suppressed a smile. Good thing Elise was flying. If he'd been at the controls, he'd be tempted to set the plane down hard and hope the bastard shit his pants. "We'll descend a little faster than normal, but you won't notice a difference. It'll be just like any other landing."

"Where are we?" Vincenzo leaned forward and shouted over the engine. His weak voice cracked.

"Nebraska. We're landing at a small airport. Everything will be fine." Satisfied they weren't involved in the current predicament, he closed the curtain.

"We're about ten miles out," Elise said.

Once he'd found the UNICOM frequency, Eric pressed the radio button. "Albert Springs traffic King Air November six-six-two-eight Charlie is about ten to the south. We're going to enter at a forty-five for a left downwind. Runway three-two." He scanned for aircraft and listened to other pilots flying in and out of the airport.

With the runway in view, Elise turned on the landing lights. "What's the plan once we're on the ground?"

"You take the passengers. I'll find a technician to look at the plane." And remove the bug and transmitter.

Elise set the approach flaps while he checked the landing gear. They touched down with a gentle bounce. She applied reverse thrust to decelerate the plane.

His gaze snagged on the cocky smile that spread across her face. A feeling of warm admiration flooded his chest and made his heart beat faster. He'd known this assignment would test his resilience as an agent. He'd never guessed it might also test him as a man.

Chapter Nine

Elise got the passengers settled in the customer lounge, then passed out the lunches and spoke to Peter about their options for continuing on to Jersey. Now to find Eric.

The Albert Springs Municipal Airport terminal consisted of a lounge, a lobby, and a diner. There were only so many places he could be. Eager to make a decision regarding their next move, she headed over to the maintenance hangar, only to discover it closed for lunch.

She'd only known the guy for a few days, but based on his eating habits, he was probably getting food in the diner. Striding up the short sidewalk from the tarmac, she drew open the door, stepped inside, and stopped.

There he was. Elbows propped on the counter of the information desk, leaning forward, a playful smirk dancing across his lips. Her gaze shifted from Eric to the object of his attention, the female information desk employee. Elise's vision tunneled. Her feet wouldn't move.

The young woman twirled a lock of hair and smacked her gum. A black bra peeked out from the edges of her low-cut blouse.

Elise glanced at her uniform. Boring, bland, and unattractive. No wonder he hadn't given her a second glance.

No, no, no. She wasn't going there. They were colleagues. Nothing more.

And yet, she found herself frozen in place, unable to look away. Jesus, what was wrong with her? Sure, he was attractive. She'd noticed that the first time she'd seen him. And yes, he had a certain brand of charm a lot of women probably found irresistible. But she barely knew him, a fact that made her behavior even more perplexing. She didn't fall for guys she just met, especially ones who were colleagues.

What she needed was a good slap in the face, something to knock some sense into her stupid brain. She should have put up a bigger fight, tried harder to get out of working with him.

Oh, who was she kidding? None of this had anything to do with Eric. It was that damned phone call with Jack. He'd gotten in her head, made her question her decisions, and now she found herself drawn to a guy who was the polar opposite of her bossy brothers.

Eric and his new friend hadn't seen her come in. Maybe she could leave the same way. She'd slip around the outside of the building, enter through the front, then sneak back into the lounge. He'd never know she'd been there. Or how she reacted when she saw him with another woman.

Gently, she leaned her back into the door to open it. Propeller noises carried by the wind drifted into the entry. *Dammit.* They both looked. Eric's gaze found hers. He straightened and motioned her over. She shuffled forward with heavy feet and steeled herself for the dreaded introduction.

He rested his hand on her shoulder and a jolt zinged through her, stealing her breath. "Elise is the better half of our team." He directed his attention to the other woman. "Bethany works here part time while taking classes at the junior college."

Elise shook the woman's hand, trying to appear unbothered by both the situation and her reaction to it.

"Bethany says the diner has the best pork tenderloin sandwich in the state. Apparently, in Nebraska, that's saying something." He winked at his new companion.

Elise wanted to barf. "You didn't get enough potato chips?"

He flashed one of those smiles that made her knees weak. "There are three other food groups."

Bethany's body drifted closer to Eric. He didn't seem to notice, but Elise saw it for what it was. The woman was staking her claim. Good luck with that. They weren't going to be here for more than a few hours. Less if Elise had anything to say about it.

Ignoring Bethany, she leaned against the desk and looked up at her coworker. "Were you able to talk to the mechanic?"

Eric guided Elise to the side and out of earshot. "He said the fuel sensor went bad. He fixed it, but in the process found a problem with our avionics. They have to order the parts. The plane won't be ready until tomorrow—at the earliest."

Getting stuck with Eric in Nowhere, Nebraska was the last thing she wanted. The more time she spent with him, the more confused she became. They needed to get out of here, stay on schedule. "Peter says he'll pay to put the clients on a different charter or we can wait for him to send another plane, but I think we need to ask the passengers if they have a preference."

"Let's go talk to them." He flashed another

megawatt smile.

Elise scowled and followed him into the lounge. Mr. Alario stood in the corner talking on the phone and gazing out the window. Rocco and his friends lounged in the club chairs, eating their lunches, and watching a home improvement show. It seemed a strange choice, but who was she to judge?

The easiest way to handle this would be to get everyone's attention and lay out the options. She took a breath, eager to be able to take the lead on something, to prove she was still a professional, and show that her reaction to the scene in the lobby was a one-time occurrence.

"Here's the situation." Eric's voice boomed across the small room, and five sets of eyes shot to look at him. Hers included.

The little spot above her left eyebrow throbbed. She'd been flying these people across the country for the last few months. They were her clients. She should be the one to explain the choices.

Eric scanned the room, no doubt confirming he had everyone's attention. "The plane needs a part, but it has to be ordered, which means we're grounded for the time being."

She stepped aside to fume but paused. There was something mildly aggressive about the way he spoke to the passengers. The strangest sensation that he hadn't been completely forthright with her worked its way out of her gut.

"You have two options—continue on a different Rocky Mountain Charter flight or we can try to get you on an aircraft operating out of this airport."

Rocco wiped his mouth with a napkin. "How long

will it take to get another plane?"

"Best guess? A few hours."

Nicky stood and stretched. "When do we leave if we go with another company?"

Eric frowned. "We still need to check availability. I'm not sure who's operating right now."

Mr. Alario stepped closer. "If we decide to wait, who will be our pilot?"

They hadn't talked about it, but it didn't matter because Eric spoke before she'd had a chance to consider the possibilities. "One of our other pilots will fly here. He and I will continue to the final destination while the first officer waits for the repair."

The old man shook his head, his expression tight. "If it's all the same, I think I'd prefer to fly with the first officer."

Relief and gratitude filled her. Perhaps she wasn't so irrelevant after all. Eric pursed his lips and gave her a look that said he had no intention of being the one left behind. She ignored the pang of hurt feelings and focused on Mr. Alario. "I appreciate that, sir, but it's Captain Erickson's command. I'll stay here and fly back to Denver when the plane is ready."

Mr. Alario focused his attention solely on Elise. "Where will you stay?"

She shrugged. "Probably a local motel."

"Are those our only options? Wait for a plane or go with another carrier?"

Again, Eric didn't give her a chance to speak. "Yes, aside from spending the night and continuing with the original plane."

She drew back, surprised. Was he for real? She couldn't think of a single reason to linger here any longer than necessary.

Mr. Alario gave a crisp nod. "Then that's what we'll do too."

Rocco's head whipped up. "Hey, Pop, I'd rather be on a plane that doesn't have problems."

Mr. Alario shot his son a hard look, then returned his attention to Elise. "Considering the emergency landing, I'd rather stick with a pilot I know and trust." He rotated his gaze to Eric. "No offense, Captain."

"Guess we're all staying." Eric relaxed his stance. "We'll call the company and tell them not to send a plane. We'll wait out the repair."

Mr. Alario nodded to his son and the other two men. "Go get the bags."

A chorus of unhappy grunts filled the room as the men started to stand. Elise held up her hand. "I know you like to handle your own luggage, but as passengers, you're not authorized to enter the maintenance hangar. Captain Erickson and I will get the bags." Tamping down her annoyance, she focused on Eric. "We'll need to check with Peter, make sure he's okay with this."

He clasped his hands behind his back. "You take care of that. I'll get the scoop on lodging and transportation."

She sucked in a quick breath. One night in a motel. Maybe two. No big deal. She could handle that.

****

A four-hour flight had just turned into an overnighter, and Eric intended to make the most of it. His heart raced, his muscles tingled, and there was a happy heat in his chest. It was finally happening. He was going to get Vincenzo Alario.

Slow down. Think.

There had to be a common denominator. Why would Vincenzo rather spend the night in this podunk town than catch a flight home? Eric clutched the transmitter in his pocket. He'd snagged it from the plane while waiting to talk to the mechanic. Maybe it held a clue.

He leaned on the information desk and waited for Bethany to return. Elise's face when she found him talking to the young woman had sent delight coursing through his body. The situation had been totally innocent, but he'd seen jealousy sketched all over her features.

He thrust the thought aside. It didn't matter. If the situation were different, who knows what might happen. But some things just weren't meant to be. Still, Fate had played a cruel trick, putting both Vincenzo and Elise within reach at the same time.

He'd discarded the idea she might be connected to the mobster. But what if he was wrong? Vincenzo's unusual attachment. His insistence on staying in Nebraska. His unknown reason for using this airline.

Eric's stomach sloshed as if churned by the blades of a propeller. She wasn't involved. Couldn't be. There would have been signs. Looks. Signals. Something.

So why the nagging feeling there was a connection?

Bethany rounded the corner, a broad smile spread across her face. Sauntering behind the counter, she batted her eyes. "What can I do for you?"

Words stuck in his throat, and he fidgeted, not wanting Elise to stumble upon them and get the wrong idea. "Looks like we're going to be here for another day or so. I'm looking for some hotel recommendations."

She chuckled. "You're in luck. I know just the place."

Eric returned to the lounge with the low-down on lodgings and a promise from Bethany to arrange transportation. What awaited him made his hands curl into fists. Elise sat on the couch, socializing with the number two man in the Alario crime family. Surely, she had better taste than that. Rocco angled his body toward Elise, and heat sliced through Eric like a lightning bolt.

She couldn't possibly find that Neanderthal likeable. Her wide smile and laugh said otherwise. A pang of jealousy stabbed Eric in the chest. She should be looking at him like that.

He tilted his head back and looked at the ceiling. Thoughts like that needed to be put in a cage. Still, he didn't have to like watching his copilot joke around with a guy whose picture belonged in the post office. He watched for a few more moments, then slowed his breathing and unclenched his fists. "Here's the deal." His voice thundered through the space.

Everything stopped. One of Rocco's thugs muted the television.

"The good news is that the airport has a courtesy car and we have rooms for the night. The bad news is the car is in the shop and there's only one motel in town." He scanned the group of curious faces until his gaze landed on Elise. "Luckily, the desk clerk made us reservations for the night and has arranged for a friend to pick us up."

She stood to address the group. "Captain Erickson and I will get your luggage and wait for the ride. We'll let you know when it's here."

Dammit. There went his opportunity to strike up a conversation with Vincenzo. But maybe he could still get a look at their bags. "I don't mind taking care of the luggage."

"There's too much for one person to manage."

"I'll do two trips. Burn off the extra chips."

"It'll go faster if we're both there." Her voice was clipped. End of discussion.

Defeated, he trailed Elise out the back door of the terminal and onto a short sidewalk leading to the tarmac. They weaved between aircraft and across the ramp to a hangar where their King Air sat parked in a back corner. She climbed straight into the plane without giving him a second glance.

He waited for her to hand down the bags. Taking the luggage—two suitcases and one duffel, he couldn't miss her frown. "Did I do something?"

"More like what you didn't do." She returned to the luggage compartment without explaining, then reappeared with another suitcase.

"You're going to have to be more specific."

Her expression hardened. "I didn't like the way you treated me back in the lounge."

What was she talking about?

"Did it ever occur to you that you should have consulted me before giving the passengers the options? Or when you decided you'd be the one to fly to Jersey while I waited for the repair? And maybe I wanted to be the one to explain the situation." She poked herself in the chest. "I'm the one they know. I'm the one they trust."

Shit. She was right. He'd been so focused on Vincenzo, he'd not considered how he should have acted. "I'm sorry, but I promise, ignoring you wasn't my intention. Next time we'll decide together what we want to say and who's going to say it."

Her body relaxed like a sailplane just released from its tow. "I get frustrated when things don't go as planned." She twisted a lock of hair. "That's on me."

"Seems to me you're doing fine."

She waved her hand and looked away. "It got worse when my dad died, and I just wanted things to go back to the way they were before."

There was an emotional charge to her words. He wasn't sure what to say but suspected she'd prefer a change of topic to any platitudes he might offer. He opened his mouth to speak, but she cut him off. "So, what's with you and the desk clerk?"

Not the direction he'd expected her to take the conversation. "What do you mean? There's nothing going on with Bethany."

Elise grunted, raised her brows, and looked decidedly unimpressed.

"She got us a ride, didn't she?"

"Remains to be seen." She handed him another suitcase. "I mean, it's not like you're going to start up a relationship while you're here. I'm curious what you get out of it."

His cheeks burned. He suddenly needed her to know he wasn't that guy. "I didn't get anything out of it, and I didn't lead her on."

She said nothing, simply waited for him to continue.

"Maybe she's just a nice person. Sometimes people do nice things for other people, even ones they don't know."

"So, you manipulated her?"

"What? No." He shifted. He hadn't, had he? "Of course not."

"You don't look so sure." Her eyes narrowed. She handed him the last of the passenger bags. "Have you tried to manipulate me?"

"I would never—"

Leaning out of the plane, she stared down at him. "So, I don't have anything you want?"

He opened and closed his mouth, but no sound emerged. Was she screwing with him? She smirked, then disappeared into the plane while he stood mimicking a goldfish.

When she reappeared, she had two bags slung over her shoulder. "I grabbed your overnight bag." She tossed his to the ground, then folded up the stairs, closed the aircraft door, and grabbed a suitcase.

Eric picked up his bag and the duffle, heaving one over each shoulder, then took a suitcase handle in each hand and followed her through the terminal to the front entrance. He set the bags on the sidewalk and tried not to stare at his perplexing copilot. Most people wouldn't have the audacity to question him like that. He admired her frankness and her honesty.

"Oh my God. I hope that's it." She clapped her hands and let out a delighted laugh. "This is too perfect."

He followed her gaze to the end of the parking lot where a big, yellow school bus rolled their way. *Please, no.*

Her smile was both beautiful and annoying. "And I was worried we wouldn't fit. Bethany really came through."

The bus continued its steady approach, brakes screeching as it stopped in front of them. The door flung open. The driver leaned forward. "You Eric?"

****

Bethany's cousin, Yolanda, drove the bus. One of three bus drivers in the school district, she'd just finished her afternoon route. The plump woman had a friendly face and a loud laugh. Elise liked her immediately and took a seat near the front.

She'd hoped proximity to their boisterous chauffeur might keep her mind off Eric. Unfortunately, after hearing the story about his dad, he'd taken up permanent residence in her brain, ignoring all attempts at eviction. She gritted her teeth. If his attitude in the lounge with the customers hadn't kicked him to the curb, she feared nothing would.

Soft country music played on the radio. The gentle breeze of the fan mounted above the windshield caressed her face and hair. Elise leaned her back against the metal wall. It had been a long time since she'd ridden a school bus. The seats were harder and narrower than she remembered. She ran her fingers over a patch on the vinyl cushion and stole a glance at Eric.

His behavior since they left the airport had been curious. When they boarded, he'd been his usual charming self, calling Yolanda his hero and making her blush. Now, sitting a couple of rows back with his legs stretched into the aisle, he'd grown quiet.

She'd enjoyed giving him a hard time about the bus but couldn't deny everything had worked out for the best. Even Vincenzo seemed appreciative. He and his companions took seats near the back.

If only she had some sort of guide for understanding this man, so unlike any she'd ever met. He somehow managed to be commanding, arrogant, vulnerable, and kind all at once. He was a puzzle—a sexy and intriguing puzzle.

One she shouldn't be trying to solve.

And yet, she couldn't help herself. Like an archaeologist excavating a site, she wanted to dig—a little at a time, until she uncovered the truth.

There was something about him. Several things, actually. The way the right side of his mouth ticked up at the corner when he was about to say something snarky. Or the raise of his eyebrow when she did or said something that amused him. And then there were all his enticing physical attributes—

She gave herself a hard shake, willing the needless thoughts to crash to the ground like apples from a tree. It didn't matter how attracted she was to him or the fact he'd revived her dead-and-buried libido. He'd already said he couldn't get involved. She needed to remember that.

He rubbed his chin and jaw. If only she knew what had him worried, maybe she could help. Earlier, he'd seemed happy to stay overnight in a motel. Was he second guessing the decision?

Yolanda drew Elise's attention away from Eric. "A natural spring a few miles outside of town is what attracted settlers to the spot. The population has gone up and down over the years. These days we have about two thousand residents. That includes outlying areas not technically within town limits."

Endless farmland sped past the window. "Have you always lived here?"

Yolanda beamed. "Yep. Born and bred. It's small, but a good place to grow up."

"Sounds nice." Elise's gaze drifted to Eric again. The sunlight caught his hair, and she itched to comb through it, skimming her fingertips against the short bristles on the back of his head.

"Of course, we're missing a lot of the variety you get in the city, but we've got the basics—a couple of restaurants, a hardware store, a supermarket. The Wal-Mart went in a couple of years back."

They must have entered the Albert Springs city limits. Small houses with chain-link fences lined the road and continued for a few blocks down side streets. The condition of the homes varied. Perfectly manicured lawns and freshly painted houses sat next to yards of dandelions, busted porches, and car bodies.

An intersection marked the abrupt change in scenery. Retail replaced residential. On both sides of the road were shops—the old-town kind, built next to each other, but with different facades. An ornate red brick building and clock tower presided over the end of the street.

"Here's downtown." Yolanda motioned to the businesses, then pointed to the building at the end of the street and its expanse of dark, green grass. "That's our city hall and city park, where community events take place."

Elise took in the quaintness and the small-town aura. It reminded her of a cozy mystery series she enjoyed. "It's wonderful."

"If you're around tomorrow night, the Corn Festival is starting. It's the biggest event of the year."

It would be nice to stay, to take some time to drink in the charming town and its people, but this wasn't a vacation. "We'll probably be gone by then."

At the stop sign in front of city hall, Yolanda turned right. In another block and a half, she took a left at the big, yellow Hidey Hole Motel sign. "Here we are." The bus stopped in the gravel lot.

The navy and white, one-story motel was set against a thicket of trees. Ropes and buoys hung on the wall, although Elise couldn't remember seeing any bodies of water on the approach. Other than an old, but immaculate pickup parked next to the office, the parking lot contained a single car. *Vacancy* flashed from the lobby window.

Eric hoisted himself from his seat, lifted his bag to his shoulder and announced he'd be back. She watched through the window, noting the way his pants squeezed his ass all the way from the bus until he disappeared into the office.

"Whew." Yolanda whistled and stared at Elise from her giant rearview mirror. "You two got it bad."

"Excuse me?" Elise's attention snapped to the woman in the driver's seat.

"The amount of effort you spend looking at each other while trying not to be seen would wear me out. Why not just tell him how you feel?"

Elise's mouth opened, then closed. "I only just met him. We're coworkers. Nothing else.'

"Uh huh." Yolanda clearly wasn't buying Elise's denial. "If it helps, he's into you. too."

The comment caught her attention, and Elise wanted to ask more, but really, this woman had a lot of nerve. And she couldn't have been more off base. "There's nothing going on."

"I get a feeling about these things. Give it some time."

Elise crossed her arms and stared out the window. Yolanda didn't know what she was talking about. She and Eric could enjoy one another's company, but that was as far as it would go.

"Men are a dime a dozen. I should know, I've got three ex-husbands." Yolanda leveled a sage look at Elise.

"Go after that one. A sweetie *and* a looker? Those kind don't come around every day."

Elise stood. "I'm going to unload the bags."

If she sat here listening to Yolanda's pronouncements long enough, she might start to believe them. A few days ago, she'd been satisfied to grow old alone and become one of those women with too many cats. Now her brain was filled with thoughts of strong arms and a warm body, and that wasn't going to get her anything besides a broken heart.

Chapter Ten

Eric stared at the six keys.

The motel owner tugged his bushy, white beard. "I've got three available rooms in front and three around back."

Knowing half of the group would be on the back side of a motel butting up against the woods didn't sit well. It made surveillance much more difficult and room distribution that much more important.

"How does the numbering work?"

"First door outside here is one, and it goes sequentially. Around the corner starts with six. The last room is number ten."

Eric sighed. With this being the only lodge in town, it wasn't like he'd had a choice. Tactically, the front worked best for him. He could keep tabs on cars coming and going, while also keeping an eye on Vincenzo. And he wanted Elise close—for her own safety, of course.

He took a deep breath to quiet the roar of worries filling his mind and decided Rocco and his goons would get the rooms in the back. He scooped up the keys and nodded.

No bus awaited him when he exited the office. Instead, Elise and the four men stood on the gravel drive with their luggage at their feet. "Yolanda couldn't wait around. She needed to pick up her granddaughter from daycare," Elise explained. "She said she'd give us a ride back to the airport when we're ready."

Pocketing the key for room number two, he distributed the others. To Elise, he gave number one. To the mobster, he handed number five. This would put her next to the office and farther from Vincenzo. He distributed the other keys, placing Rocco in the room directly behind his own. Everyone grabbed their bags and headed to their quarters.

Eric watched them go, then unlocked and entered his own. Stale, hot air that smelled of musty blankets assaulted him upon entering the small, tired-looking motel room. He stepped past the single queen-sized bed, ignoring the door beside the nightstand, and set the thermostat at sixty-eight degrees. The air conditioner rattled and clanked before settling into a loud whirr.

He needed to get his bearings, regroup, and come up with a plan to engage Vincenzo.

Then his gaze fell to the first thing he'd seen when he flipped on the light, the thing he'd avoided looking at since he entered. *The adjoining door*. The old man hadn't said anything about connecting rooms. On the other side, she could be showering. Naked. Lathered with soap.

Footsteps carried from her room to his, the sound drawing his attention as if she were the object of his surveillance. He strained to listen. There were real criminals here. They needed to be his focus, not the woman next door. And yet, he sat still, hoping to hear more.

The bed in the other room creaked, the effect like a jolt of electricity. The image of Elise stretched out beside him almost had him knocking on her door, but he detonated the thought in a puff of smoke.

He sat on the bed and dropped his face into his

hands. The job should have been easy recon, but his body betrayed him. High stress situational training had been drilled into him both in the Air Force and the FBI. And yet, he'd felt disconcerted all day. Mobsters he could handle. Adorable copilots he could not.

Opportunities like this didn't come along often. Blow it, and it would be goodbye career. Undercover work already came fraught with risk. He knew that but couldn't seem to corral his shameless emotions.

He'd spent two months prepping for this assignment, and it hadn't been enough. Hell, who was he kidding? He'd had more than two decades to prepare. Maybe that was the problem. A lifetime devoted to the pursuit of one man.

The lack of progress was maddening. Despite physical nearness, he'd not learned anything about Vincenzo's business in Colorado. On the bus, he'd strained to hear the hushed conversation, but it was impossible. The men were up to something, and he couldn't imagine what their plans had to do with spending the night in this tiny-ass town.

Digging into his pocket, he fished out his change and piled it on the bedside table, noting the coin-operated machine bolted to the nightstand. Again, he found his gaze going to the door to the adjoining room. Elise.

To say she'd become a complication would be an understatement. Throwing out mixed signals hadn't been his intention. And yet, he couldn't stop himself. Riding to the motel, he tried to ignore her, but found his gaze drawn back to her time and time again.

Unsure what else he could do, he called Grant to explain the situation. Expecting the walls to be thin, he spoke quickly, quietly. "I got the bug, but monitoring

Vincenzo and Rocco from this location will be a challenge."

The case agent grunted. "Remember, we're playing the long game. It's not going to happen in one night."

"I know. Would've been nice to have something new to report."

"It'll happen. Relax."

Eric took a deep breath. Or rather, he tried to. His chest might as well have been gripped in a vise. "I've been thinking about your theory that Elise is involved in whatever is going on, and I'm not buying it. Vincenzo has a definite interest in her—there's something not quite right about the way he's always trying to be near her, but I don't think she knows anything."

A disappointed sigh sounded on the other end of the line. "I'll run the whole family through the federal database and get back to you." He disconnected.

That damned door beckoned. Eric stood and paced. *Focus on the case, not the woman in the next room.* At the window, he parted the thick curtains. Vincenzo and his men strode across the parking lot toward the diner next door.

When opportunity knocks…follow the gangsters to dinner.

Knowing it would look more realistic if he didn't walk in on his own, he again found himself staring at the connecting door. Coworkers would share a meal. It would help his cover.

If only he could convince himself that was all there was to it.

The Glock still strapped to his ankle, he dug out the transmitter and bug and put them in his bag. Then, he grabbed his wallet, room key and phone, stepped outside and journeyed the six-feet-or-so to Elise's room. *It's now or never.* He rapped his knuckles against the wood.

She opened the door, now wearing jeans, a gray t-shirt, her classic red basketball shoes, and a pink hoodie. Her hair was wet, and his earlier thoughts of her showering came roaring back to him. His stupid body dared him to touch her. Instead, he clasped his hands behind his back.

Her expression softened and delight flashed in her eyes. "What's up?"

"I noticed you didn't eat lunch. I thought you might be hungry." He motioned over his shoulder. "There's a diner next door."

For a long moment, she didn't speak. His muscles twitched, his mouth became the Sahara Desert, and a nervous ripple roiled his stomach. Another mistake. She didn't want to have dinner with him. Why would she? He never should have asked.

And then she spoke. "Based on your eating habits, I'm surprised you're not dining at the gas station."

His posture relaxed. He sagged into the door frame and gave her a long, slow grin. "A man needs more than just potato chips."

****

He winked, and Elise's knees went wobbly. Just looking at him made her pelvic muscles contract. What would he be like as a lover, pushing her onto the bed, pressing his hard body into hers? *Shit*. Okay, so maybe her sex drive wasn't DOA after all. Fantastic. But geez, this wasn't the time, the place, or the person. And yet, something about the way Eric slouched against that door frame, watching her with a mischievous smile, made her think he wasn't nearly as relaxed as he appeared. What were the chances he was experiencing a similar struggle?

She gave her brain a mental slap. He'd given her no reason to think he was interested—in fact, he'd even said the dreaded words, "It's complicated." She shouldn't read too much into anything he said or did. He was just a regular, incredibly handsome, somewhat obnoxious guy. As long as she could remember that and treat him like any other colleague, everything would be fine. She took a deep breath and somehow managed to make her voice casual. "I could eat."

He shouldered himself from the door jamb. "Let's go."

The restaurant looked like most diners. Shaped like an L, booths lined the outer wall. A spattering of customers sat on round stools at the long and narrow linoleum counter. The aroma of fried onions greeted them when they entered. According to the chalkboard affixed above the kitchen pass-through, the restaurant served breakfast all day. The sign in the foyer said to seat themselves.

With plenty of options in the almost empty diner, Elise headed toward the second table from the door. Eric's hand flattened against the small of her back. "Let's go further down."

He removed his hand, but the imprint of his touch pulsed with a warm, heavy awareness. Her stomach rolled. She'd eaten only a small breakfast and nothing since. That *had* to be it. But did a calorie deficit explain her elevated heart rate too? She followed him deeper into the restaurant.

"Be right with you." Dressed in a retro blue uniform, the waitress carried a pot of coffee and approached Vincenzo and the other men only two booths from theirs.

Rather than take a seat on the teal-colored bench, Elise swerved. "I'll be right back. I'm going to say hi."

The tension in Eric's jaw was so slight most wouldn't have caught it, but Elise had started to learn his tells. When her brother Nate taught her to play poker, he'd schooled her in the art of reading faces, and Eric's expression had a lot to say.

Nearing the group, she noticed how they huddled together, faces tight, and realized they were in the midst of a serious discussion. Oh God. Intruding hadn't been her intention. She should have just sat down and dealt with her nerves about Eric.

"Hi, Elise," Nicky said with his nasal New York accent.

Christopher gave a toothy smile, but a look passed among the two men. Goosebumps prickled up her neck in warning.

Mr. Alario twisted in his seat. "Are you eating alone?"

She motioned toward Eric sitting two booths away. "I'm here with Captain Erickson."

The man held Eric's stare for a long moment, then looked at Elise. "I get a feeling about people, and there's something about him that rubs me wrong." He gave a decisive nod. "You can do better."

For some reason, Rocco decided to chime in. "Looks like a use-'em-and-lose-'em type if you ask me."

She bit her lip. Her face grew hot. "We're just coworkers."

"If you say so." Vincenzo's lips wrapped around his straw and slurped his soda down to the ice.

An uncomfortable silence settled on the group, and it seemed like a good time to bail on the conversation. "I didn't mean to disturb you. I'll let you know if I hear anything about the plane. Enjoy your dinner." She returned to the booth and slid in across from Eric, a slight whoosh of air escaping as she settled on the stiff cushion.

"How'd it go?" He picked up his iced tea and nodded at the glass of water in front of her. "I didn't want to order for you."

"Water is fine." With a slight shrug, she took a sip and went back to his question. She wasn't about to tell him what they'd said about him and her. "It was weird."

"How so?"

She didn't know how to put it into words. Would she sound strange if she said it just didn't feel right? "It felt like I interrupted something."

"Did you hear what they were talking about?"

She picked up the menu insert with the daily specials and shook her head. "No, just a feeling. I'm sure it was nothing. Probably my imagination."

He leaned to the side, looking over her shoulder at the men. His eyes narrowed.

Could he be any more obvious? "What is wrong with you?" She swatted at him. "Stop that."

He raised a brow as though he'd seen something unexpected. Curiosity got the best of her. She leaned forward. "What are they doing?"

"They just got their food." His voice was a whisper, his tone conspiratorial.

Her face flushed. "You don't have to be a smart ass."

"I don't *have* to be—" He laughed.

That smile of his would be her undoing. She didn't know if she wanted to smack him or kiss him. Unwrapping her knife and fork, she spread the napkin on her lap. "Does that smirk ever get you in trouble?"

"All the time." He touched a finger to his nose. "Where do you think I got this?"

She leaned forward, then to the side, studying his perfect profile. After a moment, she spotted an almost imperceptible bulge. "And?"

"High school. Broken nose." His finger moved in languid circles over the bump. His eyes brightened. "Jeremy White told me he was going to wipe the smile off my face once and for all."

"You probably deserved it." She gave a pointed look. "What did you do to piss him off?"

"Don't quite remember. Something about a girl."

She snorted.

The waitress approached. "I see you've found the daily deals." She nodded to the grease-stained card in Elise's hand. "What'll it be?"

Elise pointed to the evening special—meatloaf, mashed potatoes, and green bean casserole. Eric ordered a burger and fries.

Their server stepped behind the counter, clipped their order onto a rack at the kitchen window and gave it a spin.

"So, you got your ass kicked and your nose broken. Did anything change?" She ran her finger over a chip in the table veneer, grateful he'd given her a reason to openly stare at his handsome face.

"Who said I got my ass kicked?"

"Look at that massive deformity on your nose. What other conclusion is there?"

He grinned again. "I realized I loved the rush and started looking for fights. I begged my mom for boxing lessons, but she said no. Eventually, I found my way to underground fighting."

Her mouth dropped. "Like a fight club?"

"Kind of. Just a bunch of random people with a shared interest."

"A shared interest in hitting one another?" Filled with a mixture of revulsion and fascination, she stared. "People do that? For fun?"

"That's why I did it. Some were in it for the money. Illegal betting is surprisingly sophisticated."

"I wouldn't know. My brother Nate's poker habit and nickel slots are my only references." A scar above his eyebrow drew her attention, as did the ones on the knuckles of his right hand. He gave his nose a self-conscious rub.

"Is that when you started boxing?"

"Yeah. My mom gave in and bought me a gym membership."

The aroma of fried food wafted their way, and the waitress placed two steaming plates in front of them. Maybe now they could both stuff their faces and stop talking. An uncomfortable realization threatened to zap her appetite. The more he spoke, the more she liked him. If she had a checklist, he'd be ticking off almost every box. Funny? Check. Interesting? Check. Easy to talk to? Check. Attractive? Her face warmed. Check.

Eric squirted ketchup onto his burger and on the plate next to his fries. "What about you? What are your passions? Other than apartment consultations, of course."

She swallowed a bit of meatloaf. "You mean besides flying?"

"Yeah. You must have other interests."

"I shoot archery. I used to compete."

His eyes twinkled, smiling at her from behind the burger. There was that feeling again. Months without a tingle of attraction, and now out of nowhere, her body was reacting to even the most mundane of gestures. What was it about this guy?

"No kidding. Recurve?"

She shook her head. "Compound."

"I've shot firearms," he said. "But never a bow."

"My experience with guns is limited, but there are some similarities."

He tilted his head and chewed. "What got you into archery?"

Heat crept up her neck. He would have to ask that. "My brother Nate and I watched the movie Robin Hood—the one with Kevin Costner. I became obsessed with the flaming arrow." His grin encouraged her to continue. "I pestered him enough he bought me a cheap recurve bow and took me to a local park with a range. I kept practicing, found a coach, and switched to compound."

"Did you ever get to shoot a flaming arrow?"

"I did. Got into quite a bit of trouble for it, too." She laughed. "Not as much as Nate, though. As the oldest, he was expected to know better."

"Sounds like a good brother." He sipped his tea.

She nodded. "He is. I forget sometimes because he's such a control freak. It's one of the reasons I left home, to prove I can make it on my own."

"What are the other ones?"

"Other what?" She picked at the cracked veneer. This wasn't a topic she wanted to talk about. How long could she pretend she didn't understand his question?

"Reasons you left home."

She didn't talk to anyone about her dad's death or how she felt afterward, but something about Eric made her think she could trust him. "My dad did some bad stuff. We learned about it after he died. My brothers basically shrugged their shoulders and moved on. It wasn't as easy for me."

He didn't say anything, but the sympathetic look on his face encouraged her to keep going.

"I was just so fixated on him not being the person I thought he was. And Nate and Jack were so indifferent. I couldn't stand being around them and thought leaving might give me some perspective."

He tilted his head, leaned forward, and offered a sad smile. *Crap.* She didn't want his sympathy.

"Everyone is different. You can't compare yourself to your brothers. Just be you. You're perfect, just the way you are."

Unable to break eye contact, she sucked in a breath. Her melting heart spread warmth through her chest.

A shadow fell over the end of the table.

"I wanted to thank you both for your willingness to humor an old man." Mr. Alario patted Elise on the back and extended a hand toward her coworker. "I know keeping us here wasn't ideal."

"It's our pleasure." Eric took the man's hand. "Please let us know if you need anything."

Mr. Alario waved the comment away, his face pleasant and warm. "I can't speak for these boys, but today has held more excitement than I'm used to. I think I'll watch some television and turn in." He gave a slight nod, and with a wink at Elise, joined Rocco and the other men waiting by the door. "Goodnight to you both."

Elise followed Eric's scowl out the window. He'd

seemed at ease talking to the older man, but she sensed his dislike. The men crossed the parking lot. Mr. Alario disappeared into his room and the others around the back of the motel.

Now they were alone. Her stomach fluttered like an anxious butterfly. Too wound up to go back to her room, knowing Eric would be on the other side of that door, she offered an alternative. "How do you feel about dessert?"

One side of his mouth quirked up. "Let's get some pie to go."

Chapter Eleven

The tiny hotel towel barely wrapped around Eric's waist. It fell to the floor as he dug through his bag for a pair of boxer briefs. After wearing that thick, stifling uniform for hours, the cold shower and clean clothes felt like heaven.

A strange sense of anticipation settled over him. The way his nerves bounced around like a pinball, he might have been a teenager getting ready for his first date. Only this time he wasn't an awkward sixteen-year-old kid hoping to make it to first base. No, he was a grown man with a job to do. And a mob boss three doors down.

But, like Grant said, they weren't going to figure it out in one night. The investigation could go on for months, and that meant he needed to learn to deal with his feelings for Elise. Ignoring the attraction hadn't worked. If anything, it only intensified the temptation.

He rifled through his bag. The khakis and Rocky Mountain Charters polo had been meant for the flight back when it would be just him and Elise, but since his standard uniform had failed the smells-clean test, those were going to get called into service sooner than planned. Besides, work clothes seemed too formal. He yanked out an old T-shirt and tossed it on the bed. Stepping into a pair of jeans, he savored the feel of well-worn denim. His attention wandered to the adjoining door. She knew he wanted to shower, and he'd said to give him ten minutes.

He stepped forward, unlocked the door on his side and opened it a crack. Hers was still shut tight.

He bent, retrieved the towel, and dried his hair. A swipe of deodorant. The smell of soap. He glanced in the mirror. Not bad. Certainly presentable enough for a piece of pie.

Why did he even care? Nothing was going to happen. It couldn't.

Resetting, he closed his eyes. At least Vincenzo had turned in. One less thing for him to worry about.

God, how he hoped she wasn't messed up with whatever was going on with Vincenzo and the airline. Other than a wink at the diner, there'd been no signs she had any relationship with the gangster beyond that of pilot and passenger, but she clouded his judgment. What if he saw only what he wanted to see?

Truth be told, at dinner, he'd wanted to drag her into the most secluded corner where they could be alone, and he almost did, but at the last second, regained his wits and steered her to a table close to where the gangsters sat. Not that it mattered. He still didn't have even the tiniest hint of what they were up to.

And when Elise had wanted to talk to them? He'd thought he might lose his mind.

At least he had the bug. When they got back to Denver, the computer forensics team would take possession. If they were lucky, there'd be something that might give his surveillance direction.

By the time they returned to the motel, his thoughts had swirled—almost every one about Elise. Kissing her. Pressing into her. Those provocative lips and how they looked when she smiled, the sparkle in her eyes when she laughed.

He wanted her. More than he should. More than he cared to admit.

Jesus. This had to stop.

He knew what he needed to do. Distance himself from the temptation next door. Give her the pie and send her on her way.

He'd raided drug dens and tracked killers. Avoiding one female couldn't be that difficult.

A quiet knock and the soft creak of the door startled him. He shoved his gun and ankle holster under the wad of dirty clothing on the table.

And then he saw her and knew. He was fucked.

****

The door swung wider than Elise had intended. Eric whirled in her direction. Transfixed, she froze in place. His bare chest drew her attention to a V-shaped torso and the ripple of hard muscle on his abdomen. Her inspection traveled to broad shoulders, strong arms and back down to where the waistband of his underwear was visible above the jeans that sat on his hips. He really did look like an underwear model.

She swallowed and entered. His gaze bore into hers, daring her to speak. "I didn't mean to barge in."

He smiled but hesitated as he reached for a shirt. Sinew stretched as he slid the T-shirt over his head and pulled it to his waist. "Ready for pie?"

She took a seat on the bed. He handed her a small Styrofoam box and plastic fork, then sat in the chair next to the tiny table. His gaze burned into her as she considered the red, gooey mess of cherry pie. Mindful of being watched, she stabbed it with her fork and withdrew a heaping pile of crust, fruit, and syrup, then moaned as the glob of sweetness hit her tongue.

The way he stared made her feel as naked as if she'd stripped off all her clothes. "Sorry. I forget my manners when pie is involved." She took another bite, then several more. "Aren't you going to eat? I've been waiting for a verdict on whether you can get decent Key lime pie in Nebraska."

He opened his container. "You grew up in the Keys. What makes the Key lime so special?"

"I wouldn't know. Real Key limes aren't even grown in Florida anymore."

When he took a bite, his lips closed around the fork and slid from his mouth.

"It's good." He held out his container. "Want to taste?"

Dear God, yes. She shook her head. "I think it would be too sour after the cherry."

They finished eating in silence.

Eric rose and took her container, which he crammed into the small garbage can beside the dresser.

"What's it like living in the Keys? Is it all flip-flops and beach bums?" He returned to his chair and leaned forward. "Is every day a Jimmy Buffett song?"

She couldn't control the bitterness creeping from her stomach into her throat. "I don't know, did Jimmy Buffett write one about drug-running dads?"

Her pulsing heart beat like a jackhammer in her ears. What was wrong with her? Wincing, she crammed her hands into the pockets of her jeans.

Why were these feelings coming out now? And with him?

He leaned forward, elbows on thighs, hands clasped, waiting.

Her muscles tensed, and for a moment she wanted

to be anywhere else. "There are some issues I need to deal with."

"Want to talk about it?"

"Not really." She studied him. He looked sincere. "But maybe I should."

"I'm happy to listen."

Her chest compressed with the need to get it out. Strange. She'd held it in for months, but now it wanted to explode out of her. "My dad disappeared on a trip back from Jamaica."

For a long moment, he didn't respond. "What happened?"

"They said he was flying below radar when he ran out of gas. It was weeks before we knew what happened. Scuba divers found the wreckage." She inspected the worn bedspread, avoiding his stare. "It didn't make any sense. He'd never take off without refueling. It happened eight months ago, but the crash is still under investigation." He didn't say anything, and somehow that made her want to continue. "After he died, we learned he'd been smuggling drugs from Jamaica to the United States. They found cocaine in the hold."

He rubbed his brow, still not saying a word.

"The DEA still has our plane." Flooded with the sudden onslaught of emotion, she held her hand against her mouth. "I don't know what's wrong with me."

He gave an understanding nod.

"How do I accept he wasn't the person he pretended to be?" A tear rolled down her cheek.

He averted his gaze for a moment, a gesture that made her think he might be weighing what to say next. "Maybe he wasn't pretending. Maybe it was too complicated to explain."

Her caustic laugh sounded harsh in the quiet room. "You talk like quite the expert."

"The only thing I'm an expert at is avoidance. It's one of the reasons fighting had so much appeal. Physical pain was better than the alternative." He gave a what-do-I-know shrug. "I'm beginning to think maybe I was wrong about that."

****

Even after all these years, talking about his dad still felt like a punch in the gut. Considering so much of his life revolved around his dad's death, the irony wasn't lost on him. For some reason he didn't understand, Eric wanted Elise to know what happened—at least as much as he could safely tell her.

He stared at the old tube television bolted to the dresser. "I was nine when my dad responded to a shooting at a bar in Queens. Walked into ground zero of a mob war. He'd worked as a beat cop in the neighborhood and probably never even knew what hit him." His stomach clenched. Why did it still hurt so much?

She gasped and her eyes became dark little orbs, a mix of horror and compassion. "Did they catch his killer?"

He shook his head. "They never made an arrest, but not because they didn't know who did it."

"No?"

"The mob. Scumbag had members of the police force on his payroll. Men who were supposed to have his back." His tone was sharper than he'd intended. Twenty-three years later and the anger surged like it was yesterday.

Other than a few slow blinks, she sat still as a statue.

"You're talking about mobsters? Like in New York?"

He nodded, knowing his dad's story sounded too fantastical to be real.

"I thought they only existed in the movies."

"Nope." He studied her features for any indication this reference to the Mafia had personal significance. She'd have to be one hell of an actress to fake that level of surprise.

"Are you named after him?"

"I don't have a middle name, so everyone called me Eric."

Her chin quivered. She wiped her nose. *Please don't cry.* He didn't think he could handle it right now.

"Aren't we a pair?" She blinked away tears, dried her eyes, and surveyed the room. Her sad gaze landed on the machine attached to the bed. "Magic Fingers!"

She shot him a teasing look, an obvious attempt to lighten the mood, then grabbed a quarter from his nightstand and dropped it into the machine. The bed groaned and lurched, then started to shake.

"So relaxing." Her voice pulsated with the bed, making her giggle.

The oscillation created a soft jiggle, the bounce of her breasts both captivating and alluring. His muscles turned to jelly. *Don't stare.* An impossible task.

"You've got to try this." She drew out her words, letting her voice vibrate.

Without conscious thought, he found himself taking long, determined strides toward her.

Her lips parted and her pupils widened at his approach. He sat next to her, touched her cheek, and tilted her chin. The bed shook. Though she'd been laughing, anguish flickered in her wet eyes.

"What are you doing to me?" He searched her face, trying to understand the closeness he felt to this woman. Was it because they'd both just bared their souls?

She raised her hand and grazed her fingertips against his jaw in a light caress. His body thrummed. How he longed to give in to his desire. To lose himself in her. But that was the last thing—

Oh, fuck it.

He leaned forward. Her eyelids fluttered shut at the same moment his lips brushed hers. The soft, tender meeting of mouths turned hungry. Tongues dueled, moving in gentle, then agitated circles. She tasted sweet. Was it the pie or was she always this delicious?

She slid her hands underneath his shirt and traced the grooves of muscle on his stomach and chest. Every spot she touched blazed with fire. Pushing her flat on the vibrating bed, he pressed kisses along her collarbone. Then her neck. He gave a gentle tug on her ear with his teeth. Her heart pounded in unison with his until he couldn't tell where his stopped and hers began. The scent of her shampoo and her sweet, fragrant skin was like an opioid injection, and a delightful feeling pulsed through him when he skimmed the skin beneath her shirt and discovered her braless. He cupped a small, firm breast. His arousal hardened again. Trailing the curve of her waist, he let his hand linger on her hip. "More?"

"Oh God, yes." Her answer rumbled against his neck.

With a happy growl, he finessed open the button of her jeans and slid his hand under the waistband before returning to her chest. He pushed up her shirt, caressed her breast, then gently bit her nipple.

She mewled in a way that nearly drove him wild,

and when she laced her fingers into his hair, he prodded her legs apart with his knee and fit his body to hers. Grinding into her, he couldn't control the long, guttural moan that erupted, denim scraping denim. Their breaths heaved, the rhythm matching the thrust of his still clothed body. Kissing her again, he slid his hand beneath the small of her back and arched her toward him. He couldn't remember the last time he hadn't been distracted by his own thoughts. Thinking only of the moment liberated him. Not the past. Not the future. Now.

Make every second count.

Little whimpering sounds escaped her lips as she writhed against him. Nothing had ever felt so right. Touching her. Tasting her.

The bed jolted and stopped. She tore her mouth from his, her voice raspy. "Wait." Her chest lifted with each uneven little gasp.

He panted. "What's wrong?"

"Stop. Please stop."

Pushing himself onto his hands, she remained caged between his arms, her hair mussed, lips red and swollen. She placed one hand on his chest, the other against her cheek and averted her eyes.

He peered at her face. "Did I do something?"

She took a deep breath. "I just . . . I don't know what I want."

One look at her squished eyebrows and the way she sucked in her cheek said it all. He couldn't blame her confusion. It never should have happened.

She rolled out from under him, stood and smoothed her shirt. "I'm sorry. I think I need a minute."

Her gaze flittered around the room, and then she stepped outside. The door clicked shut with a soft thud.

He stared at it for several moments. Goosebumps ran up and down his arms as the sweat on his skin evaporated. His breath rasped in his throat.

What had he done?

His life, constructed around a single goal, had been blown to bits in less than a day.

His phone rang. He answered, his breath still ragged.

Chapter Twelve

Oh. My. God.

Elise gripped a fistful of hair on each side of her head and paced in an agitated circle, all the while, her pelvis throbbed with need. What the hell just happened? Surely, she'd hallucinated that entire encounter, because otherwise, it didn't make any sense. One minute she was talking about Dad and trying not to cry. In the next, she was inviting Eric to sit beside her on the bed.

His hands. His kisses. His musky cologne. All of her rules about getting involved with colleagues? Forgotten. Her disappointment in the male half of the species? Irrelevant. Because in that moment, he was the only thing she wanted.

Her muscles tightened, locking up as if she'd just run a marathon. But then, her body relaxed, the tension evaporating like sweat on a dry Colorado day. She'd not been the only one in that room. Eric had also been affected. She'd felt the evidence pressing against her leg.

She took a calming breath and gazed at the stars. Since her dad's death, she'd cut ties and avoided attachments. The rift in her relationship with her brothers. Old friends she'd avoided or lost touch with. Better to shut people out than take the chance they'd leave too. Now, for the first time in a long time, she actually craved the safety and intimacy of another person.

She inhaled and let the night air fill her lungs.

Looking at the sky grounded her. She'd seen similar views from the cockpit of a plane but couldn't remember having ever seen the stars so clearly with two feet still on the ground. A peaceful calmness washed over her.

A couple more minutes and maybe she'd be able to face him without turning an unflattering shade of red. Unlikely. Still, he deserved an explanation for the way she'd rushed from the room. She could go with the obvious and tell him it wasn't a good idea to get involved with a coworker, but she suspected he'd see through that lie. The truth was, she wasn't prepared to deal with something quite so real.

The trees surrounding the motel shook. Elise shuddered. Was it the cool breeze or her creepy surroundings? She drew her arms close and strolled to the other end of the building. Rounding the corner, she collided with what felt like a tank.

Nicky.

Warm, calloused hands gripped her upper arms, stopping her in place. "What are you doing out here? You look cold." His voice sounded polite, but his tone held an edge. A shadow fell across his face. Why had she never noticed his heavy brow or those fleshy jowls? Something about the man projected danger. Feeling silly, she shook her head. These were her customers. No, they weren't friends, but she knew them. They were kind and generous. She'd let Eric's mention of the mob get to her.

She tried to retreat, but he didn't release her. The pounding of her heart beat out a slow, heavy rhythm against her chest. She felt a sheen of sweat on her forehead. "I came out for some fresh air. I'm about to go back to my room." She tried to step away from the big man.

His grip tightened. "I was on my way to get you. Mr. Alario wants to have a word."

"Is it about the plane?" She glanced at his hands, still jabbing into her soft flesh. Her pulse throbbed beneath his thick fingers. "There's not much to report. The repair shouldn't take long, but they have to get the part." Her voice sounded louder, shriller than she'd intended. She turned, longing to be back in the safety of Eric's embrace.

"Where do you think you're going?" He still held one arm. "I said the boss wants to see you."

The boss? Internal alarm bells wailed. Something wasn't right. "It's chilly. Let me grab my sweatshirt."

He shook his head, placed his hand on her shoulder and guided her to the back of the motel. Her gaze swept the area. No one to help. Nowhere to go. *Scream*. The words wouldn't come. She dug in her feet, but the momentum of his push resulted in short, halting steps.

Think. The situation required calmness. "What does Mr. Alario want to talk about?"

"He's in Rocco's room."

A couple of inadequate light fixtures attached to the building cast shadows. The trees groaned and the leaves whispered. A wild screech cut the air. An owl?

Nicky rapped on the door. Christopher opened it and smiled in that familiar way. Happy, friendly Christopher. She relaxed. *It's fine*. She'd let her imagination get the best of her.

When she stepped inside the room, Nicky herded her among the other men. Her heart raced as she rotated, scanning each of the angry faces.

****

Eric punched the talk button and rasped, "Hello."

"Did you go for a run?" Grant's tone filled with curiosity.

The ethical part of Eric wanted to tell the truth, but his practical side shoved that idea down deep. At some point, they might have to discuss what happened, but confessing now benefitted no one. Besides, Grant had handed him the perfect excuse. Almost.

"Uh, no. No workout clothes. Went to check the perimeter and forgot my phone. Had to run when I heard it ringing."

"Dude. Are you really that out of shape?"

He ignored the question and stared at the open door to Elise's room, listening for her return. "How'd the background check go?"

"That's why I called. Usually, we don't check education earlier than high school or college, but I went back further this time and noticed something strange."

Eric's heart climbed into his throat. "Which was?"

"The dates of birth connected to these Social Security Numbers don't line up with the kids' ages when they first enrolled in Monroe County Public Schools."

"What are you saying?"

"Elise, Nathan and Jack Hughes don't exist."

The words landed like a sucker-punch. Eric swallowed back bile.

Grant continued. "Tombstone identities. It's almost impossible these days, but twenty-five years ago, if you had enough money? Easy. Purchase the birth certificate of a dead kid and register for a social security number."

Eric clutched the phone, reminding himself to breathe. "When does the discrepancy appear?"

The flipping of pages traveled through the phone line. "Twenty-three years ago. Started school in August."

Eric's blood went cold. *The same year Dad died.* That couldn't be right. "So, what's the connection?"

"Not sure," Grant said. "Based on what I saw, the Hughes siblings are upstanding citizens. No criminal records. They aren't on any watch lists. They have a loan on their business but make all their payments on time. No unusual bank deposits. Nothing of note really, other than appearing out of nowhere and having a drug smuggler for a dad.

Talk of Elise's dad reminded Eric of what she'd said about his death—and the fact she'd not known about his smuggling. "Elise told me about her dad's plane crash. She's still struggling to come to terms with the circumstances. Got pretty emotional."

"You believe her?"

"I do." A sinking feeling invaded Eric's stomach as he said the words. Did he truly have the clarity to make that determination?

"We'll keep that in mind, but you can't discount her just because you like her. This happens all the time. Undercovers form a relationship with a charismatic criminal and refuse to believe the worst."

"Yeah, I've done the training." Eric gritted his teeth. She wasn't involved. She couldn't be. "We know the Alarios deal in drug trafficking. Maybe her dad did business with the family. He double crossed them and they're looking for revenge?"

"Too soon to know," Grant said. "Keep up the good work and keep her talking."

Eric's chest tightened. He'd been anything but a model agent.

"Remember, staying under the radar is priority one. This is only the beginning of what could be a long investigation."

He nearly laughed aloud at the suggestion he keep a low profile. Making out with Elise had been a major breach of protocol. He'd done it anyway.

They disconnected with a promise to get in touch if either learned anything new. He lay back on the bed and stared at the ceiling.

The revelations about Elise and her family swirled inside him like a gathering storm. Either Vincenzo wanted her for revenge, or he planned to use her for leverage. At this point, he lacked any information suggesting Elise's involvement one way or the other. He hated anyone and anything connected to the Alario crime family. No way was he attracted to someone associated with the man who killed his father. He couldn't be.

But what if he was?

All the more reason he needed to keep her close.

Good God. Those sweet, creamy lips. The silky-smooth skin of her breasts. The clean fragrance of soap. This had to stop. He had a job to do. She might be involved.

Voices rumbled through the thin walls.

He stilled.

Standing, he called her name and shoved through the adjoining door to her room. Empty. He stopped and listened. The sounds came from the back of his room.

Rocco.

With his ear close to the bathroom mirror, he concentrated on listening to what was being said on the other side.

The commotion grew louder. Angrier.

Was that where Elise went? And if so, why?

****

Despite the room being the mirror image of the one she'd left, it couldn't be more different. In Eric's room, she'd been disoriented by emotions, unsure whether she should listen to her body or her head. Here, a different kind of confusion invaded her senses. Four men, she thought she knew, demanded answers she couldn't give.

They guided her to the end of the bed, looming above her with angry glares, a transformation so dramatic she couldn't believe these were the same men she'd ferried across the country for the last several months. Her gaze shifted from one man to the next. These were not the typical rich, self-indulgent charter passengers she'd become accustomed to. These men were dangerous. Criminals—like her dad.

The thought erupted inside her. Did this have something to do with him? Had he known these men? And now that he was gone, they were coming after her?

She wasn't involved in his smuggling operation, hadn't even known about it. Whatever they wanted, she had nothing to give them, and Dad wasn't here to help. If she was going to figure out a way out of this, she was on her own. As soon as they let down their guard, she'd run for it.

And then what?

An eternity passed while the men stared. No one spoke. Finally, Mr. Alario leaned forward. "Tell me about your mother."

She almost scoffed at the question. He must be joking. She'd been four years old the last time she'd seen the woman. Elise swallowed and studied the man's face. Nope. Not a joke. "She left over twenty years ago. We haven't seen or heard from her since."

His face reddened. Beads of sweat appeared on his

forehead. "Not the bullshit story your grandfather made up. Tell me where she is."

Grandfather? What was he talking about?

Loud, angry breaths pricked at her face as he leaned closer and bared his teeth. "Now."

A dark cloud covered Elise's vision and blood rushed to her head. She had to stay calm. "I haven't seen her in years. I swear."

He leaned forward, the smell of menthol heavy on his breath. A cough drop clacked against his teeth. "Give her up or I'll make you regret it."

Her heart rumbled in her chest like thunder. Why were they asking about Mom? Dad was the criminal. Unless . . . *Shit*. She'd thought she knew her dad, but look how that turned out. She couldn't even remember what her mom looked like. What did she even know about the woman? "I told you, I'm not in touch with her."

"I'm supposed to believe your mother walked away? No phone calls? No secret meetings? No birthday presents?"

She forced her shoulders back. Why was it still so hard to accept the truth? Her mother left and never looked back. "That's exactly what happened."

"Where is she?" His steady voice didn't mask frustration as he paced in front of the bed.

How many times did she have to say she didn't know? "I'm not even sure she's alive."

"I'm an old man whose days are numbered." He stared at her with cold, hard eyes. "Your family owes me a debt."

Elise leaned away from the man's glare, once again angry at the absent mother who left before she'd learned to read. Who hadn't been there when the training wheels came off her bike. A no-show at her high school graduation and every other milestone. Now to discover she might have had two selfish criminals for parents? It was too much.

Rocco put a hand on the older man's shoulder. "Give me a shot, Pop."

Vincenzo stepped aside. The younger Alario leaned into her face. "Give us her location. Where is Irina Koslov?" Drops of spit misted her nose while his sour breath warmed her cheek.

They had her confused with someone else. *Thank God.* "I don't know who that person is. My mom's name was Gloria."

Spittle built at the corners of Rocco's mouth. His nostrils flared as he jabbed a finger in her face. "Don't make me hurt you. Where is she? You owe us that much."

Vincenzo motioned for Rocco to settle down. "She doesn't know anything. Let's get someone out here that does."

"Contact Cook," Rocco instructed Nicky, then turned to his father. "He's the guy running that gambling operation out of Omaha. I spoke with him earlier. He has a place if we need it."

"Get him on the phone and figure something out." Vincenzo gave an impatient nod, then motioned to Christopher. "Get the zip ties."

She shook her head. Her breaths coming quick and shallow. Her vision darkened. No. She couldn't let them take her to another location. If she'd learned anything in that one-day self-defense class at the rec center, it was that. She'd fight with everything she had to make sure that didn't happen.

Christopher lifted a duffle bag from the floor to the bed. "On it, boss."

The good-natured man flashed her his usual smile. Elise had always regarded Christopher as a sort of gentle giant. Simple, but sweet. Something else she'd been wrong about.

She gawked at the men. Her chest hurt. She couldn't seem to haul enough air into her lungs. *This isn't happening.*

Vincenzo looked at her, then leveled his gaze on Nicky. "Call Koslov. Tell him we have his granddaughter."

From where she sat on the bed, she scanned the room. Both Nicky and Rocco were on the phone, their backs turned. Christopher ripped open a pack of zip ties, then dug through his bag. Vincenzo retrieved a firearm from the bedside table. Elise gulped back a hard lump. The old man slammed a magazine into the gun, cycled the action and crammed it into his waistband.

It was now or never.

She steadied her shaky legs and sprung, her feet barely touching the worn carpet. Three steps to freedom. She scarcely registered a ruckus behind her, focused only on the doorknob and her fingertips grazing the cool metal.

Almost there.

Her body jerked backward, yanked into something hard. A large arm wrapped around her chest and squeezed. Nicky's big hand gripped her face, crushing her cheeks and chin. The vise pressing against her chest kept air from getting into her lungs. She clawed at his forearm, but he only tightened his grip.

"I'm not fucking around. Decide if you want to do

this easy or hard." A heartless laugh rumbled against her ear. "But I promise, what's easy for me will be very unpleasant for you."

Chapter Thirteen

The indistinct boom of male voices triggered Eric's internal warning system. How long had Elise been gone? Damn it. He never should have let her leave.

Propping the door with his foot, he peered outside. Nothing. Not a sound other than the soft whooshing of the wind. Back inside his room, he pushed open the adjoining door and saw her phone on the nightstand.

A sour taste burned his throat. He strapped the holster to his ankle, slid his Glock inside, and scanned the two rooms. Wallet. Elise's cell phone. He slipped those into his pocket, grabbed his own cellular and opened the door.

Barefoot.

No time for socks. He shoved his feet into his shoes and stepped outside. A short distance across the parking lot, the bright lights of the diner beckoned. He raced across and barreled through the door. *Ding*. Heads turned. He dashed up and down the aisle. No sign of her.

Moving to the back of the restaurant, he stopped a woman leaving the restroom. "Anyone else in there?"

She shook her head and hurried away.

If something happened to Elise, he'd never forgive himself. He left the diner and sprinted back to his room. *Please let her be there.*

His key clicked in the lock, and he shoved the door open, making a quick survey of his room and hers. Still empty. He went back outside.

Loose rock crunched beneath his feet, the sound loud and hollow. Pacing the length of the motel, his gaze landing on Vincenzo's room. A soft, blue light pulsed through the curtain.

A muffled cry rose over the wind. The hairs on the back of Eric's neck came to attention. Behind the building, a car engine roared to life. He sprinted around the corner.

Every part of his body tensed. Nicky had a hold on Elise and was cramming her into a black SUV. Though her hands were tied behind her back, she struggled against him, twisting and kicking. Her feet braced against the door frame.

Eric let loose a roar and raced toward the vehicle. "Hey!"

Contorting her body, Elise managed eye contact. "Eri—"

Nicky slapped his big, meaty hand over her mouth. She squirmed and bucked, but was no match for her captor. He shoved her into the backseat.

The door slammed. Wheels spun. The car sped past. From the front passenger seat, Vincenzo gave him a bland look. Wedged in the middle, Elise peered out, eyes wide and wild.

Fuck!

Adrenalin coursed through him. His limbs tingled. His hands shook. He wanted to hit something—or someone. If any of them hurt her— Consequences be damned.

He tore around the motel, barged up to the lobby and tugged on the handle. Locked. Inside, the motel owner puttered around, probably going through his closing routine.

He banged. "Open up!"

The man waved. "Go away. We're closed."

"Open. Up." Eric pounded so hard he thought he might put his fist through the glass. He didn't stop, even as the owner started his slow saunter to the door.

"Lookie here, young man. We are closed."

"I need your car," Eric said, breathless.

The man flinched. "Is this a robbery?"

"Official business." Already distraught, he didn't think he could maintain control much longer. He opened his wallet and shoved it against the glass.

"F-B-I," the old man read slowly. "Well, I'll be." He unlocked the door.

Eric held out his hand. "Keys. Now."

"How exactly will this work? Do I get some sort of compensation?"

Eric rolled his hand in a hurry-up motion, worried about the minutes being lost. He followed the man to his office, pacing and muttering while the proprietor rummaged through a desk. Finally, a Cornhuskers key chain dangled in front of him.

The man snatched it away before Eric could grab it. "This is my spare key. It's that brown truck right out there." The man pointed to an older model pickup. "Take care of her."

Eric snatched the keys and held the other man's gaze. "Call 9-1-1. Report a kidnapping. A woman named Elise Hughes was forced into a dark SUV, headed north on highway two-eighty-one. Can you do that?"

The man's eyes widened. He bobbed his head up and down.

Eric ran to the parking lot. His heart pounded. His

body coursed with energy. His hand shook and he fumbled with the key, finally sliding it into the keyhole. He wrenched the door open and climbed inside, his foot hitting the gas the moment the engine turned over. The back wheels spun, kicking up dust and rock before digging in and shooting him onto the highway.

****

Restrained. Pushed into a car. Kidnapped. Elise couldn't believe it.

Wedged between her captors, she peered from Nicky to Rocco. They ignored her, their stoic expressions never changing. The faint aromas of fried foods and musky cologne filled the backseat.

Vincenzo glanced at her from the front seat. His profile revealed a jagged scar jutting across his neck. Something else she'd missed while flying this stranger across the country.

The driver never even glanced in her direction. He must be connected to the local guy they mentioned. She didn't know who he was, but that hardly mattered. She didn't know any of these men.

The SUV hit a bump. Her body rocked into Rocco's big meaty shoulder. His leather jacket stuck to the sweaty skin of her arm. With her hands secured behind her back and little room to maneuver, she couldn't avoid the press of his large body against hers. The bitter tang of bile filled her mouth. She swallowed it back. The jacket peeled away from her skin as he straightened with a grunt.

"Where are you taking me?"

No one spoke.

The restraints on her wrists dug into her skin. She wiggled numb fingers. Why was this happening? Damn it. She deserved answers.

Her voice shook when she spoke. "Who is this Koslov guy?" No response. "You've got the wrong person. I'm not who you think I am."

Sweat trickled down her back, yet she shook with cold. She exhaled several times to regain control, but the sides of the car collapsed around her. Why were they sitting so close? *Move over!*

"Where are we going?" Her voice sounded raspy and small.

Silence.

She glanced over her shoulder. Christopher waved from the back seat.

"Can one of you untie my hands? Or open the window?"

No answer.

She blinked. Don't cry. Keep it together. Figure out a way to get loose.

If she could get out of this car, she might have a chance. "I have to go to the bathroom."

Nicky's cheek twitched. At least that got some acknowledgement.

She rubbed her legs together, grimaced, and leaned toward the driver. "Can we stop? I really need to go."

Rocco growled. "Pee in your pants."

A surreal acceptance settled over her. She had nowhere to go. No means of escape. At least not now. Maybe when they got wherever they were going.

Focus on something good. She closed her eyes and pictured Eric. They'd worked together only a few days, but it seemed like a lifetime.

He saw them take her. He must've called the police. They were probably looking for her right now. All she had to do was stay alive, and everything would be okay.

Chapter Fourteen

Eric knew what the Alarios did to their enemies. Torture, strangulation, gouged-out eyes, severed limbs. Vincenzo liked his murders symbolic. One cooperating witness was found with a dead canary crammed down his throat.

Not to mention the wreckage of two .22 caliber shots to the temple—Vincenzo's favorite method for finishing off his enemies. Powerful enough to go in, but not come out, the bullet bounced around the skull, tearing up bone and brain tissue, destroying the slug in the process.

Had Elise been Vincenzo's target all along? Was that why they were on her flight? Eric didn't know what she'd done to attract their attention, but he wasn't about to let her become another gruesome crime scene photo.

The pickup careened around a bend at top speed, the tires barely gripping the asphalt. He turned wide, directly into the oncoming lane, barely missing a motorcycle. His heartbeat pulsed in his ears. He swerved into his lane and peered ahead. No sign of the fleeing SUV.

Calm down. Think.

He tapped a nervous rhythm on the steering wheel. Vincenzo, Rocco, and Elise were long gone. Fortunately, the motel owner's truck had some serious horsepower. Maybe he could catch up—assuming they stayed on the highway. And he didn't crash. He jammed the pedal to the floor. At the same time, he punched Grant's number into the phone. A sleepy voice answered, but as soon as Eric explained Elise had been taken, the other agent became focused and alert. "I'm going to ping your phone so we can keep tabs on you," he said. "I'll contact the Omaha field office and get you some backup."

Eric flattened his lips into a thin line. He couldn't care less about backup. Getting Elise back was the only thing that mattered.

He disconnected. Talking with Grant had been a distraction, but now he had nothing to think about but the colossal mess he'd made. Had he really suspected she might be in cahoots with Alario? And why had he believed Vincenzo was watching television?

He never should have let her out of his sight. *Stupid, stupid, stupid.* He punched the steering wheel with the heel of his hand. If he saw her again—he shook his head—w*hen* he saw her again, he would explain everything. She deserved the truth.

A faint glimmer of taillights appeared in the distance. He held his breath. *Could it be?* The lights brightened. Brakes.

Eric slowed and doused his headlights. The SUV swung onto a dirt road. He followed. With no illumination, navigating the road proved difficult, but he was grateful for the cover of darkness. Seconds later, he hit a deep, water-filled divot so hard the impact bounced him from his seat.

****

The SUV bumped over uneven ground. The driver turned again, the tires rumbling over washboard. Jostled into her captors, Elise leaned into something hard near Nicky's hip. Was that a gun? If only she could figure out a way to get a hold of it.

They zig-zagged through a maze of country roads, finally rolling to a stop before an old farmhouse with worn paint and a rickety porch. Bugs swarming the lightbulb beside the door were the only sign of life. A large tree loomed over the dwelling.

"Let's go." Rocco gripped Elise's arm and dragged her from the vehicle. Christopher and Nicky went to the back of the SUV and withdrew rifles.

She trembled and gasped for air. *I have to get out of here.* Her gaze darted across the yard. Before her was nothing but darkness. No street lights. No neighbors. Nothing.

Rocco dragged her along the side of the farmhouse toward a similarly dilapidated barn. She peered around, observing her surroundings. Grass grew around the deflated tires of an old rusty tractor. This place had been abandoned for a while. No one would ever find her out here.

A small building with a weathered wood frame and a narrow door located on the other side of a rise caught her attention. Probably a chicken coop. Might be a place to hide if she could get free.

What would they do if she ran? Would they shoot her?

She needed to try.

Digging her feet in the soft ground, she leaned against the forward momentum, but it wasn't enough to slow their progression to the barn. "Please don't do this."

"Move." Rocco shoved her forward.

Wiggling her shoulders, she struggled against his grasp, but it only made him tighten his grip.

Nicky, Christopher, and Vincenzo followed on foot. Tires crunched as the SUV continued down the road.

Alone in the middle of nowhere with armed men and her hands tied behind her back.

An eerie quiet enveloped the property. No horses, chickens, or cows. Just silence. She halted and again sunk her heels into the ground. Rocco pushed her forward, then turned to Nicky and Christopher. "Stay outside and watch the perimeter."

The men nodded like dutiful soldiers. For the first time, she noticed the handle of a handgun extending from the waistband of Christopher's pants. Had he always had that?

Rocco dragged her into the dark barn through tall double doors. Straw crunched beneath her feet. The disconcerting smell of dirt, dust and rotten produce filled her nostrils.

He yanked her to the side and flipped a switch. One lone fixture hung from the ceiling, its dim illumination casting shadows and creating dark corners.

Elise scanned the space looking for weaknesses. The foundation appeared to be made of stone, but the rest had been constructed of wood. Joists formed the vaulted ceiling and perpendicular planks completed the roof. A window and door were visible at the far end of the barn.

Rocco put a hand in the center of her back and propelled her further inside the room. The unexpected shove, combined with the thin layer of straw covering the concrete floor made her feet slide. Grabbing the restraints at her wrists, he jerked her backward so fast she saw spots. The sharp plastic of the zip tie cut into her skin. He nudged her toward a chair in the middle of the room. Dark smudges stained the ground. How many others had been brought here? Before she could say or do anything, Rocco cut the ties binding her hands.

Sweet relief. "Oh, thank God." She shook her hands and massaged her shoulders, but the freedom didn't last. He forced her into the chair and yanked her hands behind her again. She cringed at the zipper-like buzz of new cuffs being cinched around her wrists and bound to the chair.

Her chest tightened. She strained against the shackles, then stilled. Useless efforts. She should conserve her energy in case she got a chance to run. In the meantime, she'd have to endure whatever they threw at her. A bead of sweat ran down her face.

She closed her eyes and imagined Nate and Jack back home in Florida, arguing over decisions for the business. Would they even know what happened to her?

No. She couldn't think like that. She was going to get out of this, and when she did, she'd never take her obnoxious brothers for granted again.

****

Several minutes passed. Eric peered through the windshield at the decaying building. Nicky and Christopher flanked the entrance to the barn but going in the front had never been an option. He scanned the layout of the property. There had to be a way inside.

His heart rate spiked. Like an athlete preparing for competition, he wanted his nervous system ready. But too much too soon, and he'd be fatigued before he even started. He took a few deep breaths.

His phone vibrated.

"We've got your location. You're about one hundred miles northwest of Omaha," Grant said. "The property belongs to a local criminal named Billy Cook."

Alert and looking for any sign of Elise, Eric studied the door of the barn, now illuminated from inside.

"What's his connection to Alario?"

"He's small potatoes, so he's probably looking to step up. Looks like his operation focuses on the basics—gambling and drugs. Might be hoping to expand. A big boss like Vincenzo could be the jump-start he needs."

Eric didn't care about a low-budget gangster operating out of the Corn Belt.

Grant continued the update. "Agents from the Omaha office are en route. They should be there in an hour."

Too long.

"Tonight might actually be our chance to take Vincenzo and Rocco down." Grant's voice held a hint of excitement.

Eric sighed. Funny how the personal vendetta he'd carried for so many years had lost some of its importance now that he'd found Elise. He wanted Vincenzo behind bars, but not if it meant anything happened to her. Men like this didn't care about collateral damage. "I can't wait an hour."

Grant drew a deep breath. "Be smart. You can't take them on without backup. This is the closest we've gotten to the Alarios since I joined the Bureau. You've done good work and I want you to continue doing good work."

More praise. Another knife in the gut.

"We can't have you blowing your cover now."

Why couldn't Grant understand the urgency? "We don't know what they're doing to her."

"I don't want anyone getting hurt, yourself included," Grant said. "They took her for a reason. There's something they want, and they don't have it yet. So, unless you see an immediate threat, I need you to meet and debrief the Omaha team when they get there."

Eric didn't reply. He wouldn't make a promise he couldn't keep.

"I'll be in touch. Don't do anything stupid." Grant hung up.

Waiting was torture. A few more minutes passed as Eric wrestled with his options. From what he could see, the local guy hadn't provided any extra manpower. If he could come up with a diversion, maybe he could get to her.

Movement along the fence caught his eye. He stilled and focused his attention on the shadows. A figure dressed in black prowled at a brisk pace. Something flashed in the moonlight—maybe a gun. The figure disappeared around the back of the barn.

It was too soon for the Omaha backup team to have arrived. Eric unholstered his own gun and summoned his training.

Swift. Silent. Deadly.

Chapter Fifteen

The stench of manure lingered, conjuring memories of the petting zoo Elise and her brothers visited every summer as kids. It had been years since their trips to the small farm along route A1A near Florida City, but she could almost feel the weight of the grain pellets in her hand.

A lump rose in her throat. She'd been such a fool. Why had she let the falling out with her brothers fester? Compared to her, both had come to terms with their father's crimes with relative ease. She didn't understand how they could forgive him when all she felt was anger. The way they'd dismissed her pain, told her it was time to get on with her life, hurt almost as much as Dad's lies. They'd argued. She left. Nate called and told her to come home. She said the most unforgivable things.

They hadn't talked since.

Vincenzo positioned another chair across from her, but he didn't sit. "It's time for me to enlighten you about your family history."

She nodded, the muscles in her arms twitching against the restraints.

"Your mother's name is Irina Koslov. Her father is Aleksander Koslov. Those closest to him to call him Papi, though he is known by many names." A vein throbbed in Vincenzo's thick neck. "I call him my greatest enemy."

Elise swallowed. Those names sounded Russian. "My mother's name is Gloria Hughes. Her maiden name was Russo."

Vincenzo's laugh never reached his eyes. He leaned forward, held a switchblade in front of her face and popped it open. "Don't interrupt."

She pressed her lips shut.

Back and forth, he paced between Elise and the empty chair. "Twenty-three years ago, my beautiful daughter Sophia rendezvoused with a Koslov associate. Our families had been at odds for some time, and she wanted to strike a deal. To make her papa proud." He stopped and stared. His eyes glistened. "They executed her."

She stared at her lap and blinked. What were all those stories about his daughter? What did any of it have to do with her?

"The day I learned she was dead, I wanted to hurt someone, and I did. Many people. But my vengeance was hollow." He jabbed a finger at Elise. "Do you know why?"

She shook her head and swallowed the cry inching up her throat.

"Those deaths didn't mean anything. Ultimately, they weren't the ones who needed to pay. Only one man has her blood on his hands." His voice rose. His back stiffened. "Until he suffers the pain I have suffered, there will be no justice." A rumble of understanding shook her. This man had hunted her, carefully and methodically. Alarm pumped through her body. Going to war with the zip ties, she twisted and struggled. The sharp plastic cuffs cut into her flesh.

Vincenzo bared his teeth and stalked toward her.

"Her death has haunted me for more than two decades." His face contorted into an ugly scowl. His voice shook. "My daughter died. Aleksander's should, as well." The old man came closer and curled a lock of her hair around a fat finger. "It's only fair."

Elise yanked back, but he caught her hair between his thumb and index finger. His face almost touched hers. She twisted her head and leaned as far back as the stiff chair would allow. The hard slats dug into her back, and she flinched as his hot breath grazed her cheek.

"Your grandfather knew what was owed. He helped his daughter, son-in-law, and grandchildren escape. New identities. New lives."

She couldn't look him in the eye. "I don't believe you."

"Your father started a new life while your mother disappeared."

Her chin quivered. Was it true? Could her whole life be a lie?

"The time has come. You will draw your mother out of hiding. Otherwise, righting wrongs falls to you, Elisa."

A hot tear squeezed through her lashes and trickled down her cheek. "My name is Elise."

The man gave a wicked smile. "Are you sure?"

****

Eric crouched beside the truck and watched the figure creep along the fence behind the farmhouse. Hairs on the back of his neck stood on end. Something told him it wouldn't be as simple as one guy. Motion across an open field caught his eye. He stiffened, scanning the black night for others.

Working in the dark could be problematic,

especially with unfamiliar terrain. It could also be an asset. New arrivals skulking around in dark clothing meant they planned to use the night to their advantage.

His guess? An ambush of Vincenzo and his men.

He didn't know who they were, why they were here, or whether they cared about a hostage caught in the crossfire. Adrenaline hummed through him. *Focus.* Short on time, he'd have to improvise.

Eric eased open the truck's passenger door and searched for a flashlight under the seat. Without the dome light, which he'd extinguished before exiting the truck, he had to rely on touch. His hand landed on a hard plastic cylinder. He withdrew it and tested the feel of it in his hand. Too big and bulky. Rifling through the glove box, he found a Swiss Army knife and shoved it in the front pocket of his jeans.

He should notify Grant.

No. He'd deal with the fallout later. He silenced his phone and stuck it in his back pocket.

With one careful foot in front of the other, Eric slipped from the road to a row of bushes, his gaze sweeping the ground in front of him. Once secure in his cover, he went slow, taking deliberate steps. At the end of the hedge, he stopped. Nicky and Christopher were talking.

"I like Elise," Christopher said. "I hope Mr. A. doesn't ask me to hurt her."

Nicky grunted. "We do what we're told."

Christopher shifted his rifle in front of his body. "It doesn't seem right. She's not responsible for things her family did."

"I'm not talking about this with you."

Eric recalled Christopher Maldonado's file. Of

Spanish descent, he could never hope to be more than a family associate. Still, he'd worked hard to prove his worth and become a member of the inner circle. He might have a soft spot for Elise, but that wouldn't matter. Soldiers did as they were told.

Still crouched, Eric crept along the hedge and cut through the yard to the farmhouse, staying in the shadows. He paused, removed his gun from its holster, and flicked off the safety. Not his first choice for a weapon, but as much as he disliked the feel of the subcompact handgun, it was better than nothing. He flattened himself against the siding and tip-toed his way to the back of the house. The stillness troubled him. Where had the figures in black gone?

Staying in the shadows between the house and the thick forest lining the back of the property, he sprinted across an open patch of grass to the outbuilding where they held her. Inching along the side of the barn, he located a window several inches above shoulder level and stretched to peer through.

She was tied to a chair, her hair messy and posture slumped, but appeared unharmed. Without seeing her face, it was hard to know for sure.

Vincenzo hovered over Elise. Eric couldn't remember wanting to hurt another man so badly. His hand curled into a ball as he imagined Vincenzo's nose breaking beneath the force of his fist.

Breathe.

Rocco moved toward his father and Elise. Eric craned his neck and listened.

"Can we cut to the chase, Pop?" Rocco stepped forward and got in Elise's face. "My sister is dead," he said. "Your family is responsible. Your grandfather has twelve hours to turn over his daughter. If that doesn't happen, you will be sacrificed to pay his debt."

Eric's vision blurred.

Grandfather. Daughter. Debt.

His muscles twitched. He wanted to pummel every man standing between him and Elise. He closed his eyes and visualized a stop sign. *Think*.

The gravity of the situation landed on him like a weight. Could Elise be a Koslov? A member of the family Vincenzo considered his archenemy? A strange feeling invaded Eric's stomach.

Vincenzo and Rocco had stalked her. They let her fly them halfway across the country while they learned her habits and gained her trust.

His body pulsed. He braced himself against the siding of the barn. Elise had the blood of a gangster and was a hostage in a mob war. This changed everything. No longer was he looking at some racketeering scheme. Now it was personal, and there was nothing more dangerous than a sociopath out for revenge.

****

False identities? A family connected to the mob? As fantastical as it sounded, Elise knew it was true. The signs were there. The over-protective older brother. Her father's strict rules about where she could go and with whom. The absence of any extended family.

Damn them for keeping this from her. Deep down, she knew they'd done what they thought best. Unfortunately, ignorance had only made her more vulnerable. Had she known, she might have kept a lower profile. Instead, she'd been stupid. An oblivious sitting duck, unaware and unprepared for the predators lurking in the shadows.

It was time she learned the truth.

"What's my real name?" She wiggled her wrists. A pointless effort against the plastic ties.

"Elisa Reyes," Rocco replied.

She stared at him for a moment, then repeated the name, letting it roll around on her tongue. It didn't feel right. "You're wrong."

Rocco's laugh contained genuine amusement. "My God. I thought you were playing us, but they didn't tell you anything, did they?"

She shook her head.

"After World War II, your grandfather's family emigrated from the Soviet Union to Venezuela. He was born in Caracas."

"So, my family speaks Russian?"

"And Spanish. I believe that's your grandfather's preferred language. And of course, your father was from Honduras."

Something else Dad lied about. It explained why Dad spoke Spanish. Nate was also fluent. How much had her oldest brother known about their real identities? An angry heat rushed through her. She'd deal with that later.

"Your grandfather came from Venezuela where he'd worked as a member of the armed forces." Rocco sat in a backward facing chair, his arms propped against the top. "He learned the ins and outs of drug trafficking when he was stationed at the Colombian border. When he settled in New York, he set up shop. Part Colombian mafia. Mostly Russian."

So many lies. If her father were here, she'd scream at him. Dying was one more item on a growing list of grievances.

Rocco's predatory gaze sliced into her. She resisted

the urge to squirm. *Think.* The more information she had, the better off she'd be. She needed to keep Rocco talking.

"So, my grandfather started with nothing?"

He nodded. "He runs a very successful operation. My father and your grandfather might have been allies had the situation been different. My sister died trying to make it happen."

Dozens of questions about her own family tumbled through her brain, but if she focused on Rocco and his sister, maybe he'd trust her enough to take off the cuffs. "Your sister wanted to be allies with the Koslovs?"

"She'd arranged to meet a captain in the Koslov family to discuss an alliance. She had a crazy idea the families should network."

"She sounds like a pioneer." *Or a drug lord.* "Ahead of her time." *For creating a cartel.*

Rocco's face slackened, as if struck by an unexpected idea. "She was, wasn't she?"

Keep him talking. "How old were you when she died?"

"Six. She was twenty-five. We had different mothers. I barely remember her. I feel bad for that."

Pretend you care. "You were only a little kid."

He gave a sad nod.

Pop. Pop pop. A series of loud bangs interrupted their chat. Her muscles tensed and her head whipped toward the sound.

The doors crashed open. Christopher banged into the barn with one of Nicky's arms slung around his shoulder. Nicky gripped his side with the other hand and grimaced. Blood seeped through his fingers.

Christopher eased him onto a bale of straw as the big man's breathing grew labored. The blood oozed from a stomach wound, glugging like water from a forgotten garden hose.

"Shots came from two directions." Christopher's words came between agitated breath. "They might have us surrounded."

"How did they find us? Cook swore this place was off the mat." Rocco peered out the window, gun drawn. "We only just sent word we had her."

Vincenzo gestured to Elise. "We weren't the only ones watching."

Her heart hammered against her ribs. They were already dangerous men. Now they were panicked. None of this would help her situation.

One way or another, she had to get away.

"We need to get her to another location," Vincenzo said.

"There's a truck in a shed around the back of the house. Cook told me where to find the keys." Rocco loosened his collar. "But first, let's figure out what we're dealing with."

If they relocated her, they'd have to remove the restraints. At least temporarily. Maybe she could make a run for it. What's the worst that could happen? She gulped.

Christopher stayed at Nicky's side, ripping the sleeves from his jacket, and crushing it against the man's thick, muscular torso.

"Do you see anything?" Vincenzo asked.

Rocco shook his head. "I know they're out there."

Christopher muttered, alternating between pacing and mopping up the sweat on the injured man's brow. The way he tended to his friend was surprisingly gentle and compassionate. Nicky let loose one last torturous howl of pain and passed out. His chest rose and fell in time with his ragged breaths.

The rapid escalation had left Vincenzo, Rocco and Christopher disoriented. They appeared completely unprepared for this new hostility. Who shot Nicky? Were they here for her?

With a grimace, Christopher stood and cracked his knuckles. Clenching and unclenching his hands, he paced in agitated circles, glaring at nothing in particular. "Are we just going to sit here and let them attack us?"

Vincenzo glared out the window and drew his gun. "We need a plan."

"Nicky needs a doctor." Christopher's voice was raw with pain.

Vincenzo gave Rocco a decisive look. "Call the local guy. Tell him we need reinforcements. And soon." He nodded to the second level of the barn. "Christopher, get up there and look for places to perch."

Christopher scrambled up the ladder. Elise followed the sound of his heavy footsteps.

"We've got windows," he yelled.

Rocco disconnected his call. "Cook says he's got a few guys in the area. They'll be here soon."

Vincenzo motioned to the roof. "Let's get upstairs and see if we can spot these bastards."

"Should we take her with us?" Rocco waited for his father to climb the ladder before beginning his ascent.

Vincenzo paused, glancing down at Elise. "Leave her. We have the advantage of higher ground. They won't get near the barn."

Were they really going to leave her defenseless and alone during a gunfight?

The footsteps from upstairs sounded more like an

army of thirty than a mere three men. Dust shook from the floorboards with each chaotic footfall. Now, she just needed to figure out how to get herself loose.

She wiggled and twisted and made her hand as narrow as possible, crushing her thumb against her palm. Pain exploded in her tender wrist. She winced. If she couldn't get her hands through the cuffs, maybe she could wear them down. She rubbed the plastic tie against the wooden rods forming the back of the chair. A splinter sliced into her hand.

She wasn't giving up. Sure, her first two ideas were a bust, but maybe she could break the spindles. Her hands would still be bound, but at least she could run. She leaned forward and slammed against the back of the chair. *Fuck*! The damned things wouldn't budge.

She took another deep breath. Since they hadn't secured her legs to the chair, perhaps she could take it with her. As a test, she pushed up onto her feet and took a few short, quick steps, then dropped back down. Useless. Even if she could get out of the barn, how far would she get tied to a chair?

Her heart thudded in her chest, her body suddenly too heavy to move. She bit down on her bottom lip. It was no use.

She was trapped.

Chapter Sixteen

Breathe. Barging through the door wouldn't help anyone.

Eric peered through the dirty window. They'd secured Elise's hands behind the spindles of a wooden chair and pulled her arms into an unnatural position. Her attempt to escape had only gotten her a few inches closer to the door.

I'm coming.

Shouting and commotion erupted from the loft.

It's now or never.

The door hung on a rail and slid to the side. He edged it open just enough to slip through. Alert to the sounds from above, he hugged the wall and eased his way to the center of the barn.

Pop. Pop.

Hay shifted through the cracks in the planks overhead. Footfalls and clomping echoed through the rafters.

Elise yanked against her shackles. The chair wobbled under her desperate tugs. If she wasn't careful, she'd end up on the floor.

Close enough to grab her, Eric waited until the frantic movement above subsided. After several seconds, he resumed his slow journey.

"Aghhh!" A phlegmy groan erupted from the direction of the hay bales. Nicky struggled to sit. Eric stilled and held his breath. The big man strained to rock his body into a sitting position. A deep red flush colored his face. He shook, then fell back, his arms hanging limp and loose.

Eric took another step sideways. He couldn't risk appearing out of nowhere and startling her. With silent movements, he sidestepped into her periphery.

She startled. Her brows lifted. Her mouth fell open.

Holding a finger to his lips, Eric eased forward and peered up at the second level. No sign any of the men were watching. A few more steps and he was there. He grasped her chin and peered into her eyes.

"What are you doing here?" she whispered. "Did you call the police?"

"I'll explain later."

He tucked the gun in his ankle holster and removed the knife from his pocket.

"Where'd you get a gun?"

"Later." He moved to the back of the chair and saw her bloody wrists. His hands shook, but in one smooth motion, he sliced through the plastic manacles.

She leaped up, rubbed her wrists, and shook her arms. He wanted to hold her—to haul her into a tight embrace—but gripped her hand instead.

They weren't out of danger yet. Far from it. Her solid warmth and soft skin reminded him how close he'd come to losing her. He squeezed tighter than necessary. No way was he letting go now.

****

Elise clutched Eric's hand, his grip confident and familiar. She had no idea how he'd found her, but thank God he did. She followed his lead along the interior walls to the back door. Once outside, she scurried to match his pace. They sidestepped along the back of the building, moving through the shadows, her breaths quick and shallow. On shaky legs, she raced over the wet, soft ground. Her heart pounded into her throat.

They approached the back corner of the barn. He raised one hand.

Pop.

Another gunshot. More shouting.

She squelched a cry.

Something hard pressed into her palm. She glanced down. Her phone.

"In case we get separated," he whispered.

Before she could reply, he crushed the bones of her hand in his firm grasp and yanked her out of the shadow. Her instincts shrieked to find cover, but he dragged her forward across the open field, her feet bumping against each other.

The soft earth gave under her toes and her ankle turned. Groaning, she fell forward. A firm hand grasped her upper arm and lifted her back to her feet. "Keep going. We're almost there."

She peered into the dark. *There* looked to be the dark shadow of the grain silo. Eric slid behind the structure and stopped. Momentum sent her crashing into him. In one quick movement, he peered around the storehouse and jerked back. His gaze found hers. "How's your ankle?"

"Don't even feel it."

"That's the adrenalin. You will later." His face tightened. "I'm sorry, but right now we need to move. Can you do that?"

"Ye—" Everything tilted. Breathing became a struggle, each panicked gasp for air met the one trying to come out, none of it reaching her ravenous lungs. She braced herself against the steel silo. *This isn't happening.*

He grasped her shoulders. "You're in shock. That's normal. We're going to get out of here. I promise." The lines of his face hardened. A fierceness flickered in his eyes.

She believed him. She trusted him. "I'm ready."

"I've got a truck down the road."

Where'd he get a truck? She started to ask, then shook her head. It didn't matter. He towed her across an open space to a battered old fence. She crouched in the shadows as instructed. The crack of gunfire echoed through the night. He withdrew his gun from its holster. "Keep close. Stay low and be as quiet as possible. Once we're in the truck, we'll call for help."

Another deep breath steeled her to continue.

"Next stop, those bushes over there." He pointed toward a hedge running down the side of the yard. "Ready?"

She gave a decisive nod.

Once they reached the shrubbery, he crept in the same crouched position, slowing as they neared the end of the hedge. He motioned for her to stay put, then stood to peer around the last bush.

A second passed. Then he reappeared, hands up. A man in a dark shirt held a gun to his chest. Eric released his own weapon, letting it dangle from his finger. The man took the firearm and tucked it into his waistband.

Elise wanted to melt into the brush. Her heart beat like a bomb about to explode. She put a hand on her chest as if she could slow down the out-of-control organ.

Keeping his gun trained on Eric, the shadowy figure patted him down, then removed the knife from one pocket, his cell phone from another. He tipped his chin toward Elise. "She's coming with me."

"Not happening." Eric backed up protectively.

She took several shallow breaths and squeezed his hand, as if the harder she held him, the safer she would be. She leaned into him and peered around his arm at the man with the gun. He had tawny brown skin and dark hair, similar to her own. The shadow of a moustache darkened his upper lip.

The stranger gestured with his gun for Eric to move aside. "I don't think you get a say in that."

Eric tightened his grip on her hand.

The man stepped closer, eyes blazing. "Do you know who I am?"

The insincere snort Eric offered in response suggested he did.

The stranger narrowed his eyes and pointed a finger at Eric. "Here's what's going to happen. Elisa is coming with me. In that SUV." He pointed in the direction of the road. "I'm taking her to our grandfather. As for you, you can crawl back into whatever hole you slithered out of."

Elise rotated her gaze back and forth between them. The two men stared at each other, not bothering to mask the hate. It seemed they spoke a different language—one in which she had no fluency.

She crouched behind Eric's powerful body, unwilling to lose his protection. The other man spoke in a gentle voice. "Elisa, I'm your cousin Sergei."

She shook her head. "My name is Elise."

"My apologies." He smiled at her, while still pointing his gun at Eric. "I'm here to protect you."

She firmed her voice. "I don't believe you."

Eric positioned himself in front of her again. "You

heard her. She doesn't want to go with you."

"Back down, FBI."

Elise gasped. "FBI?"

The memory of Eric talking to their clients in the Albert Springs airport crashed over her like an ocean wave. Had he known they were dangerous all along? Was he here because of them?

He spun to face her, his expression pleading. "I can explain."

The man named Sergei grinned. "Ah. She didn't know?"

The guilty look on Eric's face said it all. She stiffened and he released her. "I'll tell you everything. Later."

She took a step back and shook her head, her teeth biting into the fleshy insides of her cheeks. Was anybody on that godforsaken plane who they said they were?

Eric followed her retreat, holding his hands as if trying not to scare a frightened animal.

Her gaze ricocheted from Eric to the scary man holding the gun, then back to Eric. The pieces fell into place. His vagueness. Not answering questions. Lenny's retirement and Eric's mysterious appearance as her new partner. It made sense. A deep breath of cool night air steadied her. This was good. If Eric was with the FBI, someone would be coming for them. They were going to be okay. He stood just out of reach, his hands in his pockets and his gaze lowered. Between the guy with the gun and the FBI agent, the choice was easy.

And then all hell broke loose.

More gunfire.

Out of nowhere, an SUV veered onto the grass. Sergei ran toward the car. "Get in!"

Elise shook her head. "No."

"We don't have time for this. Get in the car. Now."

She stepped to Eric's side. He'd rescued her from Vincenzo. He'd keep her safe. "I'm not going with you."

Sergei pointed his gun at Eric's head. "Does this change your mind?"

Chapter Seventeen

Eric tensed at the sound of Elise's wobbly voice. "You wouldn't." She stepped closer.

Sergei's glare stayed fixed on him, but he spoke to Elise. "Are you willing to take that chance?"

"Don't do it, Elise." Eric kept his voice quiet, but firm. He grasped her hand. "Don't listen to him."

Sergei's expression tightened. "I'll count to three."

Indecision flashed across her face. She scanned the woods behind the house, then the dark street. Eric could almost hear her thoughts, calculating the chances of escape.

"One."

"Once you get in that car, you're theirs," he whispered.

Her unblinking gaze squeezed his heart. "What other option is there?"

How had this happened? He clutched her hand. "Forget me. Just run. Save yourself."

"Two."

"I can't let them hurt you." Her voice came out strained, weak. She squeezed her eyes shut and, with a pained expression, wrenched free and darted for the back seat of Sergei's SUV. Damn it. Eric lurched after her, but a bulky man with a gun and an over-sized forehead stepped in his path.

Sergei spoke in Russian and tipped his head to the

man, then swung into the front passenger seat. The Cro-Magnon jammed his gun into Eric's kidney, steered him toward the vehicle, and forced him inside.

Eric sat cramped, knees bent at an awkward angle, as the driver veered off the lawn and onto the gravel road, not slowing for the turn onto the highway. He braced a hand against the ceiling and leaned into Elise's shuddering form. On his other side, the henchman pressed against his hip and arm. "Where are you taking us?"

Sergei twisted in the passenger seat and casually held his gun on Eric. "I'm not sure I'm taking you anywhere. I may still put a bullet in you and leave you on the side of the road."

Elise gasped. A hysterical pitch crept into her voice. "Can you put that thing away?"

The desperation in her tone made Eric's muscles quake. He longed to fight back but couldn't protect her if he was dead. If only they'd been quicker and gotten to the truck.

"Where are we going?" Her voice crescendoed with a tremble.

Sergei held up Eric's Bureau-issued cellular, rolled down the window and hurled it onto the highway. Eric's heart sank. His only connection was gone.

"I need your phone too, Elise." The man sounded almost apologetic. She set the cellular in his palm, and he tossed it into the dark void. "We're going to a private airstrip where we will get on a plane and go to the family compound in upstate New York."

Elise's hand rested on her thigh. Eric reached for it, his fingers brushing hers.

No. He had no right. Not when he'd failed to keep

her safe. All he had to do was look around to see how screwed they really were. After everything that happened with her father, he could only imagine what she must think.

She probably hated him.

His heart ached. He pulled away.

Elise shifted her weight and huddled against the door, head back, eyes closed. He was losing her.

The guy to Eric's left rested his gun on his leg, the barrel pointing at Eric. He was big and bald, his face scarred by pockmarks. Their gazes met and the large man's lips quirked into the sinister smile of someone who enjoyed inflicting pain.

Elise punctured the silence, a quiver in her voice. "How did you know where I was?"

Sergei angled to look into the backseat. "We've been watching you for your entire life but kicked things up when we realized Vincenzo and Rocco had retained your services as a pilot. We knew it was something to keep an eye on."

Eric let his head fall back, finding the knowledge someone had been paying attention to Vincenzo's interest in Elise strangely reassuring.

"You've been watching me my whole life?"

The man smiled. "Well, not exactly. We had a PI who recorded business transactions, where you lived, where you went to school. Stuff like that. All on paper. No one physically kept tabs."

"You had no right."

"Of course we did. We protect our own." Sergei didn't flinch under Elise's hard, unblinking stare. He shrugged. "I was only a kid when you left."

Eric tensed when he felt Elise's body go rigid.

"How'd you know we were in Albert Springs?" she asked.

"We tracked the tail number of your plane."

Eric caught Elise looking at him but couldn't read her expression. Did she blame him for their current predicament? She should. He was the one who encouraged them to stay the night. Not to mention his grand rescue that failed to accomplish anything. He'd gotten her away from one criminal and led her straight to another. He prayed she'd be better off with the Koslovs than with Vincenzo.

She folded her arms across her chest. "And the farm? How'd you end up there?"

"Just as we arrived at the motel, we saw Dick Tracy here tear out of the parking lot in a brown pickup. He led us right to you." He smiled over his shoulder. "Thanks, by the way."

Eric's chest constricted. He'd had a tail and missed it. When had he become so careless?

"We would have gotten you. Pretty boy should have stayed out of it."

Eric clenched his jaw but didn't take the bait. "Could Vincenzo have had a hand in the mechanical problem that forced us to land?"

Sergei shook his head. "Not his style, and I doubt he has the know-how."

That had been Eric's thought too. It had been a coincidence. A big, stupid coincidence. Unless…. "What about your organization? Were you involved?"

Sergei turned cold, flinty eyes on Eric. "We'd never put her in danger like that."

Eric snuck a glance at Elise. She stared at her lap, a stricken look on her face. "Why not just grab her on the first trip?"

The other man pursed his lips. "My guess? They were formulating a plan—maybe even toying with her but decided they could use the plane's mechanical issues and the unscheduled stop to their advantage."

Eric nodded. It made sense.

Elise wrinkled her nose. "Who shot at the barn?"

"Our guys." Sergei smiled. "Like I said, we were going to get you out one way or another."

Eric's voice shook. "How was shooting into the barn in her best interest?"

"I don't owe you any explanations." Sergei peered at Elise. "You were never in danger. We shot the guard to show we meant business. Everything else was a diversion."

She leaned back and took a shaky breath. Eric's hand twitched, the impulse to reach for her almost too much to resist. Again, he denied himself the gratification. Eventually, he'd make her understand how much he cared. Yes, he'd been doing his job, but he'd do anything to keep her safe. Protect her with his life if it came to that.

She spoke again, this time a hard edge crept into her voice. "Vincenzo said my mother went into hiding because a Koslov killed his daughter, and he wanted revenge. An eye for an eye."

Sergei threw a quick glance into the backseat. "Grandfather will fill you in."

The SUV turned onto a dirt road. After several minutes over bumpy terrain, they stopped. Looking out the window, Eric saw a large, private jet on a gravel runway. There were heads of state who couldn't afford luxury like this. The magnitude of the Koslov wealth and power came into sharp focus. He gave a rueful sigh and glanced at Elise. Pushing her to talk to him wouldn't help. It would be difficult—maybe the most difficult thing he'd ever done, but he needed to give her space.

****

Elise climbed out of the SUV and ascended the stairs to the plane. A mob plane. Tightness filled her chest. With no other choice, she stepped forward into the cabin and scanned the space. Her gaze darted from one extravagance to another in this luxurious prison. The rich fabrics and shiny surfaces barely registered after everything else that had happened. Her jaw ached from clenching it. She wouldn't be surprised if she ground her teeth into powder before this was over.

"Sit wherever looks good," Sergei said. "Get comfortable. Relax."

She suppressed a snort. Relax? Not a chance. She clasped her hands and held them against her chest to control fidgety fingers. She hated these people and their ridiculous aircraft.

A creamy white sofa decorated with polka dot throw pillows sat positioned opposite the hatch. On the other side of the aircraft were two leather captain's chairs and a foldable table attached to the wall. She limped deeper into the plane and found more seats.

Shifting her weight to relieve the pain in her ankle, she glanced at Sergei sprawled on the sofa. God, she hated the way he watched her every move. Chin held high, she made a quick decision and chose a forward-facing chair. She sank down, letting the plush leather hug her body.

Maybe she should elevate her foot. Take off her shoe and prop it on the table. She caught a glimpse of

Sergei, still staring. Maybe not. She didn't want to do anything that might suggest she was comfortable with any of this.

Eric walked toward her, escorted by two men—one of whom had been with them in the SUV. They led him toward her, but she couldn't pull her gaze from his wrists, now bound in front of him with zip ties. The raw abrasions on her own wrists throbbed in sympathy. "Take those off him," she demanded.

They ignored her, turned him to the left and pushed him into the seat across the aisle. These men weren't any better than the ones she'd just escaped. Maybe worse.

Heat flooded her insides. Her eyes found Sergei. "Is that really necessary?"

Her cousin met her stare, then made sure to hold it. "Despite what you think, he's not on your side."

His calm demeanor sent her heart into a frenzy. She glared back at him, hatred pulsing through her veins. "This isn't a game."

Sergei laughed. "You'll figure it out."

Elise fell silent and dug her fingernails into the palms of her tight fists. Why was this happening? Families didn't do this. They didn't hold each other hostage.

Sergei smiled. "I know what you're thinking." Condescension threaded his voice. "But I'm not your enemy. The sooner you figure that out, the better off you'll be."

She swiveled to Eric. His stony expression revealed nothing.

The men who'd escorted him into the plane sat across from Sergei. The one from the SUV had the enormous arms of a bodybuilder and a nose that looked like it had been flattened one time too many. The other appeared thin and wiry. His mien communicated ruthlessness, and something about the way he leered made her shiver.

She peered at Eric again, willing him to look at her, hoping he'd give her a chance to apologize for getting him ensnared in her screwed-up life. Even if she hadn't known anything about it.

Instead, his stare remained fixed on the window. Twice on the ride to the plane, she'd thought he might take her hand, but then he didn't. Would he forgive her for going with Sergei? It had been her only choice. He couldn't expect her to just stand there and let them shoot him.

When she pictured what could have happened, a sharp pain drew her hand to her chest. The muzzle flash. The bang. Eric going limp.

He might be a prisoner. He might blame her, but at least he was alive. She'd never regret that.

"Speak up if you want something to drink." Sergei said. "Soda, water, beer, wine? If you're hungry, we've got chips and pretzels."

She gazed at Eric. Again, he didn't speak. Was he okay? Why wouldn't he look at her?

A sinking feeling filled her stomach. Betrayal had been her first reaction when she learned his real identity, but she understood. He'd only been doing his job, and now he was the prisoner of a crime family. Because of her. She swallowed the lump in her throat. The only reason he was even here was because he'd rescued her from the barn. Who knew what her mobster family would do to him?

The high-pitched whine of the engines came to life,

and the plane began to roll, bouncing over the runway and picking up speed until it had enough lift to leave the ground. Elise gripped the armrests. She squeezed her eyes shut, trying not to picture the type of reject pilot who'd work for the mob.

She glanced at Sergei. She needed to know about Jack and Nate. Would they be kidnapped too? "Are my brothers safe? Do they know what's going on?"

"Someone from the family will be in touch," he said.

"I need to see them. Tell them I'm okay."

He nodded. "That's the first thing we'll do after you talk to Grandfather. If it makes you feel any better, we know they were visited by law enforcement, so they are aware of your kidnapping."

She was about to respond but saw Eric tense. She glanced over and noted his clenched fists.

He fixated on her, his eyes fierce. "Don't listen to him. The family won't let you talk to anyone. Controlling contact with the outside world is one of the ways they plan to manipulate you."

Was he right? Elise frowned and waited for Sergei to contradict the statement.

"Settle down, Deputy Dawg."

An animal-like sound rumbled from deep in Eric's throat, and even though she'd not gotten any reassurance about her brothers, changing the subject seemed like the best idea. She shifted her attention back to Sergei. "You said we were cousins?"

"Your mother and my father were brother and sister. Our grandfather raised me after my dad died."

She pursed her lips. It all seemed a little too convenient. "Why should I believe you?"

The man shrugged. "I think you'll find plenty of

evidence at the compound."

The throbbing in her ankle distracted her for a moment. She shifted in her seat and untied her shoe, sliding it off to inspect the swelling.

"Looks bad." Sergei rose and brought her a can of coke and dropped two pills into her hand. "Anti-inflammatory."

She stared at the pills, then at him.

"Take them or don't. Doesn't matter to me."

She placed the pills on the table and sat back. She'd live with the pain rather than trust a kidnapper. "How did Sophia die?"

Sergei didn't look at her. "I wasn't there."

She folded her arms across her chest. "But you know?"

He regarded her for a long moment and sighed. "She set up a meeting with our cousin Carlos. Some sort of networking idea. Her father had forbidden her from working in the family business, so the little rebel took it upon herself. Vincenzo had her followed. Carlos spotted the tail and thought he'd been set up."

"He shot them?"

Sergei nodded.

"What happened to Carlos?"

Her cousin gave a humorless smile and shook his head. "When you kill another boss's daughter, your life expectancy is significantly reduced."

Elise frowned. "But why kidnap me after all this time?"

"It is strange this has all come up again," Sergei admitted. "There's been an unofficial truce for years."

"Cancer," Eric said.

Sergei's eyebrows raised. "Come again?"

"Vincenzo has throat cancer. Supposedly stage four. Rocco will take over the business when the old man is dead. If not sooner."

Sergei nodded. "Unfinished business and nothing to lose."

Elise looked from one man to the other, fascinated by the shift in tone—a weird mutual understanding pulsed between the two.

"That would be my guess," Eric said. "Going to jail probably doesn't seem like a huge threat if you know you're going to die."

The men kept talking, but her ability to concentrate on the details disintegrated. She leaned her head against the seatback. The events of the last day were an absolute whirlwind—with more to come. What would happen when they landed in New York? She'd soon be in the home where her mother grew up. A mother she barely remembered.

The hum of voices blanketed her. She sank lower into the soft chair. Her eyes closed. Her head bobbed from side to side, the slow rise and fall of her chest the only thing she could concentrate on—until a sudden sensation of falling jolted her upright. She scanned her surroundings. Still aloft in the Koslov plane.

Eric scrutinized her. "You okay?"

"How long did I sleep?"

He shrugged. "Maybe an hour."

She yawned and rubbed her eyes with the back of her hands.

He leaned over his arm rest and into the aisle. "Can we talk?"

She ran her fingers through her messy hair. There were things she wanted to say too. But did she dare?

"This isn't good." He kept his voice low and nodded to the men in the front of the cabin. "I don't like it."

She peered at Sergei, then at Eric's bound hands. She couldn't let them do this to him.

"I need to explain." His voice came out hoarse and ragged. "About the assignment."

Elise caught a glimpse of Sergei, pretending not to listen.

Eric opened his mouth, but before he could speak, the cabin pressure changed. Elise's ears filled, followed by the familiar light-headedness that meant they were descending. "What will happen when we land?" she whispered.

His body went rigid. "I don't know."

"It'll be okay." She bit her fingernail. "Won't it?"

Her stomach tensed. She waited for his reply.

There wasn't one.

Chapter Eighteen

The plane slammed into the runway and lurched to the right. The pilot braked hard. Eric gripped the left armrest with his bound hands, but still jerked forward, his right shoulder dipping low. Crosswind landings could be tough, but the guy came in way too fast.

Elise raised her eyebrows, and Eric knew she'd had the same thought. "Where'd they find this guy?"

Her question didn't require an answer. He gave one anyway. "Probably a smuggler who worked his way up."

They taxied to a private hangar.

Sergei stared at Elise. "Stay here." He opened the hatch and dropped the stairs. The two thugs followed.

"There are so many things I want to say." Elise's voice cracked.

Eric's heart felt like a stress ball, squeezed and crushed by the situation. "Me too." He tugged at his bonds. He wanted to touch her, hold her hand. But first he had to figure out how to keep her safe.

Sergei and the two men reappeared, now with rifles slung across their backs.

Eric studied the weapons. M4 carbines. He'd known things could get worse, but seeing his fears become reality was something else entirely. With that kind of firepower aimed at them, what sort of protection could he offer?

"Elise, come with me." Sergei waited for her to undo

her seatbelt and slip on her shoe.

A knot formed in Eric's stomach. He'd never felt so helpless.

She gave him one last look, her expression tight, before turning and limping off the plane. The thin, wiry man followed.

The giant from the SUV glared at Eric. "I'm not sure why you're still here. If it was up to me, I'd have shot you in the stomach and left you for dead."

Eric's heart thrashed in his chest, but he forced a smirk onto his face and spoke with mock concern. "Dude, that much anger is *not* healthy. Mental wellness is a real thing. Your healthcare provider might have some treatment options."

"Do you ever stop talking?" The man growled. "Guys like you make me sick."

"I don't think it's me. Again, you might want to check your HMO."

The colossus cracked his fingers. "Hurting you would be so much fun." He sneered. "First, I'd cut out your tongue. Then I'd pull out your teeth. One tooth at a time."

Eric fought to keep his expression impassive, well aware he was provoking a man with a gun and a short fuse. "Guess it's a good thing you're not the boss." He held up his hands and smiled. "Looks like I'm not the only one whose hands are tied."

"Shut up." The man gave a derisive snort, unfastened Eric's seatbelt, and yanked him to his feet.

Talons dug into Eric's biceps making him wince. He pulled against the strong fingers, but the pain drilling into his arm only intensified.

The gangster guided him down the stairs. Eric

stepped onto the smooth, polished concrete of the hangar and scanned the surroundings.

"Where does he want him?" the giant shouted.

The thin guy from the plane pointed to an open door on the other side of the garage. Eric scanned the space as they strode past the nose of the aircraft. He didn't see Elise anywhere.

They neared the door. Eric pushed against his captor, but the big man was immovable.

"Get in there." He shoved Eric forward, causing him to stumble.

The room contained wooden pallets and several large wooden crates. Elise and Sergei stood among the cartons. Sergei held a gun on her.

Eric lunged for Sergei, but a beefy hand held him back.

"Relax," Sergei said. "Elise and I were just negotiating proper behavior. My cousin forgot her manners. Rather than thank us for our hospitality, she tried to make a run for it." The man gave a self-satisfied smile. "At least now we both know where we stand."

Too shocked to speak, Eric's jaw went slack. Did she have a death wish?

"So now, since I don't have time to babysit, the two of you are going to stay right here while I find out what Grandfather wants to do about our uninvited Fed." He leveled a stare at Eric, then turned to Elise. "And of course, let him know you're safe and secure."

Sergei stepped away from Elise and used the gun to motion for Eric to move into the room. He repeated the gesture until they stood side by side.

"Don't go anywhere." He smirked and the door clicked shut. The lock engaged.

Eric's body trembled, his battered heart pumping useless rage to his extremities. Damn it. He rounded on Elise. "What were you thinking?"

She shrugged but didn't look at him. "It's an airport. I know airports. I thought maybe I could get to the terminal building and get help."

"You could've been hurt."

She gave a belligerent snort. "Not likely."

His heart clenched, and he shook his head. How could she be so naive? Had he finally met his breaking point? Would protecting Elise be the thing that did him in? He tried again to get through to her. "Did you see the behemoth they left me with? Do you think hired killers like that are going to care who you are?"

She turned her back to him, a motion he took to mean she wasn't interested in his condemnation.

Oh, Elise. Hit by a sudden wave of exhaustion, he blinked weighted lids. He was so tired—physically, mentally, emotionally. But sleep was the last thing he should think about. He'd sleep when he was dead. A rueful chuckle bubbled up his throat. The way things were going, that might be sooner, rather than later.

Now it was his turn to avoid eye contact. He scanned the room. Shipping crates and not much else. What did these things hold? Weapons? Drugs? Crossing his bound wrists into an *X*, he curled the fingers of his right hand beneath the lid of the nearest crate and tugged. Nailed shut. They wouldn't find answers in here. All they could do was wait for Sergei or one of his goons to return. He exhaled and looked up.

Elise leaned against the wall and stared. "At least this gives us a chance to talk." Her voice was soft, apologetic.

A jolt of urgency shot through him. He needed to explain. No excuses. No rationalizations.

He took a cautious step closer, hoping she'd let him clarify his side of the story. "I didn't know anything about you when I took this assignment. I had no idea you were the reason for Vincenzo's trips to Colorado."

He lifted his bound hands, wanting to reach for her, but let them drop. As much as he wanted to hold her, it had to be her decision. She frowned. The pain written on her face was because of him, and he hated himself for it.

"Elise, I'm so sorry—"

Her brows squished together as though she didn't understand. "Eric, no—"

"Let me finish."

She crossed her arms but didn't speak.

"I lied to you, and I'm sorry." He blinked, his lids heavy and sticky. "Once trust is lost, it is so hard to get back. I know that, and I wish I could have told you, but I promise from here on out, no more secrets."

This time it was she who moved closer. "It was a shock, but I get it. You were doing your job."

"I was only there to observe Vincenzo and Rocco. We knew they were up to something, but I had no idea it had anything to do with you."

She tilted her head and spoke in a soothing tone. "I understand."

Determined to say everything he'd planned, he pressed on. "My main task was surveillance, to record incriminating conversations involving Vincenzo Alario." He paced away from her, then back. "If I could do things differently, I never would have let you out of my sight."

She hooked a finger around one of his pinkies. "I'm

not upset."

Her words, so matter of fact, drained the tension from his shoulders.

He bowed his head and sighed. "There's something else."

"More?" She choked out a strained laugh.

He could count on one hand the number of people he'd told of his dad's death. Ironic really, since thoughts of that day had consumed him for the last twenty-something years.

But she deserved answers.

He took a steeling breath. No reason to hide the truth now. "Do you remember when I said my dad died in the line of duty?"

She bit her lip and nodded.

"He was shot in a Koslov-owned bar. I believe Vincenzo went there after learning his daughter had died. He killed almost everyone in the place. My dad was the first officer on the scene."

His gaze drifted down and saw her small hand fit perfectly into his—as if it belonged there. Overcome, he perched on the edge of a crate. She settled beside him.

"He barely got through the door before being hit." He gripped her warm fingers. "It took several minutes for other units to arrive. By then he was gone."

"Oh, Eric—"

He didn't want her pity. "The investigators called it a total slaughter. Only two people escaped, a vendor who'd just completed a delivery in the alley and a customer using the bathroom. Both saw a man matching Vincenzo's description leaving the scene." He paused long enough to watch her eyes widen. "Later, both said they didn't see anything."

She leaned closer and placed her hand on his forearm.

"The official story was an angry patron shot up the place before escaping. When I got older, I tried tracking the witnesses down, but they'd vanished."

Her fingers laced between his and squeezed. Something about her touch gave him the strength to continue, to speak the truth he'd avoided for so long. "He never should have been there." He winced at the memory. "It was my fault."

"I don't see how that's possible."

"I had a baseball game later that week. My first time as pitcher. He switched shifts so he could be there."

She leaned over, forcing him to peer into her eyes. "That doesn't mean it was your fault. It just means he loved you."

He'd not realized how much he needed to hear those words. He'd never told anyone how he'd blamed himself, not even his mom. "I shouldn't even be on this case." She didn't speak, and he took her silence to mean he should continue. "No arrests and no official record of Vincenzo's involvement."

He shook his head, resenting his selfish need to chase down his dad's killer. On some level, he'd known he'd been lying to himself all along about why he wanted to work on organized crime. "Local officials scrubbed all connections between my dad's death and the mob. The Bureau doesn't know I have a personal interest. I should have disclosed it. I didn't." He'd convinced himself he was working for the greater good and not his own revenge, but that had been an excuse.

She squeezed his hand again. She hadn't let go. He stared at her in wonder.

"I've spent more than twenty years learning about the man who killed my father. My entire life is devoted to bringing him down. I've studied the crime scene photos—"

Her face twisted with horror at his revelation. "Why would you do that to yourself?"

"My dad shouldn't have died. His life mattered." He couldn't bear to see her disapproval, so he tucked his chin into his shoulder and closed his eyes.

She didn't speak, but he felt her stand and leave his side. Who could blame her? Not after learning he'd compromised the investigation with his own selfishness. He looked up, but instead of moving to the other side of the room, she stood before him, her cheeks flushed a light pink, her bottom lip tucked under her front teeth.

A primal urge crested and rippled through him. Eric sucked in a breath, and noticing how the t-shirt clung to her curves, he recalled the way her body molded to his.

She stepped forward, cupping his chin in her hands, catching his gaze, and not letting him look away. In her eyes, he recognized another tortured soul, a lost cause. Both of them defined by pasts they had no say in and decisions made without their knowledge.

He longed to hold her, to pull her near. But he couldn't—and not because his wrists were tied.

"I don't like this uncertainty, not knowing what comes next." He could see distress in her tight face and the rigid way she held herself. "But I feel better knowing you're here." She leaned forward and let her lips brush his. Her kiss was slow and sweet and far more than he deserved.

A sweet, earthy smell conjured visions of rolling fields and livestock—and Elise tied to a chair. Reality slammed into him and made his head spin. He turned from her, dragging her lips against the corner of his mouth. He couldn't protect her at the farm, and he couldn't protect her now. A sharp pain sliced through his chest, carving up his hope and leaving only harsh truth. "I'm the last thing you need."

She didn't argue, and somehow her silent acknowledgment was like a blade cleaving his heart in two.

Muffled voices sounded from outside. The door slammed open. The time had come. The closer they got to Aleksander Koslov and the compound, the sooner he'd find out what the family planned to do with them.

Chapter Nineteen

The rosy glow of the sun peeked through the trees standing guard along the roadway. Bright fall colors whizzed past. Elise turned away from the window. Mother Nature was a tease, using her beauty to instill a sense of hope. A great big setup for disappointment.

An arm's length away, Eric sat, a reminder that good still existed. He'd not said a word since Sergei took them from the storage room. She worried her bottom lip, hoping he'd be safe once they got to the compound.

The compound.

Her stomach churned. Soon, she'd meet her grandfather. She tugged the neck of her shirt to her nose and sniffed. Yikes. Her clothes and shoes—the same ones she'd changed into at the motel, were soiled with dirt and sweat. God. Had that only been last night? She glanced at Eric. He lifted his still-shackled wrists to scratch his nose. While lacking outward grime, his face carried the strain of their ordeal. The pulsing jaw, lowered brow, narrowed eyes.

There were so many things she needed to say, starting with how sorry she was for getting him involved in her screwed-up life. And yet, just knowing he was beside her gave her the strength to face her grandfather.

She gazed over her shoulder. They were in the second of three vehicles. All black with dark-tinted windows—a mafia motorcade. A new guy drove their

SUV, while Sergei sat in the front passenger seat. Neither talked.

The silence was maddening.

Just as the SUV crested a hill, the morning sun broke through the leaves of the tall maples. The sudden flickers of light reminded her of the unexpected turn her life had taken. She stared at her tightly clenched hands. The long-hidden granddaughter of a crime lord. What would her dad say about her current predicament? Would he tell her to trust this man—a crime boss, but also family?

Thinking of her father filled her with bewilderment. It had been one bombshell after another. First, it was his cocaine business. Now this. In some ways, she still found it hard to believe he wasn't the man she thought he was—the man who'd loved spending time with her, often volunteering to help with her home improvement projects on her place back in Key Largo. The back deck. The cinder block shed in her carport.

But the evidence continued to grow, and as the rolling New York countryside passed, so did her curiosity. How much of a sacrifice had it been to say goodbye to his wife and his identity? He'd given up everything to protect his children. Maybe he wasn't the best father. In some ways, not even a good one, but he'd loved his family.

A wave of warmth enveloped her. Her heart swelled. *He loved me.* How could she have thought otherwise? She fought the tears, not wanting Eric or Sergei to see.

She swiped the moisture from her eyes and glanced at Eric again, reminded of what he'd told her about his father's death. Every step forward with this man preceded two steps back.

Of course, this wasn't a normal situation.

Surrounded by criminals, all of them armed, some on their hips, others using shoulder straps. She'd seen him studying the men who transferred them to the SUV and had no doubt Eric had mentally catalogued every visible weapon and knew who carried what.

She'd never felt so helpless. Somehow this was worse than being kidnaped by Vincenzo and his goons. At least then, she thought there'd be an end. Dead, rescued or traded in a bizarre hostage exchange.

This was different. Uncertain.

She sat on her hands and bounced her legs on the balls of her feet. No point denying it, she was curious about her grandfather, but after everything with the Alarios, she felt fairly certain her old-man gangster quota had been met.

But Aleksander Koslov was blood. Allegedly. And he had a lot to answer for, especially since her father couldn't speak for himself. If only she could hear her brothers' voices. Maybe that would calm her?

"Can I have a phone, please?" Her heart pounded as she waited for the inevitable reply. "I want to call Nate."

"Sorry, no dice, cuz." Sergei threw her a grin over his shoulder. "Just wait to see what Grandfather says about things."

Damn it. She huffed and slouched deeper into her seat. So much for getting in touch with her brothers. Or anyone else, for that matter.

Eric was right. The promise of outside communication was nothing more than a rabbit meant to keep her running in circles. She'd been kidnapped and tied to a chair, but knowing these men—who supposedly cared for her—controlled her ability to communicate, made her feel more trapped than Vincenzo and Rocco

Alario ever could.

****

Eric fought the impulse to look at Elise. It would only distract him, and he needed to figure out a way to get a message to Grant. He thought of his phone, probably crushed to smithereens on a Nebraska highway. At the present moment, he had zero options. He stared out the window, reminding himself how many men rode in each vehicle and the weapons they wielded. In reality, all he could do was wait and see how things played out.

This whole mess-up of a mission would probably end with him in a shallow grave. No one would ever know what happened to him.

His stomach churned. His death would kill his mom. She'd endured so much already. The thought she might never know what became of him took his breath. Two men she loved. Both gone. Because of the mob.

He scrubbed his hand against the stubble on his chin. She'd been against him going into law enforcement, but he'd insisted. Justice was in his blood, he'd assured her. Now, he might never get to apologize for all the worry and heartache he'd caused.

Outnumbered and outgunned, any attempt to escape would be futile. Truth be told, they'd treated him well, all things considered. And, if you could ignore the weapons—which he couldn't, you might think the situation wasn't that bad. Koslov's men were polite and considered Elise a queen, but it didn't make this any less of a prison. The SUV idled at a light. He yanked the door handle. Locked. Like he knew it would be.

Twenty minutes or so later, they turned onto a long drive lined with tall evergreens. Behind the trees peeked a stone wall. To his surprise, it sported no defense turrets and not a single head on a spike.

At the gate, they rolled to a stop, and the driver lowered his window. A guard armed with a semiautomatic rifle approached the car. Eric needed to remember every detail on the off chance he made it out of this hellhole.

After a brief exchange in Russian, the guard motioned with his hand and the massive iron gate opened. They followed a curved driveway past manicured hedges and large trees before arriving at an enormous two-story house.

He'd seen drone and satellite images of the Koslov compound, but with all of his energy focused on Vincenzo, he'd not paid much attention to the layout of the stronghold. *Big mistake.* His short-sightedness became more evident with every minute.

He studied the estate from the car window. Lush, neatly trimmed ivy twined around the doorways and shutters, and crept up the stone facade. He caught sight of Elise out of the corner of his eye. Her gaze swept in all directions, taking in the world beyond the SUV windows. Did she recognize this place? Had she been here before?

More men with guns came forward to surround the car. His heartbeat slowed to a hard thud. To his knowledge, no other FBI agent had ever set foot inside the compound—at least none who lived to tell the tale.

The car door opened. "Let's go." A man with an angular face and hard eyes, his weapon slung across his back, motioned for Eric to exit the car.

With slow, deliberate motions, Eric set his feet on the ground and stood. The man grabbed his shoulder, spun him around, then felt up and down Eric's back and legs. Considering they'd taken his gun and knife earlier, the pat down seemed unnecessary.

"How 'bout buying me dinner first?"

The man grunted and shoved him forward toward the house. Elise, looking small and tired, waited on the steps next to Sergei, her eyebrows knitted together. As he approached, her lips parted as if she had something to say, but she closed her mouth before any words emerged.

Whatever happened here, however restricted his movements, he'd find a way to protect her. To his last breath if that's what it took.

He joined her at the entry and followed her through the front door. An open, airy foyer and the smell of fresh-cut flowers greeted them inside. Not at all what he'd expected from a mob boss.

He scrutinized the surroundings as they traveled deeper into the house. The walls were white and topped with ornate crown molding. A dark wood floor stretched into the belly of the house, and a staircase with a wooden handrail curled into the entryway. Through the room, he spotted a wall of French doors.

Men in dark, tactical clothing, likely coated with Teflon and carrying military-style rifles, tried unsuccessfully to blend into the furniture. The implication was clear. This was a fortress. No one got in or out without the king's approval.

Eric glanced at Elise. She'd spoken little in the car and hadn't said a word since they arrived at the house. He wished for a few minutes alone, but he didn't know when—or if—they'd get any privacy.

"This way." Sergei led them beneath the second-story gallery and into the back of the house. The guy from the driveway flanked them from behind. "I expect

Grandfather will want to meet with Elise first."

An angry rumble rose from deep in Eric's chest. "Not a chance—"

Elise lifted a defiant chin. "He goes where I go."

"Yeah?" Sergei shook his head, as if humoring a child. "We'll see about that."

They went through an arched entryway, into a lavishly furnished living room and stopped at a heavy wood door. Sergei rapped on the door while Mr. Frisky put his hand on the back of Eric's neck and squeezed. "Give the man the respect he deserves."

Eric curled his lip. The guy was a hot head and not worth the effort, especially when he was armed, and Eric wasn't.

"Enter." The voice resonated from behind the door. Eric could picture Mr. Koslov, but hearing his voice was something else entirely. Strong. Commanding. Authoritative.

Sergei stepped inside and shut the door. A moment later he reappeared, motioning to Elise and Eric. "He'll see you both."

"Told you." Elise smirked as she stepped past her cousin, but the light in her eyes faded the moment she entered the room.

Eric followed into an oak-paneled study lined with bookshelves. A woodsy cigar smell hung in the air. Aleksander Koslov—a man known as Papi because of his fatherly demeanor—sat behind an enormous desk. He stood and came around the massive piece of furniture. "Excellent." The old man gave his grandson an affectionate smile.

Sergei nodded, closed the door, and left. A short man, Koslov wore brown slacks and a crisp button-down shirt. Wispy, white hair stuck out from under a newsboy cap. He removed the hat and flattened the thin layer of hair on his mostly bald head. "I was out with the dog." His attention jumped to a basset hound lounging on a bed in the corner of the room. He smiled, extended both hands and moved toward Elise. "*Cariño de nieta*," the old man said, grasping Elise's hands. "You look just like your mother."

After listening to so many of Koslov's men speaking Russian, it was easy to forget the man's unusual background. Born and raised by a Russian family in South America, Aleksander Koslov was fluent in three languages and familiar with criminal tactics from both the Bratva and the Medellín Cartel. He was a dangerous man who couldn't be trusted. The mere sight of him with Elise sent adrenaline coursing through Eric's body, but he resisted the urge to yank her away.

"Hello, sir." Her voice trembled.

"Please, call me Papi. Or Grandfather."

Everything about the man seemed genuine, grandfatherly. Just like his nickname implied. No hint of the thug Eric knew him to be.

Elise gave an uncertain nod and brought a shaky hand to her forehead. Her grandfather motioned for her to have a seat. She glanced at Eric and took a tentative step toward a leather chair.

"First things first," Koslov said. He glowered at Eric. "What do you want me to do with him?"

Eric took a deep breath. The moment of truth. He glanced at Elise's pale face. Who would she choose? The wealthy and kindly-looking grandfather standing in front of her? Or the FBI agent who'd failed to keep her safe?

Chapter Twenty

Elise's heart pounded. She couldn't let anything happen to Eric. Her gaze snapped from her grandfather to the FBI agent she'd grown to care about. The seriousness of the moment hit her like a brick. Eric stood with his legs wide. Beneath bound wrists, his hands clenched into fists so tight the skin between his knuckles had turned white.

She gawked at the man who claimed to be her grandfather. "I won't let you hurt him."

His eyes went cold. "He's not one of us. That's a problem."

"I'm not one of you, either."

The old man stepped closer. His calloused hands brushed her cheek. "But you are, *mi nieta*."

She flinched away from his touch.

"It's been a long time, but you once sat on the floor of this very office, playing with your dollies."

"What difference does that make?"

"Family always comes first." He returned to his desk and pressed his fists into the leather blotter. He glared at Eric as though he had a personal grievance, but spoke to Elise, his words short and clipped. "I ask you again. What do you want to happen to him?"

The muscles in Eric's forearm tensed. Physically, there'd be no contest. Even with his hands tied, she was certain Eric could easily best the gangster. Of course, in a house full of armed guards, it would be a death sentence.

A bemused smile flickered across Papi's lips as if he could read her mind.

"Nothing." Her voice rose. Her feet moved without thought, and before she knew it, she found herself standing at Eric's side and sliding a possessive hand beneath his arm.

Her supposed grandfather gave a heavy sigh. "Very well. I do this against my better judgment, but I can't say no to you, *mi corazón*." He touched a hand to his chest. "Not when I just got you back."

Papi dug around in his front pants pocket, withdrew a folding knife, and walked around the desk. He flipped it open and sliced through the plastic ties.

Only a small victory, but a sense of triumph—warm and wonderful, flowed through her veins. Eric was safe. For now.

He rubbed his wrists and stared at the other man in a way that conveyed a mutual dislike.

Her grandfather motioned to the chairs in front of his desk. They sat, and Papi scrutinized Eric for a long, torturous moment. "My granddaughter has apparently developed an attachment to you but understand this. You are a visitor to my home and that comes with certain expectations. Don't think for a second you are free to go and do whatever you want. Your freedom here is relative. Make no mistake, you will be watched."

Eric's posture went rigid. "Understood."

"Good. Because you aren't here to snoop or whatever it is you do. You're a guest. I expect you to have the decency to respect my home and my hospitality." He poked a short, stumpy finger in Eric's direction. "Misbehave and you'll regret it."

Elise's stomach crumpled like a balled-up piece of paper. The men scowled at each other until Eric leaned back, an insincere smile on his face. *Let it go, dammit.* She prayed he wouldn't antagonize her grandfather. She couldn't bear for something to happen to him.

Corded muscles appeared on Eric's neck. "And just so we're clear, if anything happens to Elise and it's your fault, you answer to me."

"Will you two stop? I have questions that deserve answers." Elise's gaze shifted from one man to the other. It wasn't the time for a testosterone-fueled pissing match.

Papi shook his head and gave Eric a sad smile. When he spoke, the hard edge had gone from his voice. "I know who you are, *pana*. I'm sorry about your father." He took a deep breath. "I always felt bad about what happened to him. Even donated to the Widows and Children's Fund in his name."

Eric sucked in a breath beside her, but his expression remained inscrutable.

Papi's attention returned to her. "What do you want to know?"

"Where's my mother?"

"I have no idea. It's safest that way."

She studied the old man's expression, unsure if he could be believed. "Don't you give her money?"

"Filtered through anonymous offshore accounts."

The dull throbbing in her temples made it hard to think. "Vincenzo said you helped my mother go into hiding. He also said you were responsible for Sophia's death."

"I had nothing to do with what happened to Sophia

Alario, but Vincenzo believed because he lost his daughter, I should lose mine as well." He paused and rubbed his hand over his heart. A pained look crossed his face. "My daughter may still be alive, but I've lost plenty."

She couldn't summon any compassion for this man. "Was my father a criminal?"

"Depends on how you look at it."

Elise's heartbeat chugged. She shook, struggling to keep her voice level. "What's that supposed to mean?"

Capitulation speared the old man's sigh. In a flash, he showed his age. An obsolete Al Capone. "Your father flew for a global trade company. That's where he met your mother. She worked in the office and manipulated information on the shipping manifestos. He never did anything illegal, but he knew the grift." He eyeballed Eric. "He also knew how to keep his mouth shut."

"So, my mother engaged in fraud, and my father let it happen. A love story for the ages." Her voice shook with bitterness. She shouldn't have asked. What she wouldn't give to return to her invisible existence and her boring, nothing-ever-happens life.

After a long pause, Papi spoke, his voice quiet. "You can't know the sacrifices they made because of their love for you and your brothers."

For a moment, she let herself reflect on the pain written across his face, then forced herself to look away. She wanted nothing to do with this family of criminals.

Her instinct said run. *Leave. Don't look back.*

But that wasn't an option. Her old life was over. And now, she had only one choice. Adapt.

****

Elise's grandfather's story left out details and

ignored the truth. Eric folded his arms in front of his chest and leaned back into his chair. There was more to it than two men losing their daughters.

How many other lives had these families ruined? How many had died? All for a senseless feud? His racing blood heated his face and pounded in his ears with a deafening thunder.

First, Vincenzo took Eric's father. Now Papi wanted Elise.

His Elise.

His fingers tightened around the arms of the chair.

The man's comment about his dad seemed genuine, but Eric had no way of gauging his sincerity. He was surprised to realize Papi's research had been so thorough. Of course, one look at the date and location of his dad's death, and the old man would know exactly who was responsible. Eric shook his head to remind himself not to be fooled by fake sentimentality. The fact Koslov brought it up now only proved he had no qualms about exploiting the memory of Eric's father, and the comment was most likely an attempt to appear compassionate in front of his granddaughter.

Eric wasn't falling for it. He didn't think Elise would either.

He studied the books lining the shelves behind the old man. Tolstoy, Twain, Dickens. Props. Nothing about this family was as it appeared. And neither was their interest in Elise. He needed to remember that. Just because he wasn't locked in a room, didn't mean he wasn't a prisoner.

Elise fidgeted with a paper on Papi's desk—some sort of news article. "Are my brothers in danger?"

The old man leaned forward. "They're fine."

"How do you know?"

"I have eyes on them. Just like I did on you."

Her face paled. Eric set his jaw and stifled the desire to jump over the desk. Throttling the man would accomplish nothing. Cooperate now. Figure out how to get away later.

Kozlov kept his attention on Elise. "You must think me a coward, watching you from afar, but protecting you meant keeping my distance."

"I don't know what to think." She spoke in a voice so soft, Eric almost didn't hear her next question. "When can I go home?"

Tension rippled through him at the sight of Elise cowed, her voice quaking.

Her grandfather sighed, and Eric knew he was going to evade her question. "I'll send word later this morning that you are safe so your brothers don't worry."

Another non-answer. The manipulation continued. Offering small concessions in exchange for endless patience. As long as Elise remained in this house, she'd be a fish on a hook, baited with empty promises.

Eric clenched his jaw. He could only take so much. "She wants to know when she can leave."

Papi narrowed his eyes. "The sooner you leave, the better." He motioned to Elise. "I'd like Elisa to stay until the situation with Alario is resolved."

"That's not my name!"

Eric touched her thigh. Her leg bounced under his hand. She took a deep breath and stilled, but he felt her muscles constrict.

Papi ignored Elise's outburst. "For however long you stay, I hope you'll think of this as your home."

She snorted and looked away. Again, Papi pretended

not to notice.

The dog, lying in a round bed next to the desk, yawned, stood, and stretched. She ambled toward her owner, feet flopping and ears nearly dragging on the floor. Papi leaned over and scratched her between the shoulder blades. The dog's foot thumped, and she leaned into Papi's hand. He lifted, then set her on his lap. "This is Clementine. She's the real boss around here."

Clementine nuzzled the underside of Papi's chin. Her long tongue flicked, catching the old man on the mouth. He let loose a booming laugh. Eric couldn't help but shake his head. A psychopath and a dog person.

Papi pushed the button on an old-school intercom and asked the woman who answered to come to his office. "I've arranged for you to shower and have clean clothes."

Within moments, the door opened, and a short, older woman entered.

"Miranda runs my household. Tell her what size you wear; she'll take care of getting clothing."

Eric looked down and groaned. He still wore the T-shirt and jeans he'd dressed in last night at the motel. It seemed so long ago now.

"Mr. Erickson will also be staying." Papi's tone was sharp. "Please find him a room."

"Of course." Miranda gave a nod, then smiled at Eric and Elise.

Papi focused on his granddaughter. "I know you'll probably want a nap, but I've got some targets on bales in the backyard if you're up for it. You look tense. It might help to shoot a few rounds."

Elise frowned. "Archery?"

"I know how much you enjoy it. I thought it might

help you relax, make you feel at home."

****

Petite and efficient, Miranda's heels clicked on the wood floor as she led Elise and Eric to their rooms. She stopped, glancing at Elise. "Your grandfather has looked forward to seeing you. Being separated from you and your brothers has been a real trial. It's such a blessing you're finally here."

Elise rolled her eyes and wished everyone would stop pretending this was a fun family reunion. She studied the other woman's face. Despite the smooth skin, her gray hair and the wrinkles radiating from the corners of her eyes hinted at her age. She'd probably been with the household for a long time. "How long have you worked for my—"

"Grandfather?"

Elise nodded. She still couldn't bring herself to say the word.

"I've been with him for almost thirty years. He's a wonderful employer. A good man."

Elise expected a sarcastic comment from Eric, but he stayed silent, scanning their surroundings like he needed to commit to memory every doorway, corner, and dust ball.

Miranda waved. They followed. "The house was built in the 1920s and originally had nine bedrooms. Some of the upstairs rooms were converted into an apartment for your parents. Mr. Koslov added a first-floor suite about five years ago. He rarely comes upstairs anymore."

Would anyone else be up here with them? She didn't dare ask for fear it would lead to the real question. Would she be alone with Eric? The thought sent a shiver down her spine. She caught him staring and blushed, certain he could read her mind.

At the top of the stairs, they emerged into an open space. French doors lined the back wall. An enormous glass chandelier glittered in the natural light. "When they built the house, these three rooms were meant to be used as a ballroom." Miranda swept her hand indicating the arched entryways that led to additional large rooms on either side of the dance hall.

Elise could almost hear the music playing.

The woman motioned them through to the large doors at the back of the house. They stepped onto a long, stone balcony. The scent of wet vegetation rose from the river visible through the trees at the rear of the property. Elise inhaled pine from the nearby forest and spied a gardener trimming a hedge, the buzz of his landscaping equipment carrying on the wind.

Elegant, comfortable, and…ordinary. Exactly how she'd expect any wealthy person to live. But Papi wasn't any other person. He was a criminal.

"We also have a theater, a library, a billiards room, and a gym. Once you're rested, you can explore all you want." Stepping inside, Miranda pointed to a wide hallway on one side of the stairway. "Sergei's suite is down there. You'll be over here."

She led them into another room with black and white marble tiles. "Mr. Koslov once held his annual holiday party in these rooms." Miranda turned in a circle, a slight smile spreading to her face, as if basking in the memory. She shook it off. "That ended a long time ago."

Elise watched the woman stride toward another arched entryway and realized Miranda had worked in this house since before her birth. "Did you know my mother?"

The woman stopped. "I did." Miranda squeezed her eyes shut for a moment. "She wanted a little girl so desperately. You meant the world to her."

The words hit like an electrical current, and hot, angry blood surged to Elise's muscles, causing them to contract. She put a hand to her throat, hoping to corral the indignation in her voice. "Is that supposed to make her leaving okay?"

Miranda came to her, arms outstretched and grasped Elise by the shoulders. "Oh honey, she never would have left if there were another way. Originally, she planned to take you and send your brothers with your father. In the end, they decided against splitting you from your siblings."

Elise's heart went taut as a bowstring. *Don't tell me this. Not now. Not after I've hated her all these years.* She couldn't conceive of a life without Nate and Jack. She sniffled and wiped her nose. Miranda drew her into a hug, and over her shoulder, Elise spied Eric, his stance tight, ready to spring.

Then, just as quickly, the woman pulled away, tears in her eyes. With a sad smile, Miranda gestured them into a wide hallway lined with impressive artwork. They stopped at the first room. "Your mother's room before she married." Pushing open the door, she revealed a plush bedroom with patterned walls and a bed piled with so many pillows it looked decadent. Miranda strode across the room and opened glass-paneled doors to reveal another balcony. "You can see the river from the veranda. She loved spending time here even after she and your father moved to the other side of the house. She'd sit on the balcony every night with you in her lap and watch the sunset."

Elise stepped inside and surveyed the room. Maybe she'd find a connection to her mother here, something to help make sense of everything.

Miranda continued, once again the responsible hostess. "Make yourself comfortable and take a shower. I'll find something for you to wear."

Elise stepped to the threshold and watched Miranda take Eric to a door at the end of the hall. It wasn't a motel room with an adjoining door, but it was private. Perfect for plotting their escape.

Perhaps other things, as well.

Chapter Twenty-One

Refreshed and clean, Eric turned off the shower, wrapped a towel around his waist and pushed his hands through his hair. It felt as if he'd washed away weeks of grime. In reality, it hadn't even been a day.

His last shower was just before the encounter with Elise on the vibrating bed. Kissing her smooth lips, touching her soft skin—*Don't go there.*

Too late. His cock throbbed and a warm tingle spread to his abdomen. He dropped the towel and wrapped his hand around his erection, stroking its length. Slow at first. Up. Down. Up. Down. Then quicker. He moaned. Bracing a hand against the shower wall, he closed his eyes and imagined the warm tightness of Elise's mouth. *Oh fuck.* He exploded onto the wet tile.

Dazed, he shook his head. Relieving tension was one thing, but geez. What was he thinking? He was a captive. In a mobster's house.

Not to mention the other problem. Even here, he couldn't shake his attraction to Elise. It had grown like a weed, fast and sure, climbing and twisting and sprouting into his heart. He scrubbed his hands across his face. The attachment was real. No reason to pretend otherwise now.

The urge to be near her tugged at him. Protecting citizens came with the job, but this was different. This need to keep her safe went beyond the typical call of duty.

Towel wrapped around his waist, he stepped into the bedroom where he found a neatly piled stack of clothes. Thumbing through the expensive garments—brands he'd only ever heard associated with celebrities—he pulled out a pair of athletic pants and a black tee.

He stepped into the pants and slid the soft shirt over his head. His thoughts returned to his concern for Elise. The effects of the kidnapping likely hadn't sunk in yet, but they would. The consequences of her ordeal—anything from denial to shock to feelings of hopelessness—might not appear right away. There was no telling which would hit her first. Or when.

He needed to go to her. Both to provide comfort, but also to check her mental state for himself. And, if he was being honest, to be close to her.

The doorknob called to him. All he had to do was step forward, turn the handle, and he'd be halfway there. Then she could be in his arms.

He didn't move.

What was he afraid of?

That she'd tell him to go away. That he'd fuck it up.

He sat on the bed, needing to clear his head. Instead, he found himself surveying his surroundings. The room was large and plush, but a comfortable jail cell was still a jail cell. He'd scoured for hidden cameras first thing. The fact he didn't find any provided only a small measure of relief. Papi might not be surveilling the bedrooms, but he'd be watching. Of that, Eric was sure.

Leaving the room would allow him to assess how much freedom he actually had.

He pressed his ear to the door. Quiet. No voices. No movement. Didn't mean no one was there. Opening it a crack, he peered into an empty hallway. He pulled the door wider, expecting an armed thug. Nothing. Strangely insulted, he took a tentative step into the hallway and realized his captors had no reason to waste manpower guarding him. With nowhere to go and no weapons, how much of a threat could he be?

The door to Elise's room stood ajar. He stopped, peered inside, and pushed it open. A disheveled bed, clothes strewn all over the floor, and used towels littered the room. It looked like a tornado had touched down. In the middle of the mess sat Elise, dressed in loose pants and a T-shirt, her hair wet from a shower, and so absorbed in whatever was on that piece of paper she stared at, she didn't even know he was there.

He stepped inside and the movement caught her attention.

She glanced up, flinched ever so slightly, then folded the paper and dropped it into the nightstand drawer, almost as if she didn't want him to see what she was doing. Where had it come from? Was it something her grandfather gave her? Miranda?

He opened his mouth to ask, but she spoke first. "You looking for me?"

"I wanted to see how you're doing." He took a step into the room and closed the door. "It's almost dinner time and you haven't eaten since last night."

"Neither have you."

With a nod, he stepped closer. "We should have something sent up."

She held his gaze and delivered one of her radiant smiles. "When will the FBI be here?"

The question dropped into his stomach like a rock from a cliff. He swallowed the desire to tell her what she wanted to hear in favor of the truth. False hope would help neither of them. "I doubt they know where we are."

She stared with wide eyes. "Didn't you contact them when I was kidnapped?"

"They were tracking my phone."

It took a moment, but then her shoulders collapsed. Her words emerged, slow and thick. "Sergei threw your phone out the window."

"And even if it still works, that was in Nebraska." Should he ease her worry by saying there was a chance the FBI had pieced together what had happened at the farm? No, best not get her hopes up. There was no reason for them to make the connection since he'd not gotten a chance to tell Grant about Elise's link to the Koslovs. Plus, he didn't know if the FBI were aware the Koslovs had even been at the farm.

She flopped onto her back and stared at the ceiling with vacant eyes.

His throat ached with unspoken regret. What could he say? If he'd been with her at the motel, none of this would have happened.

Elise's hands balled into fists at her side. She gave the ceiling a nod, sat up and regarded him with a steady gaze. "We aren't giving up. We're going to get out of here."

If only he shared her optimism. What he wouldn't give to be able to tell her he had a plan. He shook his head, sat beside her, and rested his hand on her thigh. "I'll try to walk the property, see if I can find any weaknesses." His heart wanted to believe escape was possible but his head said it wasn't likely. Still, it didn't hurt to look. He should gather as much intel as possible on the off chance they had an opening.

Elise leaned forward and gave him a sweet kiss on the lips. His body buzzed, wanting more, but today, he needed to let her lead.

She pulled away.

"You should eat and then get some sleep." He kissed her on the forehead and headed for the door. Before opening it, he looked back and sighed. Papi's long-term plan likely didn't include keeping an FBI agent on the premises for very long, which meant time was limited. He needed to figure out where this was going.

****

The next morning, Eric woke before the sun. In truth, he'd barely slept. Thoughts of Elise and his lack of options for protecting her had tumbled through his brain all night. He got out of bed and dressed, then drifted through the ballroom and down the stairs.

The entry of the first-floor foyer was devoid of guards. Their absence made him wonder if yesterday's welcoming committee had been trotted out for his benefit.

Miranda exited a small office and intercepted him. He hadn't expected anyone to be up at such an early hour. This woman was everywhere. If he ever got back to the Bureau, it wouldn't hurt to run a background check on Papi's loyal assistant.

She gave a crisp nod. "Agent Erickson, how were the clothes? Satisfactory?"

He nodded and rubbed his jaw, surprised to find the beginning of a beard.

Miranda noticed too. "I'm so sorry I didn't think to offer you a razor. I'll make sure one is sent up ASAP."

Unsure what to make of the woman's hospitality, he searched for something to say. She'd been incredibly kind to Elise during the tour of the house and appeared to care about their comfort. Was her affection genuine?

He had a thousand questions, but none he thought she would answer. "I thought I might take a walk."

"Of course." She beamed, while motioning for him to follow to the back of the house. "The grounds are lovely. If you follow the path, you'll see several exquisite pieces of art and fountains. Make sure you stop at the koi pond in the northwest corner of the property. It's a wonderful place to watch the sun rise." She opened the door and followed Eric outside. "And definitely check out the maze garden."

He thanked her and started along the winding stone path. Once out of view, he made his way across the lawn to the perimeter wall. Standing at least ten feet tall, the solid concrete barrier was cool beneath his hand. From where he stood, it was impossible to guess its thickness, but the entire structure appeared to extend into the ground, eliminating any chance an intruder—or an escaping captive could dig underneath it. Glancing up, he spied video cameras mounted every twenty-five yards or so. Great. Papi would know he'd been out here and why. He'd have to tell Elise they were stuck. At least for the time being.

Eric covered every inch of the compound's outdoor space. Once satisfied he'd seen everything, he turned back toward the house, noting the sun's position. Mid-morning. He'd stayed out far longer than he'd planned. When he got to the stairs, he felt a presence and looked up. Miranda. "If you're looking for Elise, she's at the target range."

Eric peered through the glass doors at the back of the house. He already knew where to find the archery field but didn't want to interrupt the woman's instructions.

"Go through the garden and take the path to the right. Keep going when you reach the tennis courts. Take a left at the fountain."

Following her directions, Eric trekked through the Koslov compound, this time taking his time to note the landscaping. Topiaries, statues, a pool, and waterfall—opulence at every turn. If Vincenzo's daughter hadn't died, Elise would have grown up in this house. What if she decided this was the life she should have had?

A hollowness invaded his chest. His feet slowed. He rounded the corner, and a garish fountain loomed before him. Poseidon with his trident struck a magnificent pose at the center.

Eric gazed past the god of the sea, and his breath caught. Elise. The way the sun captured the wayward strands of hairs on the top of her head, the graceful way she moved. He remembered seeing her in the break room in her workout clothes. God, was that less than a week ago? It felt like a lifetime. The initial attraction had been instant, but also superficial. That was no longer the case. Every moment he spent with her, his admiration grew.

She stood on the lawn, a compound bow in her hands. A beefy, bald man who looked like a drill sergeant stood beside her, his biceps straining against the sleeves of his shirt.

She bit her lip, an adorable look of consternation on her face as she turned the bow over in her hands. Her lips spread into a smile when she spotted him, and he felt as though he'd been struck in the chest by one of her arrows. She waved and trotted his way, still favoring her right ankle.

He put a hand on her arm when she neared. "Is everything okay?"

Her smile faltered. "I think so."

"What's the problem? Does your ankle hurt? Is something wrong with the bow?"

In a nervous gesture, she pinched her earlobe and shuffled her feet. "It's nothing."

"Elise?"

She gave an exasperated huff. "It's just weird."

He made a rolling, give-me-more motion with his hand.

"I came out here to shoot and Craig gave me this bow." She gestured toward the hired gun pretending to be an archery coach. "It's the same bow I use at home. Same model, same color. It's even got the same stabilizers and weight." She lifted the pouch that hung against her leg. "Quiver, arrows, fletchings. All the same."

Unpleasant prickles at the base of his neck sent a warning to his brain. He stared at the Dwayne Johnson wannabe. Craig glared back with equal ferocity. "Are you sure that's not your bow?"

"Mine has a chip on the riser." She ran her finger over the smooth finish and lowered her voice. "Even the bowstring colors and serving are the same. How could they know?"

Eric's eye twitched. This went beyond a paper trail. They'd kept tabs on her every move and still were.

She swallowed. "Papi suggested archery. Do you think that was intentional? Is he trying to scare me? Make a point about who's in control?"

A good question. Eric had no answer. Was it another example of mental manipulation? Or did her grandfather genuinely want to make her happy? Either way, it was more proof the man didn't plan to let her leave anytime soon. Possibly never. He grasped her hand and squeezed.

"I hate this place," she said under her breath. "Did you do any snooping? Figure out a way to get us out of here?"

If only. "I wish I had good news, but I didn't see anything that will work to our advantage."

She let out a low, heavy sigh.

He lifted her chin and forced her to look into his eyes. "It doesn't mean we can't escape. It just means it might take some time."

****

Shooting usually made Elise feel better. She found nothing quite as satisfying as the thump of an arrow hitting its target at two hundred miles per hour. On a typical day, as soon as the first arrow left the bow, her frustrations melted away. Not today.

She shot twelve rounds of five arrows, a standard 300-point game, and kept score out of habit. Each time she retrieved an arrow, she grumbled at her poor performance. One missed the bale entirely. Several others hit the paper, but not the target. She struggled to concentrate.

Some of it had to do with the bow. Despite being identical in every way to the one she shot at home, she detested the look and feel of it in her hand. The entire situation was nothing but a mirage meant to mimic her normal life. But there was nothing normal about being held against her will. No amount of ornamentation or luxury could change that fact.

But the bigger distraction? The thing she couldn't shake? The paper she'd stolen from Papi's desk. Right there in front of her. An article about Eric's dad. She'd been certain he spied it when he came to her room last night, but he'd said nothing.

Slain Officer Laid to Rest.

She couldn't decide what was more unsettling—the idea that Papi had investigated Eric or the article about Eric's father.

The picture of a young, blond-haired boy standing among a throng of police officers squeezed at her heart. She'd memorized the entire article. It confirmed everything Eric had said. Patrol officer Arthur Erickson had responded to a shooting at a bar in Queens and was shot upon entering the premises. He'd died before first responders arrived.

Arthur. She repeated the name to herself.

Her stomach churned. Reading the article had felt wrong, like she'd taken a piece of Eric without his permission.

She drew her bow again and aimed at the bottom right of the five-spot target twenty yards down range. Her thumb twitched on the trigger, and she jerked, releasing the arrow, and sending it left of center. She squinted, locating the bright-green fletching in the gray background between the two bottom rings. *Dammit.* Why was she even bothering with this nonsense?

It was bullshit. All of it. Papi was trying to create an illusion of freedom by allowing her to walk the grounds and conveniently indulging her interests.

Good intentions or not, she couldn't live like this. This new reality was only marginally better than being tied to a chair in a barn. Eric said he hadn't found any places where they might slip away. Perhaps she could convince Papi to let them go. For the time being, her best bet might be to go along with the charade. He wouldn't cut her off from her brothers and the outside world forever. Would he?

She let out a wry laugh, glad there was no one close enough to hear. To think, she'd been under surveillance most of her life and had no idea. Shivers ran up her spine, and she scanned her surroundings for creeps hiding in bushes. Would she ever feel at ease again? Or would she spend her life looking over her shoulder?

Judging by the stoic expression Eric wore as he stood off to one side watching her shoot, he felt it too.

She wrenched an arrow from the bale as Sergei approached. Older than she, he had a friendly, open face that belied the cold-blooded criminal she knew him to be. The memory of him yelling for her to get in the SUV while threatening to shoot Eric was forever seared into her brain. If she hadn't seen it with her own eyes, she might not believe this charismatic guy with the dimples and that roguish moustache was mixed up with the mob.

Perhaps Sergei could be an ally. At the very least, maybe he'd let her talk to Nate and Jack.

"You don't remember, but I taught you to hula-hoop on this very spot." His eyes held a playful gleam. "What you lacked in coordination, you made up for with heart."

She gave him a cool look.

When she didn't respond, he cleared his throat. "Nate and Jack know you're safe."

"When can I talk to them?"

"We can't risk it just yet. We're keeping things on the down-low for the moment."

She seethed. Another excuse to isolate her, to restrict access to her old life. Just like Eric said. "Do they know where I am? Or are they supposed to take you at your word?"

"They know."

"How did they react to finding out we have family we knew nothing about?"

He stilled.

Heat crept up her neck. "They knew?"

"Nate did."

Unbelievable. Her heart throttled up, fueled by anger. Another person who'd lied to her. Was this why he'd tried so hard to exert control over her life? What else had he kept from her?

Sergei glanced at her hand. She looked down at her white-knuckle grip on the handle of the bow. She took a deep breath and attempted to relax, but her jaw stayed clenched. This was her chance. "Do you think you'll talk to him again soon? I think I'd feel better if I could hear his voice."

Her cousin's gaze softened, the lines of his face loosened, and he put his hand on her shoulder. "No promises, but I'll see what I can do."

The smile pasted on his face didn't quite reach his eyes. She sensed bad news was coming.

"Papi wanted me to invite you to a family dinner tomorrow night at eight."

She frowned and yanked the two remaining arrows from the bale and jammed them into the quiver. In her peripheral vision she saw Eric stride toward them.

"The cook is preparing an eight-course meal in your honor."

Eight courses? That would take forever. She didn't know how much of these people's presence she could actually stand.

Sergei glanced at Eric and added as if it were a huge

concession, "Your guard dog can come too."

Her stomach rumbled. She couldn't remember the last time she'd eaten a full meal. "I don't have clothes for a fancy dinner."

"Miranda's taking care of it."

She scowled. They weren't going to leave her any excuses. "Please tell Papi I appreciate the offer, but I have to decline."

Sergei let out an exaggerated sigh. "That's not an option."

"I thought you said it was an invitation. People can say no to an invitation."

Sergei started to respond but didn't get a chance.

Eric appeared at her side, glaring at the other man and his arrogant smile. "Is everything okay?"

"We're being summoned to dinner tomorrow night."

Eric snorted. "Attendance is mandatory?"

Sergei ignored him. "If you're hungry, there's a sandwich tray in the morning room every day at noon." He started to leave, but stopped, an underlying message in his gaze. "I'm not your enemy. I understand your suspicion, but Papi's right. We're your family and we love you."

****

Eric couldn't imagine living in a world where a morning room was an actual thing.

Located on the back of the house, its French doors and floor-to-ceiling windows allowed light to flood in. An ornate rug decorated the hardwood floor, while the interior featured a small table, leather chairs and couch. A tray of sandwich meats and cheeses sat atop the buffet cabinet against the wall.

They each took a plate, built a sandwich, and sat in one of the wingback chairs.

Elise chewed her lunch. "I didn't realize I was hungry until Sergei mentioned dinner." She popped the last bite of the sandwich into her mouth and stood to get more.

Her movements were fluid, assured, and he conjured an image of her with the bow. Her stance, her draw, her focus. Everything she did conveyed grace and authority. Would she devote the same attention to making love?

The hairs on his neck prickled again. Caring for Elise meant keeping her safe, getting her away from this hellhole. Indulging his sexual fantasies was the last thing he should be thinking about. He scanned the room for hidden cameras, saw none but suspected they were there. Working for the FBI, he'd seen cameras smaller than a fingertip. Concealing one would be easy.

She returned, her second sandwich bigger than the first, and peered at the plate balanced on his knee. "Aren't you hungry?"

He glanced at his untouched sandwich. "I am." Picking it up, he crammed a corner into his mouth, tasting nothing.

His entire adult life had been about catching a mobster. Now, he found himself held hostage in the home of a crime lord, cut off from the Bureau and the rest of the world. No weapons. No phone. No way out. He glimpsed Elise. No way to keep her safe.

That was the biggest worry of all. He'd already lost so much and didn't know if he could handle losing another person he cared about.

A pile of cookies had somehow appeared on Elise's plate. Chocolate oozed as she bit into the cookie, then pulled the uneaten half from her mouth. "Mmm. I could get used to this."

Her words cut like a knife. The last thing he wanted was for her to get used to this food, this house, this life. He took an obligatory bite of his sandwich, and when he finished, she took his plate.

"I'm sorry I got you involved," she said, her voice hushed.

He stood and gazed into her tired, puffy eyes. "I've been involved for a long time."

He caught her hiding a yawn.

"We both need a nap." Resisting the impulse to touch her, he let his hand hover behind the small of her back. "Maybe we'll wake up, and this will be nothing but a bad dream."

Chapter Twenty-Two

The perfect dress. Elise didn't know why she'd expected anything less. So far, Miranda's picks had been spot-on. It couldn't be luck. Or skill. Someone had been keeping notes. She fingered the soft material. Silver and raspberry-colored stripes accented a high-low ebony skirt. The dark, velvety bodice with its plunging neckline was soft and silky between her fingertips. Would it feel this decadent against her skin?

A prickle of unease worked its way up her back and neck. She could think of a dozen unpleasant things she'd rather do than go to this dinner with her new family. Retake the SATs. Get a root canal. Eat the sticky, old hard candy her elderly next-door neighbor kept on her coffee table.

A tear swelled in the corner of her eye. She wiped it away, took a cleansing breath and returned to the dress. In her old life, she never had any reason to wear fancy clothes. She took a step back to examine the gown. This might be her only chance to wear something this exquisite.

She and Eric had been imprisoned here for two full days. Enough time for reality to seep in. They weren't getting out anytime soon. At least not of their own accord. The house was comfortable, and they'd been provided with everything they could want, but it was hard to overlook being held against your will.

On the vanity she discovered everything she needed for a night out, including a small jewelry box with a note. *Your mother's favorite—Miranda*

Elise opened the small package and gasped. In it was a beautiful oval-shaped ruby pendant. Mom's birthstone. Two rows of tiny diamonds surrounded the gem. Holding the necklace against her palm, she studied the impeccable stone. Had her mother meant for her to have this?

She set the necklace aside and with a deep breath, stared into the mirror. Time to put on her armor. Never one for make-up, tonight she longed to be someone else. Someone with a normal life. Someone with the freedom to make their own decisions. A smooth line of eyeliner. A dusting of eye shadow. Mascara. Some toner, a dab of powder and a thin coat of lip gloss. She puckered her lips and gave her reflection an exaggerated kiss.

When her hair dried, she used the curling iron to add some loose, bouncy curls.

Next, she slid into a pair of black lace panties, and couldn't help but imagine Eric's fingers pushing them in the opposite direction.

Finally, the moment of truth.

The luxurious material of the gown rippled against her bare legs and torso as she pulled it to her shoulders. Once fastened, she turned to the full-length mirror and barely recognized the stranger looking back at her. She slipped on a pair of strappy black wedge-style sandals and buckled the clasp. Standing, she placed weight on her right leg to test her injured ankle. Some pain, but nothing she couldn't handle.

The ruby necklace sparkled from the dressing table where she'd left it. She picked it up and held it up to the light. By choosing to wear the pendant, would she be making a statement? Honoring a mother she scarcely remembered? Or would she feel like a fraud?

Only one way to find out. She undid the clasp and fastened it behind her neck.

With a deep breath, she took one last look in the mirror. A picture of elegance. The dress fit perfectly. Her hair fell full and shiny.

If only she didn't look so miserable.

She stretched her mouth into a would-be smile. The corners refused to turn up.

Hugging herself, she walked to the balcony. The sun had disappeared behind the horizon long ago, but the moon was full and bright. She sighed, unsure why she'd taken such pains to get ready. She had no one to impress.

What a lie. Why deny it? Only one person truly mattered.

Under different circumstances, she and Eric might go on a real date and do normal couple things. Eat at a restaurant. Go to the movies. Hike through the woods. Instead, they were hostages playing dress up. For all she knew, this might be the only night they'd ever get. No point sugar-coating it. They were looking at an evening of manipulation. Truth be told, she welcomed any pretext that allowed her to pretend things were different. Still, she had to remember it wasn't real. Papi could dress it—and her—up all he wanted. Nothing could make her forget her stolen freedom.

She'd spent half her life in the air. Up there, in the cockpit, she had power and independence. Not to mention, a literal bird's eye view. On a clear, cloudless day, she could see for miles—cities, rivers, mountains, the sea. It was magic. She prayed she'd feel that way again soon.

A forceful rap pounded on the door. She advanced slowly, pausing with her hand on the doorknob to take a deep breath. When she pulled it open, her knees nearly buckled. Freshly shaven and wearing a dark blue suit, Eric tugged on the knot of a light blue tie. He started to flash his crooked smile, but then his gaze raked over her, and his mouth dropped open.

Something in her chest loosened, and she felt buoyed by the warm sizzles that flooded her nervous system. Looking at him, an unexpected certainty grabbed hold. He was all she needed, and as long as he was here, everything would be okay.

****

Wow.

Dark hair cascaded down her back. Her dress revealed tanned shoulders and toned arms. Her body was alluring, but it was her eyes he couldn't look away from. The smoky outline accentuated flecks of copper. An electrical current passed from her hungry gaze to his body, stirring him alive, as if every neuron had fired at once. He inhaled, relaxed his shoulders, and silently counted to three.

She watched, expectantly.

Idiot. Say something. "You look great."

Biggest understatement of his life. She was an oasis—like flying over desolate landscape of desert and stone, before emerging above an iridescent lagoon. Had there not been a crime lord waiting on their arrival, he'd be tempted to peel the dress from her body and finish what they started in the motel.

"Thank you. You look very handsome too."

He wanted to smile back but couldn't. "Are you

ready for this?"

"No." The pitch of her voice rose.

Eric hated that her grandfather was making her jump through these hoops but resisted the impulse to draw her into his arms. "You'll be fine."

She gave a nervous smile. "Why do you think Papi's doing this? Making us pretend we're his guests?"

Because the old coot can. "I think he's hoping it will make you think you belong here."

"Right now, I just want to make it through dinner."

"You and me both." He dreaded the upcoming farce of a formal dinner party but hoped it might yield some answers.

She fidgeted with her necklace, sliding the dark red gem across the chain.

"Is something else bothering you?"

She stroked her collarbone, drawing his attention to the sleek curve of her neck. "I don't know who I am anymore."

"What do you mean?"

"It's all been a lie. My entire life." She bit her lip and shook her head. "Where does that leave me?"

This time, he didn't resist. He drew her near, pulling her head to the crook of his neck. He allowed himself an indulgent breath and was surprised to find her now-familiar lavender scent missing, replaced with something sweet and heady. "Your family has secrets, but that doesn't change who you are."

"How am I supposed to behave with these people?"

"When I trained to work undercover, I learned you have to believe in yourself. This is the same. Be confident in the person you are." She shivered, and he rubbed his hands up and down her bare arms. If only he could take her away from this place.

"I wish I knew where this was going." She met his stare with an imploring gaze. "When will I get to go home?"

"Hopefully we'll figure some of that out tonight." He wished he could shield her from all of this. "Are you ready?"

"As much as I'll ever be."

He followed her out the door, noting the slight limp. "How's your ankle?"

"A little sore. I'll be all right."

He looped his arm into hers to give her support. At the bottom of the stairs, a server directed them to a small, but elegant room, featuring silver walls accented with gold painted leaves and capped with an intricate ceiling.

The tableau that awaited them was as contrived as it was absurd. Papi sat on the couch with Clementine at his feet and Miranda perched behind him on the arm of the sofa, rubbing gentle circles on his back. Sergei sat in one of the plush leather chairs, sipping an amber liquid. He held his glass in mock salute as they entered.

Eric scanned the scene as if stepping into a performance already in progress. The roles they played were meant for one man. Elise had the lead as long-lost granddaughter, while Eric was pretty sure he'd been cast as the dancing monkey.

The scenario was so ridiculous, he almost laughed. But then he caught a glimpse of Elise, her face drained of color, pupils dilated. Framed photos lined the mantel above the fireplace. She'd fixated on a photo of two young boys and a baby.

He leaned over and whispered in her ear. "I'm here. You're not in this alone."

She set her jaw and stepped forward. "I'm okay."

The movement caught Papi's attention. He twisted to peer over the back of the couch. His gaze softened. "*Mi cielieto*, I'm so happy to see you again." He leaned toward her. "You look lovely."

Elise looked away. "Thank you."

Miranda grasped Papi's hand and smiled at Elise. Apparently, the old man and his secretary's relationship went beyond employer and employee. That might explain the woman's seeming devotion to Elise and her family.

A server approached with a tray of crystal stemware full of wine. Elise snatched a glass. When offered the platter, Eric declined. He needed to keep his wits about him.

"We have other options if wine isn't to your liking." Sergei motioned to a bar cart filled with bottles, glasses, and an ice bucket.

Eric held up his hand. "A glass of water would be great."

Glancing at Elise, he noticed she now held an empty glass. *That went quick.*

When the server stepped forward to take her glass, she snagged a replacement.

Eric rubbed his brow. He'd not expected this. The things he didn't know about women could fill a football stadium, but there was one thing he'd found to be consistently true. Telling them not to do something did almost nothing. Telling Elise to cool it would almost certainly have no effect. At least she looked relaxed. More so than since this ordeal began.

Papi motioned for Elise to join him on the couch. "Sit down. I want to get to know my granddaughter."

Elise bit her lip before taking a halting step forward. She gulped the rest of her wine and lowered herself to the sofa. Her gaze darted around the room, looking at Eric, then the exit, then the floor. Never at Papi.

Eric crushed the urge to grab her and run.

Somehow Elise procured herself another glass of wine. If she kept it up, she wouldn't be able to walk to the dinner table. She'd had so little food in the last few days, he worried the alcohol might hit her hard.

Papi glanced at Eric. The old man's pinched expression implied annoyance with his hovering. Eric refused to move. "Tell me, Elisa—"

"Please don't call me that." Her voice had grown huskier.

The old man's expression turned patronizing. "Sweetheart, that's your name."

"It's not. Stop saying it." The alcohol had loosened her tongue. Perhaps this wouldn't be a total disaster. He wouldn't mind seeing Elise rip into the old guy.

Papi looked annoyed but said nothing. "Is there anything you want to know about the family?"

"No." She gestured to the room with her arm. "I don't care about you or any of this."

Eric sensed the insult had hit its mark. Papi stood. "You've been through a lot. I'll forgive this behavior."

Elise made a face. He needed to cover for her before she did or said something she'd regret.

"These family get togethers are always so much fun." The sarcastic voice came from Sergei, who looked bored and amused in equal measure.

"She's nervous. This has been a lot to take in." Eric moved to the other side of the sofa and lifted her to his side. "We need to get some food into her."

Elise waved her hand in the air, clearly having found the courage to say all the things she'd held inside. "I'm not nervous. I'm a hostage."

Papi clenched his hands into fists. "After everything I've done for you?"

"Like what?" The pitch of Elise's voice raised an octave. "Turning my life into a big lie?"

Her grandfather jabbed a finger in Elise's face. "You have no idea the sacrifices that have been made to keep you safe."

"You keep saying that," she fired back.

Eric tensed and tugged her closer.

Miranda put a calming hand on Papi's arm. "Alexei, you can't force it."

He shook off her touch and stormed from the room. She started to follow but slowed to give Eric a brief glance. "Please forgive him. His intentions are good."

Sergei approached Elise and handed her a tumbler and a decanter of something dark. She poured a finger of liquor into her glass and swallowed a gulp of the amber-colored beverage. He kissed her on the cheek. "Welcome to the family, cousin. You'll fit in just fine."

He patted Eric on the shoulder. "Good luck with this one."

****

Elise peered around. Everyone had left. "What about dinner?"

"I don't think we're eating tonight."

She shrugged. Dining with her new family hadn't been high on her list anyway. Might as well have another drink. She tipped the bottle toward her glass.

Eric grabbed the carafe. "That's enough." His stony expression was resigned and weary.

"Are you going to start telling me what to do now too?"

He put the bottle down and held up his hands. Then, without a word, turned to leave.

"I don't need you anyway." The moment the words left her mouth, she knew she didn't mean them, but still savored his look of hurt as he left the room. Good. Why should she be the only one who felt like crap? She lifted the glass to her mouth but stopped. *What am I doing?*

She'd always thought of herself as independent—as not needing anyone. That was a bunch of garbage, a rationalization. In truth, she couldn't handle being hurt. She didn't give people the chance to abandon her. But Eric was different. She should thank him, not push him away.

The family didn't want him. He knew that. Everything he'd done had been to protect her. Look where it got him. She'd been so selfish. And now she was acting like a child. She needed to tell him how much he meant to her. She needed to apologize.

She whirled to the door. The room spun with her. With deliberate steps, she made her way to the staircase.

"He's out back."

Elise stopped. Miranda sat in the foyer on a small settee. The woman smiled. "This isn't my first rodeo. I can tell how much you care for each other."

"I'm sorry about dinner." Elise stood as steady as possible. "And the drinking."

Miranda waved her hand. "You didn't have that much. Let's get you some food. You'll feel much better."

Elise followed her down a long hallway that opened into a bustling kitchen. The savory smell of spice and stock made her stomach rumble. Pans banged and glassware clinked as servers and cooks hurried to clean up after the aborted dinner party. Miranda spoke in a low voice to the chef. He waved his hand and yelled something in French. Everyone disappeared.

With wide eyes, Elise took in the trays of food filling the huge counter.

"What do you want? Goat cheese crostini?" Miranda took a plate and bowl from the stacks next to the stove. "Pumpkin bisque? Duck confit? Grilled steak? Crème brûlée?" She pointed to each item.

Regret filled Elise's empty stomach. "Was this all for dinner? I'm so sorry."

Miranda shrugged as she set the dishware on the counter. "Chef is used to it. This isn't the first dinner service that didn't happen."

Elise took the plate and grabbed one of the toasted baguettes topped with tapenade and cheese. She took a bite. "Oh. My God. That is so good."

Miranda smiled and took one for herself. She pushed the bowl toward Elise. "Have some soup."

After piling her plate with duck and steak, Elise concentrated on eating. By the time the plate was clean, she felt better. And sober.

She peered at the woman who apparently knew everything. "So…are you and my grandfather—"

Miranda chuckled. "Yes. Have been for almost forty years."

Elise reached for a crème brûlée and broke the sugar crust with the back of her spoon. "Do you live here?"

Miranda nodded. "It's a lovely house. I hope you'll be here long enough to see everything."

Elise scowled and licked her spoon. "I think I'll be here as long as he wants me to be."

"He wants to get to know you. His approach is rough, but he's doing it for the right reasons."

Elise stared at her plate, unsure what to say.

"Everyone agreed your mother leaving was for the best, but it was hard on your grandfather. Family means a lot to him. He enjoys knowing you're near."

"What about Eric? Is he safe?"

"Your grandfather isn't a monster, and while he's not happy to have an FBI agent in his home, he would never hurt him."

"All the men with guns?"

"Protection is a genuine concern, but hurting people isn't what Aleksander is about. He's kind. Generous. He takes care of the people who work for him, and they love him for it." She patted Elise's hand. "I hope one day you'll love him too."

A good man running a crime family? It seemed like a stretch.

Miranda answered as if she'd heard Elise's thoughts. "He's not perfect, but he protects those he loves. You're both safe here. Even a stubborn old man can see how you feel about Eric."

Elise almost choked on the strawberry she'd just popped into her mouth. "What do you mean?"

"Oh honey. The two of you are the only ones who don't know."

"Until a few days ago, he was someone I only saw every so often. I hardly even know him."

Miranda scooped up the dirty dishes, put them in the sink, and then gave her a wink. "Why don't you go look for him? I bet he's still in the garden."

****

Eric removed his jacket and threw it on the wall

surrounding the ugly fountain. He paced like a wounded animal. Tension rippled through him.

I don't need you. Her words stung, but was she right? Would she be better off without him?

He didn't want to believe it.

Still, wasn't she safer here? Between the river, the walls surrounding the property, and the armed guards, it would take an act of God for someone to get into this place. Even Alario wasn't stupid enough to try.

He yanked loose his tie and unbuttoned his cuffs. If he and Elise were ever going to have a chance—if the woman he was coming to care about was ever going to have her freedom, he needed to get Vincenzo out of the picture. He saw one option. Get out of this house and back to the FBI.

As long as Vincenzo remained a threat, Elise and he would never have a chance at happiness. He shook his head. What a mess.

Lack of sleep and food didn't help, but he'd lived on field rations many times during training exercises in the military. An arduous experience, but one that taught him self-discipline and focus. Considering tonight's dinner consisted of a handful of mints found in a dish on a hallway table, it helped to know his limits. Right now, hunger wasn't his problem. The current complication took the form of a slightly belligerent, but hot-as-hell pilot he'd do anything to protect.

He unbuttoned the top button of his shirt and ran a hand through his hair. He had to know what happened at the farm in Nebraska. Vincenzo might already be in custody. He might be dead. With the mob boss gone or apprehended, there'd be nothing to worry about. No reason to keep Elise hidden. Until then, Papi could do a better job protecting her than he could. His stomach lurched, the realization slamming into him like a hard landing. Catching Vincenzo Alario would be a win-win. Justice for Dad. Freedom for Elise.

Leaving the compound without her was the right thing to do. So why did it feel so wrong? A hollow ache spread from his gut to his chest. It was for the best. Once Vincenzo was gone, he'd come back.

If he *could* come back, and it wasn't too late. By then, Elise might not want him. She might decide she belonged with her family. She might be glad to be rid of him. She might have found someone else to be with.

A sharp pang hit him in the chest. He inhaled, but the air didn't reach his lungs. Enough. He had no choice. To save her, he had to figure out how to leave, even if it meant losing her. He resumed his pacing. There were things to do. Plans to make.

Number one? Convince Papi to let him go. It seemed like a long shot, but maybe not. The old gangster had never wanted him here in the first place. The challenge would be making sure he didn't end up wearing a pair of concrete shoes.

Number two? Remind Papi of their common goal—protecting Elise.

First thing tomorrow, he'd ask for a meeting. Eric almost laughed. He was about to suggest an alliance with a gangster. Who would've thought?

In the meantime, he had to figure out a way to persuade Elise it was for the best.

Chapter Twenty-Three

Elise wandered along the cobbled path. Was Miranda right? Did she have something special with Eric? He was handsome. Possibly the sexiest man she'd ever seen. But physical attraction didn't make a relationship.

Not that she would know. She'd had her share of casual flings, but serious, meaningful connections had been rare. Come to think of it, she could only recall two guys she'd ever referred to as boyfriends, and one of them had been in high school.

If she really wanted to analyze her relationship history, she'd have to face the fact she'd intentionally kept people at a distance. She'd never given it much thought, but thinking back, the reason was obvious. It was one thing to be rejected by someone who didn't really know you. It was something else to let someone in, only to have them decide you weren't what they wanted.

Now here she was, suddenly compelled to seek out another person, ready to vomit out her every thought and emotion. She slowed. Was she really debating this? She'd lived a lifetime in these three days, but in reality, they barely knew each other.

She rounded the corner and sucked in a breath.

The lights from inside the fountain pool cast an ethereal glow. He paced the length of the monument—

back and forth, the god of the sea his silent sentry.

He'd set his jacket on the wall. Hair mussed, shirt sleeves rolled up, tie hanging loose, he moved with jerky motions. Working something out, he mumbled, and though she couldn't make out the words, she recognized his look of worry. She could read him. The tilt of his head. The slump of his shoulders. *I know him.* Affection snaked through her insides.

How had it happened so fast? People she'd known her whole life didn't inspire these feelings. Yet, looking at Eric, her chest swelled. She wanted to run to him, but stayed glued in place, watching. Hand on his chin, he turned in her direction. Their gazes met, and his eyes darkened. He took several long steps and grasped her shoulders. His closeness, accentuated by a woodsy, masculine smell captivated her.

The gurgle of the fountain echoed the beat of her heart. She shivered.

"Are you cold?" He rubbed rough hands along her bare upper arms.

She shook her head. *Tell him how you feel.* The words stuck in her throat.

"Elise," he said, his voice gruff and shaky.

Before she could speak, he hauled her against him, his lips crashing into hers. His tongue teased its way into her mouth, and he stroked the line of her jaw with his thumb. He tasted of sweet, sugary candy.

He wrapped strong arms around her, and for a moment, location didn't matter. This was where she belonged. She clasped her hands behind his neck and melted into him until they were soldered together like two pieces of steel. Her lips parted. Her pulse pounded.

She wanted more. Needed more.

Their mouths separated, and a moan left her throat, hoarse and needy.

In the reflection of the fountain, his eyes turned the color of clover. His gaze softened. He stepped back. "I'm sorry. I've got to leave. And you've got to stay."

She reached for him but dropped her hand when she saw the serious look on his face. "What do you mean?"

"I have to get out of here." He brushed her cheek. "I'm going to ask Papi to let me go."

"That won't happen."

"I think he understands I'm more useful out there looking for Vincenzo. And you'll be safe here."

An acrid taste filled her mouth. More useful? How was abandoning her here with her corrupt grandfather going to fix anything? She needed Eric. She needed his arms around her, his mouth touching hers.

She stared at his drawn brows, set jaw and steady gaze. "No."

"I have a job to do." She could see his determination in the way he flattened his mouth into a thin line.

She clutched her mother's pendant. Eventually everyone leaves. Why did she think he'd be different? And to think, she'd wanted to tell him how she felt. *So stupid. S*he squared her shoulders. "If that's what you think is best."

Was that reluctance in his pursed lips and hard smile?

"It is."

Her powder keg of a heart threatened to explode, but she kept her voice even, not allowing a hint of emotion to slip through. "When will you talk to him?"

"In the morning."

She turned, needing to be alone, to sort out her

feelings. The last thing she wanted was to let him see her pain. He couldn't know how much she cared, how the thought of his leaving devastated her.

"Good luck. I hope you catch him." Her feet carried her away.

"Elise," he called, his voice rougher than usual. Almost pleading.

It took all her self-control not to break into a sprint.

****

Damn it. Eric's stomach dropped at the hurt in Elise's gaze, the monotone sound of her voice clearly meant to disguise her misery. The back of her skirt trailed behind her like a cape, the bottom swishing against the stone.

Rolling his shoulders to relieve the tension, he closed his eyes and took a deep breath. He hadn't thought the night could get any worse. Stuffing his hands into his trouser pockets, he started after her. "Will you stop? Please?"

The tap of her shoes against the cobbled path increased in speed. She rounded the first corner.

"Elise?"

The slight jerk of her head said she heard him, but she didn't look back.

The walkway meandered to the right, then the left. He lost sight of her. When she reappeared, she was entering the open French doors at the back of the house. She glanced over her shoulder and hastened her pace.

Never had he chased after a woman before. Never had he wanted to. What was it about Elise? She rushed through the fancy sitting area and made a sharp turn at the stairs.

Her quick steps wouldn't do her any good here.

Taking two stairs at a time, he closed the distance. As she neared the second floor, he came up behind her. "I'll be back for you."

She stopped, took a deep breath, and tightened her grip on the banister. "Like I haven't heard that before."

"Will you look at me?" He fought—and failed—to keep the frustration from his voice. "You need to stop assuming everyone is like your mother." He bit his tongue the moment the words left his mouth.

Her back stiffened, but she said nothing. Instead, she lifted her foot to the top step, then darted toward her bedroom, clutching the folds of her skirt in tight fists.

Stubborn woman. What didn't she understand? He was doing this for her. For them. He started after her. But then, her foot wobbled. Her leg buckled. She let out a shriek of pain and collapsed, falling to her hands and knees. Easing herself into a sitting position, she grasped the ankle injured at the farm.

His heart pounded. He rubbed his chest, hit by a typhoon of frustration and concern. Dragging a hand through his hair, he growled. *Calm yourself.* He approached and stared down at her. "Are you okay? What happened?"

A tear rolled down her cheek. "Leave me alone."

He offered his hand. She batted it away. Bending over, he scooped her up. "You're more trouble than you're worth, you know that?" The words sounded harsher than he'd intended.

She kicked and wiggled. "Put me down."

"Can you walk?" He only wanted to help.

She didn't answer but tightened her hold around his neck.

He pushed the door to her room open with his foot,

kicked it closed, and set her on the bed. "I'm doing this for us. So we can be together."

She took off her shoes and massaged her ankle. "We're together now."

"You know what I mean."

"I trusted you," she said through gritted teeth.

"You *can* trust me."

"I'm so sick of being left out and left behind." A shoe sailed across the room and slammed into the wall.

He could taste his anger. Anger at the situation. Anger at himself. Anger at Elise for making this so much more difficult. His voice shook. The emotions he'd suppressed came roaring to the surface. "Do you have any idea what it's like for someone like me to be somewhere like this? Trapped? Useless? Unable to protect you?"

"I feel safer with you here. I want you to stay." Her words held a quiet plea.

He rubbed the back of his neck. "I'll be back. I swear. But I can't stay."

"Can't and won't are two different things."

"We don't even know he'll let me leave."

She got off the bed and limped in his direction, indignation and disappointment flaring in her eyes. With hands outstretched, he expected her to push him away, but her arms slid around his waist instead. Wrapping her in his embrace, he stroked her hair, trailing his fingers along her bare shoulders.

Her voice shook against his chest. "Just go. Everyone else does."

Tilting her head, he gazed into her eyes, seeing her doubts, and realizing he'd regret any decision he made. He spoke slowly, wanting to be clear. "I'm not leaving you. You're a part of me now."

She pressed her body to his, her voice muffled. "I feel that way too."

He slid his hand to the small of her back and hauled her soft curves deeper against him.

Unbalanced. The only word to describe how she made him feel.

He let his hands follow the contours of her body, tracing soft circles along her back, waist, and hips. She dragged a fingertip down the placket of his shirt, the gentle pressure of her touch, the flick of each button, sending shudders to his extremities. By the time she grasped his belt buckle, he couldn't imagine how his legs still supported his weight. Hunger surged through him.

Her hands grazed the inside of his waistband before skimming up his torso and knitting into his hair. Nails raked the top of his head, and he bent his head to her neck, kissing her collarbone. The tip of his tongue chased the moan that climbed up her throat. All the way to her soft, plump lips.

God. That mouth.

He wanted to pour himself into her, to calm her fears with his kisses, his touch. The combination of her taste and scent left him dizzy with desire. Their tongues worked together, synchronizing into a natural rhythm. His arousal tightened. He slid one hand down her lush backside, grabbed a handful of her skirt and twisted. Deepening the kiss, he wove the other into her hair. Soft breasts pressed against his chest and a jolt of pleasure echoed through his limbs. He pulled away, his focus falling on her flushed cheeks and eyes glistening with need.

"Don't ever question my feelings." He tipped her

face and ran his thumb over her red, swollen lips. "You're funny and smart. Beautiful. And this body." He trailed his hands around her slim waist. "I get hard and go weak every time you look at me."

****

"I thought you said you weren't what I needed," Elise whispered, challenging Eric with what he'd said in the storage room at the hangar.

His eyes smoldered, dark and intense. "I'm not, but I was stupid to think I could stay away."

Melting into his gaze, she forgot her wounded ankle until a sharp pain shot through her leg. She gasped as her weight settled on the sore joint.

His brows lowered, his pupils blazed. "Are you all right?"

With a hand on his shoulder, she lifted her foot and probed her ankle. "It's a little tender. I'll be okay."

In one smooth motion, Eric lifted her to the bed.

Prickles of heat danced across her cheeks. "You didn't need to do that."

"Better safe than sorry." He kicked off his shoes and settled beside her. "Do you want me to get you some ice?"

She shook her head. "FBI and a medic? What other skills are you hiding?"

"Not a medic." He leaned forward, allowing his mouth to graze hers. "But I might have a hidden talent or two."

Warmth coiled through her. Her belly pulsed with her growing need.

Holding her face in his hands, he used his thumbs to brush soft circles on her cheeks, all the while plying her with kisses. Gentle at first, then voracious. She grasped the tie that hung loose around his neck and drew him closer.

The need in her abdomen swelled, the soft tingles multiplying until her entire body hummed.

Tugging his shirt from his pants, she worked the buttons. When the last one popped free, she ran her hands over his hard chest, exploring every ridge and valley of muscle. "I guess you see some pretty naughty people in your line of work."

He flashed a devilish smile. "Some naughtier than others."

The hair on the back of her neck stood on end as he placed a gentle kiss behind her ear.

"Interrogations can be tricky." Another kiss. "Sometimes I have to get rough." He tugged her legs apart.

She shivered as his hand on her leg traveled higher. "Is your plan to drive them mad?"

He responded with a nibble on her ear.

Her nipples hardened in response. Her head lolled back. "Good cop or bad cop?"

His lips brushed her neck again. His chuckle, deep and throaty, reverberated against her skin. "They both have their merits."

Keeping his touch light, his fingers moved at a maddeningly slow pace up her inner thigh until they tickled her most intimate place. She moaned as his lips clamped over hers, his tongue igniting the heat between her legs.

His teeth tugged on her bottom lip. She bit back a moan when his hand slid between her wet, aroused flesh and whimpered in frustration until he pressed his thumb on her already-throbbing sex, stroking in circles, then back and forth.

"How's this?" The velvety baritone of his voice made her shiver despite the warmth coursing inside.

"Good." She panted. *Oh, God yes.*

She squirmed when he withdrew his hand. "Torture must be your specialty."

He stared down at her, tenderness and adoration shining in his eyes. Smiling, he bit one side of his bottom lip and raised an eyebrow.

Scarred by disappointment and betrayal, she'd guarded her heart for so long, she wasn't sure how to let anyone in. But something about Eric made her want to fling the door wide open. He'd broken through her barriers, and she'd not even realized it.

"God, you're beautiful." His gaze flashed with desire. "I can't explain how much I want you."

She wrapped her arms around his neck. "I want you too."

He kissed her again before rolling her on her side and unzipping the dress. He tugged down the bodice and cupped her breasts, bringing his mouth to her nipple and sucking. His tongue flicked back and forth over the sensitive nub. She arched into his touch.

"This dress has got to go." Grasping her hips, he yanked her to the edge of the bed. Careful of her injured ankle, he wiggled the gown down her legs and flung it across the room. His fingers slipped into the waistband of her panties. "These have also overstayed their welcome." Her underwear followed a similar trajectory.

He caressed her body, placing delicate kisses around her stomach. Dropping to his knees, he draped her legs over his shoulders and rubbed a finger through her slick folds.

Oh, dear God.

He slid his fingers inside her, twisting and stroking, all the while applying pressure to her sensitive bud. She bucked, driving him deeper, gasping at the sensation.

More.

He withdrew his fingers and slid his face between her legs, his warm breath electrifying her tender flesh. After a gentle kiss, he homed in on her sweet spot, revealing a wicked and talented tongue.

Her body convulsed as he sucked and licked and took her in his mouth.

Rocked with pleasure, she clutched the blanket and arched her back as the first wave of ecstasy hit. Euphoria rushed through her, hot and slick. With no reprieve, he pulled her still-shuddering body closer, burrowing into her heat.

She whimpered as his sensual assault continued. Still sucking. Still probing. She moaned. His mouth gratifying and tormenting in equal measure.

She climaxed again, a cry of pleasure ripped from her center.

Spent, she trembled with aftershocks. He stood, shed his shirt, and climbed onto the bed, his naked torso hovering above her. He stared down, eyes shiny with passion.

Unable to speak and unsure she had the energy to make her hands and arms work, she fumbled to undo the button and zipper of his trousers.

"Your turn," she said. Her throat was dry, her voice hoarse.

He stared down, one hand on each side of her. "I don't have protection."

"I have a contraceptive implant. In my arm." She

pressed two fingers against the inside of her biceps. "Are you clean?"

He licked his lips and nodded.

"Me too."

His forehead wrinkled. "Are you sure you want to do this?"

"Yes," she breathed.

He stood and stepped out of his pants, his erection springing free. She hadn't thought it possible, but she grew hotter, wetter.

When he climbed on her again, she reached for his arousal, rubbing her thumb over his slick tip. Lifting her hips, she guided him inside, realizing everything had changed.

For once in her life, she understood how it felt to need another person. Not only did she need him, but she wanted him.

And not just him. All of it. Everything that came with being in a real relationship.

For the first time in a long time, and in spite of their predicament, she believed she might actually be able to have it.

****

Eric drove deep and slow, savoring the pressure at the base of his cock, the gentle squeeze lighting a fuse that sent sparks up and down his shaft.

Elise grew wetter and slicker with each thrust, the ridges of her body gripping and stroking, hugging him like a glove. Nerve endings tingled, rushing to his brain, and drugging him with desire.

Go slow. *Make it last.*

Warm. Tight. Wonderful.

He pumped, changing angles, and taking

satisfaction in the flush of her cheeks and the cute little *O* her mouth made as she sighed with pleasure.

Her chest lifted and fell in shallow gasps. She let out one low, surprised moan, her muscles spasming around his cock. Then she came again.

More than passion, the pressure swelling inside him spoke of devotion, reverence—a promise. He closed his eyes and erupted, rocking with pleasure.

Breathless, he went slack. His heart raced. His body tingled. Still inside Elise, he lay atop her, feeling as if he might float away.

Incredible. Phenomenal. Amazing. There weren't enough superlatives to describe how good being inside her had felt. Better than he ever could have imagined.

He opened one eye. Her face flushed with color, setting off the sparkle in her citrine eyes. Mussed hair spread across the pillow, making her look thoroughly ravished.

He collapsed onto the pillow and let his sweaty body stick to hers.

His muscles loosened as his weight pressed into her, but he couldn't look her in the eye. Not yet. Not until he understood what had happened. His mind reeled. She trailed her fingers through his hair, massaging his scalp. This was more than sex. Something inside him shifted, a missing piece of himself found.

He'd been wrong to think tracking his father's killer would make him whole.

This. Her.

He couldn't recall a time his thoughts extended beyond catching Vincenzo. Now, he lay here, wondering what the future held, but also content to enjoy the moment.

"Tell me you won't go anywhere without me?"

"I won't." He kissed the top of her head. "I couldn't."

"Promise?" Her grip on his hand tightened.

"Yes."

She closed her eyes. "Thank you, Arthur."

"How—" He smiled, wondering when she learned his given name. But why ruin the moment? "How's your ankle?"

"Don't even feel it," she murmured. Soon her soft, steady breaths warmed his chest.

He stared at the ceiling. If this was a dream, he never wanted to wake. He kissed the top of her head and inhaled the sweet, flower-scented shampoo.

There'd be obstacles, but something told him they'd manage. Together.

His heart swelled, squeezing out the empty feeling that had lingered for so many years. He skimmed his fingers along her arm, her stomach, and the soft, smooth skin of her breasts. He curled against her, drawing in her warmth.

Maybe he'd transfer to Miami. She could be near her brothers. They'd commute, living somewhere in between. What would it feel like to have a normal life? With her?

He drew her closer. "You're mine."

Elise let out a quiet snort as she shifted to wrap her leg around his. Several long, agonizing minutes passed as he lay there, hyper aware of her body and fighting to tamp down his rising libido.

Think baseball. The original major league teams. *St. Louis, Chicago, Boston, Cincinnati, New York... Damn.* He paused. *I used to know these... Phila—*

A slight squeeze at the base of his cock drew his attention. Elise's hand wrapped around him and twisted.

"You're awake," he choked.

"I am." She applied just the right amount of pressure and began slow strokes as she touched his cheek and leaned forward for a kiss.

Increasing her rhythm, she loosened her grip, then slowed again. He dropped his head against the pillow and closed his eyes.

When she accelerated, he knew he didn't have long. Grabbing her hand, he interlaced fingers. Reaching between her legs, he found her slick arousal. "Roll over."

He positioned himself behind her. With a grip on her shoulder, he slid in with one smooth thrust.

She moaned. "Eric."

Hearing his name as she panted was a powerful stimulant. His body longed to take her, to claim her as his own, but his heart already belonged to her. Now and always.

She trembled, squeezed, and convulsed. Her climax came quickly, their bodies moving as one. He pumped once more, letting loose a husky moan as he came.

He kissed her shoulder, never wanting to let go. The impulse disconcerted him. He could lay here with her in his arms for days, and considering there was nothing else to do while they were trapped in this house, it was tempting. But he had things to sort through, feelings to figure out. He wanted to make sure he was thinking straight before he shared his thoughts with Elise, and it would be easier to examine alone, where he wasn't distracted by her warm skin and full lips.

Overwhelmed by a dreamy wistfulness, he watched her stretch and yawn. "You need to sleep." He leaned over and gave her a soft, lingering kiss. "I'll see you in the morning."

She dragged the covers to her chin. Her eyes fluttered shut. "Why don't you stay here?"

He kissed her again. "Because I need sleep too."

She responded with a drowsy nod.

Standing, he tugged on his pants and grabbed his shirt and shoes. He reached the door and stopped. The sight of her relaxed and content knocked the air out of him. For the first time in a long time, he believed things might be okay.

A few steps into the hallway, he realized everything seemed brighter—the colors on the artwork decorating the walls, the pattern in the carpet—all the little details he never took the time to notice. Still grinning when he stepped into his room, he flipped on the light.

Sergei Kozlov, smarmy grin on his face, sat on the end of his bed.

A bitter taste filled Eric's mouth. *Please no.*

"Well, well, well," Sergei said. "What have you been up to?"

Posture rigid, Eric dropped his shoes onto the floor and tossed his shirt and tie on the bed. "Why are you here?"

"You're going back to the FBI. Today."

Not the worst news. But what about Elise? "Fine. But she's coming with me."

Sergei shrugged and tossed a gym bag to Eric. "This isn't a negotiation. Get your things."

"What things?" Eric spread his arms wide.

"Whatever you want to take with you." Sergei jerked his thumb toward the bathroom. "Then shower and dress. I'll wait here."

A flash of heat rose to Eric's cheeks. He clenched his hands into fists but didn't act on the impulse. Saying or doing something impetuous could get him killed. "I need to talk to her."

Another laugh. "Nope. You'll be back in Philly in time for the morning commute."

He should be glad they were letting him go, giving him the opportunity to go after Vincenzo. But tearing him away from Elise? That was a punishment. "Why now?"

The gun resting on Sergei's leg sent a clear message. "Let's just say you've overstayed your welcome."

Chapter Twenty-Four

Elise rolled onto her back and stretched her arms above her head. She'd slept deep and content, the ache between her legs a wonderful reminder of the intimacies only hours before.

Eric. Just thinking of his hard body pinning her beneath him evoked a breathy gasp. His touch, like a defibrillator, resurrected her heart. The physical attraction was intense, but there was more to it than that. They cared for one another. She felt it woven through her body and saw it in his eyes.

If only they'd met under different circumstances. But one day this would be over. Maybe a normal life wasn't too much to hope for. She'd slept with the curtains open. Warm sun streamed in through the French doors, making the accommodations feel less like a prison. Of course, her night with Eric was largely responsible for her good mood.

She glanced at the clock and threw off the covers. Cool air rippled against her naked skin. Cupping her tender breasts, she remembered the reverent way Eric caressed her. She stumbled to the bathroom, turned on the shower and tilted her face into the stream. Her breath quickened as she replayed their night together. Touching him. Kissing him. The feel of him inside her.

The warm water ran down her back and over her hips. She caressed her curves and the tender spot between her legs. If he'd stayed the night, he might be with her underneath the spray, their bodies pressed together. Still dripping, she turned off the faucet and stepped out of the shower. She dried herself, enjoying the warmth of the bathroom but longing for the heat of Eric.

In the bedroom, she riffled through a pile of clothes, selecting a white tee and faded jeans. She slid her feet into a pair of sparkly sneakers. The appearance of her favorite footwear gave her pause. How did they know all these details? Elise shook her head. She'd think about it later. Right now, there was only one thing she wanted, and he was down the hall.

She pinned her hair into a messy bun and crept into the corridor. To think that while she slept, he'd been mere yards away. They could have been snuggled up together this whole time. Tonight, she'd make damn sure he stayed where he belonged, holding her tight, trailing kisses up and down her stomach, breasts, and neck.

The thought of sliding under the covers and waking him made her stomach flutter. Everything slowed, and a shiver ran up her spine as she approached the doorway.

Eric's door stood open, revealing a tightly made bed in an austere room.

Her body went cold.

No Eric. No sign he'd ever been there.

She checked the walk-in closet, finding unused hangers and nothing else. What about the suit he wore last night? Had Miranda sent it to be cleaned already? They'd provided other clothing for him to wear. Those items must be here somewhere. She slid open a dresser drawer. Empty, like the sensation beginning to fill her stomach.

Where is he?

She stepped into the bathroom. Vanity? Bare. Shower and tub? Dry.

She stood slack jawed in the middle of the room and spun round and round. He wouldn't—Where—Why would he—

It didn't make any sense. She shook her head, unwilling to accept what she was seeing. "This can't be."

Last night, everything had been perfect. He'd been perfect. He couldn't fake that.

Could he?

Her mind raced. He said he planned to leave. Then he said he'd stay. Now he was gone.

She bit down on her bottom lip to stop the sob migrating up her throat.

Maybe he was somewhere else?

She hurried down the stairs and flew into the morning room. Miranda and her grandfather sat at the small table eating toast and jam. Papi folded his toast in half and shoved it in his mouth before he spoke. "Good morning, Elisa.".

"Where is he?" She hated the quiver in her voice.

Her grandfather took his time, chewing and swallowing. Finally, the old bastard dabbed his mouth with a cloth napkin and looked up. "Gone."

Elise's back stiffened. *He wouldn't.*

With pursed lips, Miranda shook her head and stared at Papi.

Elise sucked in a calming breath. It didn't help. "What do you mean *gone*?"

"He left." The man wiped his hands on a napkin. "This morning, with Sergei."

"No." She took a step back, wanting to put distance between herself and her deceitful grandfather. "You're lying."

The old man shrugged.

"Why?" The word came out in a breathy, strained whisper.

"He said he'd be more useful at the FBI searching for Alario." Papi took a sip of coffee. "I agree."

Elise couldn't stop her shaking head. She didn't believe it. Not after last night.

But that was almost exactly what Eric had said to her at the fountain.

"You'll see him again." The man looked unmoved by her distress. "In the meantime, you're safe with us."

She twisted the fabric of her shirt, wanting to rail and scream and tell this old, manipulative man just how wrong he was. Instead, she let a bitter cold settle over her.

No one wants me.

"Come." Miranda held out a welcoming arm and gestured to an empty chair. "Sit and eat."

The short walk to the table felt like miles. Elise sat and forced down a few bites of toast with her coffee. She ignored all of Papi and Miranda's attempts to engage in small talk. Even here, surrounded by her supposed family, she didn't feel truly wanted.

Leaving her half-eaten breakfast on the table, she pushed back her chair and stood, then shuffled to her room unable to focus her thoughts. She flopped onto the bed and stared at the ceiling. It was no use. She'd finally trusted someone with her heart. Look where it got her.

Why would he lie?

He got what he wanted.

She clutched her stomach and squeezed her eyes shut, letting the thought settle. Something about it didn't ring true. Sure, the evidence was there. They made love. He got up and left. But the Eric she knew had integrity. He was kind. He wouldn't do this. His word meant something.

A soft knock startled her. "Come in." She didn't care who was on the other side.

Miranda stuck her head in the room. "Do you have a few minutes?"

Elise nodded and sat up. Something about the woman inspired trust. She believed Miranda's overtures to be sincere. Though God knew she'd not shown herself to be a good judge of character.

The bed dipped as the slight woman's weight settled. "How are you doing?"

She shrugged.

"You must be confused and angry." Miranda rubbed circles on Elise's back in a motherly gesture. *"Listen to your heart."*

"Hardly seems like sound advice."

"Sometimes we have to give the men in our lives the benefit of the doubt." Miranda looked out the window. The look on her face suggested she'd experienced this firsthand.

Elise's chin quivered. She blinked back the hot tears. "Who does the same for us?"

Miranda wrapped an arm around Elise and drew her close. "It's okay to cry, sweetheart."

Elise sobbed against the woman's shoulder and asked the question she'd been asking her entire life. "Why does everyone leave? Is it me?"

"Shush." Miranda gave her a tight hug. "Of course, it's not you." The older woman drew her closer. "Do you believe in Eric?"

Elise wiped her nose with the back of her hand and nodded.

"Then give him the opportunity to explain." Miranda's eyebrows knitted together. She offered a slight smile, rose, and left. Elise barely heard the click of the door.

She had a choice. Put her faith in the man who had abandoned her or trust a grandfather she didn't even know.

****

Eric glanced at the clock. Every turn of the tires carried him farther from Elise. He wanted to throttle Sergei, shove him out of the car and race back to rescue her.

But he couldn't.

Sergei had made that clear when he accosted him in his room. Eric's head fell back against the leather headrest. *You idiot.* He should have stayed in Elise's room. If he had, she'd know he had no choice. Now she'd think he left with Sergei voluntarily. Papi would tell her lies, make her think he didn't want her.

He glanced down. He wore the pair of jeans and a gray T-shirt Miranda had given him. Not knowing his true destination, he'd thrown a bit of everything into the bag.

Why hadn't he put up a bigger fuss about seeing her?

Because a gun in the back was a persuasive deterrent, and he'd been an unwanted guest in a mobster's home. He'd been paraded right past her bedroom door. He could have called out, made some noise. At the very least, he should have recognized Sergei was only posturing. He'd never have shot him.

Especially not in front of Elise.

Now, he needed to fix his mistakes and figure out a way to contact her. Convince her the lies she'd heard weren't true. Suddenly, nothing seemed more important than getting to Elise and making her understand. If she rejected him—he rubbed his chest and grimaced—he'd be crushed.

He almost couldn't bear to look at the man in the driver's seat. The man giving him his freedom while taking him away from the woman he loved. After the piercing silence for most of the trip, now he wanted answers. "Where are we going?"

"I'll tell you when we get there."

Eric clenched his jaw. This might all be a lie. But he didn't think so. If he'd learned anything working organized crime, it was that these guys observed their own twisted code of honor.

Of course, if it was a setup, he wouldn't be the first agent shot by the mob. Not the last, either. On the off chance he made it back to the FBI, he might as well dig for intel.

"How did Papi come by the idea of letting me go?"

"Something you said."

"Which was?"

"He heard you telling Elise you wanted to go after Vincenzo Alario."

Eric flinched. That damned conversation by the fountain when he'd told her he needed to go. He'd known the property was monitored and still, he dropped his guard.

"What will he tell Elise when she realizes I'm gone?"

"Probably that you went back to work."

Eric tensed. Papi had timed it just right. His words. His promises. She'd think it had been a giant lie. He wanted to punch Sergei in the side of the head. "Can you at least get a message to her?"

The mobster kept his eyes on the road.

Bile rose in Eric's throat. He'd do anything to get her back. Even this. "What do you want? Some sort of deal?"

The other man sighed. "Look, dude, this probably won't sit well, but I'm asking you to trust me."

It was so ridiculous, Eric almost laughed.

"Go back to work, find out what's going on with Vincenzo and wait to hear from me. It'll work out."

"I'm supposed to believe anything you say?"

"Way I see it, you don't have a lot of choice. I'm your best shot at seeing her again." Sergei let out an exaggerated, put-upon sigh. "My cousin likes you even if I don't. It would be nice to think at least one of us can have something we want."

Sergei guided the car off the road and into a gravel lot with an old gas station and motel. He parked in front of the pump. "We're about forty minutes outside the city. There's a pay phone on the side of the building."

Eric clutched the duffel and jacket as Sergei handed him his gun. He checked the chamber and dropped the magazine. No bullets. Next came a wallet with his badge and some cash. Finally, Sergei produced the knife Eric had taken from the motel owner's truck.

Without a word, he climbed out of the car. Sergei gave a two-finger wave. Eric straightened, shut the door, and watched the car make a U-turn onto the highway.

Kidnapped and released by the mob. He should be counting his lucky stars and trying to get as far away from the family compound as possible. Instead, his brain churned, working out the fastest way back inside.

****

Eric's stomach clenched, threatening to dislodge the small pack of powdered donuts he'd devoured. Grant's dark, government-issued sedan veered into the gas station parking lot without slowing. The car came to an abrupt stop next to the building and enveloped Eric in a cloud of dust.

"Erickson." Grant leaned toward the open passenger window. "Get in."

Eric downed the rest of his now-cold coffee and tossed it in the trash. It did nothing to wash away the hard, dry lump rising in his throat. He climbed into the vehicle. "Hey, boss."

Grant's lips squeezed into a tight line. The car careened onto the highway. Eric braced his hand against the ceiling.

For several minutes, neither man said anything. What was there to say? Eric had disobeyed orders and hadn't told the Bureau where he'd disappeared to or why. And he'd do it again. A thousand times if that's what it took. At least now he knew she was safe.

The silence of the man beside him spoke louder than words. Grant slapped the steering wheel. "When did you stop being a serious agent?"

Eric swallowed down the guilt clawing his insides. Grant was right. He'd been disregarding protocol and common sense since the moment Elise marched into that break room. Like a helicopter with no tail rotor, he'd been spinning away his career ever since.

"Do you have any idea what you've put the team through?" Grant's barely contained rage seeped through his normally ever-so-calm British accent.

Eric had never heard Grant raise his voice. This was a whole new level of agitation.

Grant stared straight ahead. "I told you agents were on their way. I told you to wait."

Eric lifted his chin with a defiant thrust. "I saw men advancing toward the barn. I needed to protect Elise."

"You should have looped me in. When the Omaha agents arrived, they found chaos and bullet wounds. You were gone." He stretched the collar of his shirt. Judging by the too-large neck hole, it wasn't the first time. "We didn't know what happened to you. If you were even alive."

Usually immaculately groomed and attired in a suit, Grant's messy hair now stood on end, a shadow of a beard grew on his jawline and a coffee stain decorated his t-shirt. Eric had never seen him so disheveled.

Unable to look at the other man any longer, he stared out the window.

"My first thought was helping an innocent civilian." There would be other opportunities to explain his relationship with Elise.

"Undercover is a different world. Sometimes you have to stand down. Or at least let someone know what you're doing." Grant leveled his attention at Eric. "Don't ever jeopardize a mission again."

"Understood."

"Do you have any idea how lucky you are? Did I not drill into you the biggest danger of undercover work?"

Eric recited Grant's number one rule, the heaviness of self-loathing filling his chest. "The agent is always last to know when his cover is blown."

"It's a good thing you ended up with the Koslovs

and not the Alarios."

Eric gripped the duffel. He'd never considered himself lucky, but Grant was right. It could have been much worse. Had it been Vincenzo and Rocco who learned his identity, he wouldn't be around to get his ass chewed. He'd be at the bottom of a lake.

Drawing a deep breath, Grant relaxed. "On the phone you said you were taken to the Koslov compound. Tell me about it."

All Eric wanted to think about was getting himself back to Elise. He cleared his throat. "There are armed guards everywhere—most carrying semi-automatic rifles. The house backs up to the river and is surrounded by a high wall. The outer perimeter appears to be patrolled at all hours."

"And the girl? Any chance she's involved?"

"No."

"Are you sure?

Hearing Grant question Elise's motives made Eric's body tense. He gritted his teeth. Reveal too much, and he'd be off the case. If he wasn't already. "She's not the problem."

Grant frowned and narrowed his eyes.

Eric rubbed his aching jaw. After his dad's death, he'd struggled with his temper and ground stress fractures into his teeth. The bad habit always returned in times of high pressure. Best to change the subject.

"Did you recover the bug from the motel?" The last few days had been so chaotic, Eric had almost forgotten the covert listening device.

Grant nodded. "Forensics is still working on it, but we hit pay dirt with the bug in Michelson's office. Turns out Vincenzo paid extra to make sure Elise was his pilot.

When she went to Michelson the other day to ask for another route, the dumbass decided it might be a way to make some extra money."

"Extortion?"

"Bingo. He wanted fifty thousand to keep Elise on their route. Rocco called him an opportunistic fuck. We're guessing he pulled a gun because Michelson backed down immediately."

"Did you bring him in?" Eric couldn't help but think if they'd known sooner about the deal between Michelson and the Alarios, Elise never would have been put in danger.

"Yes, and he's cooperating."

Eric was silent for a moment. It was all progress on the case, but none of it would protect Elise. "What happened at the farm?"

"We apprehended Christopher Maldonado and Nicky de Luca. Nicky is recovering from surgery. Christopher is at FCI Englewood."

"Has he told you anything?"

"We're holding him for kidnapping, but he's got counsel." Grant shook his head. "He's not talking."

"Did you arrest any Koslovs?" Eric guessed not, considering Papi seemed as much in the dark as he about what went down after Sergei grabbed Elise.

"Nope. Just two from the Alario crew and several connected to the local guy."

"Vincenzo and Rocco?" Eric asked, fearing he already knew the answer.

"In the wind. We're thinking they escaped in an unregistered vehicle known to be on the property."

As much as Eric hated to admit it, staying with Papi looked like the best option for Elise. Still, he'd feel better with her near. "We need to get Elise out of that house and into protective custody."

Grant shook his head. "Rocco and Vincenzo Alario are our priority. She's got armed guards, an entire organization to protect her. She'll stay where she is."

The words were almost identical to the thought Eric had last night. Leaving her with her grandfather made sense. But things were different now. *He* was different now. He hunched into his seat, his heart squeezed between doing what he was told and his need to see Elise. Realistically, it wasn't a choice. He would get her back. One way or another.

Chapter Twenty-Five

Elise spent the afternoon in her room. Her head throbbed, her heart ached, and the pain between her legs chafed at her psyche in a way that had nothing to do with the amazing sex she'd had the night before.

He'd promised he wouldn't leave. Now he was gone. It didn't make sense. Not after the way he'd kissed her, made love to her. Lust didn't explain it. He'd made her feel cherished. Cared for. He couldn't fake that. No. One of these bastards made him leave. It was the only thing that made sense. She hugged herself, remembering the tenderness of his embrace. His warm skin. His hard body.

Tap. Tap tap. She ignored the rap on the door.

Tap. Tap. The knocks persisted. Why couldn't these people just leave her alone?

"I don't want anything," she yelled.

The doorknob turned. Miranda's face appeared around the side of the door. "May I come in?"

Elise shrugged. What did she care?

Miranda held up a cordless phone. "I thought you might want to talk to your brothers."

Elise reached for the handset, hand trembling, but stopped. She pushed her shoulders back. "I thought it wasn't safe. I thought we were 'keeping it on the down low,'" she sneered, mimicking Sergei.

Miranda pressed the phone into Elise's hand. "You

need to keep it short, but your grandfather agreed there wouldn't be any harm in letting you say hello."

It was another manipulation, but she didn't care. She clasped the phone to her chest.

"I'll be down the hall. Let me know when you're finished." Miranda stepped out of the room and pulled the door closed.

Once the woman left, Elise dialed her brothers' number. The line rang. And rang. And rang. An uncomfortable lump rose in her throat, and she gripped the phone tighter. *Please answer.* Another ring. She squeezed her eyes shut, unable to pull the phone from her ear.

"Hello?" A deep voice cut through the numbness.

"Nate?" She ignored the quaver in her voice. "It's me."

He responded with an audible sigh. "Oh, thank God. We've been so worried."

Relief poured through her when she heard the timbre of his voice, so warm and familiar. Had she been standing, her legs would have buckled. "I know. I'm sorry. For everything."

"Me, too. I've been an ass." Good old, solid-as-a-rock Nate. He'd never been one to express himself with a lot of words. "You okay, Peanut?"

"I think so." She exhaled. "I'm having a hard time believing this is real."

He didn't speak.

"You knew about this. All of it." This was the crux of the problem. He knew all along and hadn't said anything. "How could you keep this from me?"

"I was just a kid." Her big brother—the one who had always taken care of her—sounded pained and uncertain.

"Dad told me people would get hurt—maybe die if I told."

She bristled. "How much do you remember about our lives before?"

"Not much. I recall living in our grandfather's house and playing football with Sergei. That's about it."

"You speak Spanish." The words came out like a challenge.

"Not well."

"At one time?"

Her brother let out a dejected sigh. "A lifetime ago."

"And Russian?"

Nate sucked in a breath. "I could follow a conversation, but I can't speak it."

"Sergei said he talked to you. He said you were friends."

"A long time ago."

"What do you think of him now?"

Nate exhaled into the receiver. "I was thirteen when I last saw him. Two days ago was the first time I've spoken to him in over twenty years."

"Can I trust him?"

"I wish I knew."

Elise bit the inside of her cheek. Despite having known their secret all those years, one thing was clear—Nate had no influence with these people. She'd spent so much time blaming him for keeping secrets, but he'd only been on the periphery.

They were both powerless.

****

Late that afternoon, Elise sat on the balcony waiting for the sun to drop behind the trees. What was she going to do? She needed to find a way out of the compound—

and soon.

But how? The stone walls were tall and armed guards circled the edges of the property. Sneaking out undetected would be impossible. Watching the sky change colors, she considered her situation. The house employed dozens of people, most of whom lived off-site. They must have a way to come and go. Maybe she could find an unhappy employee willing to help.

She let out a huff of frustration. Forming relationships, figuring out who to trust would take time. She couldn't wait for that.

Surely, Eric would try to come back for her. She recalled Miranda's question. *Do you believe in him?* God help her, she did, and for one simple reason.

Love.

It was the first time the word crossed her mind. Unexpected and unwanted, she froze. But the more she repeated it to herself, the more she understood it was the only explanation for how he made her feel. Not long ago, the idea she would be part of a complimentary set—the salt to his pepper—was unfathomable. And, as much danger as the sentiment held, she welcomed it.

No point fighting it now. She was in love.

The time had come to stop avoiding life, to start living—even with an uncertain outcome.

She remembered the gleam in his eyes as he'd gazed down at her and the strong arms that held her tight after they'd made love. What she wouldn't give to be with him now. Wherever he was.

An emptiness filled her stomach. He said he lived in Philadelphia. Had that been the truth or part of his cover? Deep in her bones she sensed their connection yet didn't know the most basic details about him.

She grimaced. Her life had been a never-ending quest to avoid attachments. Counselors she'd been trotted to all said the same thing—her mother bore the blame for her abandonment. Intellectually, it made sense. Emotionally, she couldn't stop wondering why she'd been rejected. Shallow relationships, mistrust of authority, putting up walls—she'd missed so much. And now, just when she found someone she could relate to, when happiness felt within her grasp—she was trapped by an overbearing old man who wanted her to be someone she wasn't.

It wasn't fair.

"Elise?"

She swung around to see Sergei at the door. He didn't enter, but in each hand, he carried a bottle of beer.

She rose, muscles tensing as she took slow, cautious steps toward him. "What do you want?"

He extended a bottle. "I thought we could talk."

She accepted a beer, twisted off the top and returned to the balcony.

He followed, taking a seat beside her. "How are you doing?"

"You don't have to pretend you care."

He shook his head and smiled bitterly. "I wish you remembered how things used to be when we were kids. Nate and I were best friends. You were the cute little pest who followed us around."

"That was years ago. Things have changed." She pretended to pick lint off her shirt, but a knot formed in her stomach. "Besides, if you actually knew Nate, you'd know he's blaming himself for all of this."

Something shifted in Sergei's gaze, tenderness pushing out the hardened resolve she'd grown accustomed to seeing. "Nate was like a brother to me. You and Jack were my younger siblings." He picked at the soggy corner of the beer bottle label and closed his eyes. "I lost my family—everyone who meant anything—when you left. My life was never the same."

Elise reached for his hand, then thought better of it. No. She wasn't falling for it. *He wants something.* "Why are you here?"

"You have no reason to trust me. I know that."

"But you think saying my brother's name will make me forgive and forget?" She tilted her head and took a swig of the bitter brew.

"I understand your skepticism."

She snorted. "That's an understatement."

"I want to help."

"Really? You've been super helpful so far. Pointing a gun at Eric. Bringing me here. Driving him out of town." She held up her hand. "No thanks. I'm good."

"I'm sorry about all of that. I wish I could have let you escape at the farm, but Papi's men were there too." He guzzled his beer. "You didn't sign up for this. And even though you're safest here with us, you deserve to make that decision for yourself."

A strange sensation filled her chest. It sounded like the truth. She shook her head. What was wrong with her? Did she actually believe this maniac? God. What a gullible idiot she'd become. "Would you have shot Eric if I hadn't gotten into the car?"

His face puckered like he'd just put a sour candy in his mouth. "I didn't have to make that decision."

"That's not an answer."

"Okay. Yes." He clenched his jaw. "But only because if I didn't, someone else would have—and they would have killed him."

Elise looked away, for the first time fully comprehending the magnitude of her predicament. The reality of it hollowed out her insides, but she had no choice. She'd trust anyone and do almost anything to escape. To find her way back to Eric.

Sergei set his empty bottle on the table between their chairs and faced Elise. "I never had a say in how my life turned out, but that doesn't mean you shouldn't. I'm going to do one good thing in my life. I'm going to get you out of here."

****

Another coworker scurried away. Eric huffed. Everyone wanted to hear his story, and while baring his teeth at colleagues wouldn't win him any friends, he had more important things to do than indulge his coworkers' curiosity.

He'd been at it for hours, comparing the Alario and Koslov files, trying to find a weakness. Something—anything he could use, a bargaining chip to get Elise back. He splayed his hands on the top of the desk and groaned. He was no closer to a solution than when he started.

Concentration eluded him. His stomach growled. He couldn't remember the last time he'd eaten real food. Dinner last night? Nope. Breakfast? Only if two stale powdered donuts counted. Lunchtime passed by hours ago.

He gulped his cold coffee and squeezed his eyes shut. The dim flicker of the fluorescent light did funny things to his vision. A dull throb began in the middle of his forehead, but soon hammered against his skull. The pounding in his head made him squint.

Grant Morgan leaned against the wall of Eric's cube. "Good God, man. You look like the walking dead."

Eric rubbed a hand against the stubble on his jaw, feeling like the poster child for rock bottom. "What time is it?"

"You need food and sleep. In that order." Grant frowned. "And you're going to tell me what's really going on."

Eric's cramped leg muscles complained as he stood. He followed his now-impeccably dressed manager into the elevator.

"I assume you don't object to the cafeteria?" Without waiting for an answer, Grant slapped him on the back. "Glad you're agreeable."

Anxiety gnawed at Eric. There was something he needed to do, but his brain had stopped functioning. He stumbled as he stepped from the elevator into the sparsely populated lunchroom. Grant gave him a pitying look and led him to the counter where he shoved an orange tray into his hands. Eric stared dumbly at his colleague. "Aren't you going to eat?"

His boss pulled a face. "I'm not eating this garbage. Come on. Let's get you some carbs and protein."

Eric trailed behind helpless as Grant stacked a double helping of overcooked spaghetti and an extra serving of shriveled meatballs on his tray.

"Two pieces of bread, please." Grant grinned at the server behind the counter, his British refinement on full display. He grabbed a bottle of apple juice, then faced Eric. "What else are you in the mood for?"

Eric shrugged and watched his supervisor pay for the food. Grant scanned the room, then chose an isolated spot near the window. The pounding in Eric's head drowned out the soft murmur of conversation. He swayed, barely able to stay upright.

"Drink this first." Grant pushed the drink across the table.

Eric stared at the plastic bottle gliding toward him. At the last minute, his brain remembered it had a job to do. He stuck out his hand and caught it just before it slid to the floor. He took a sip. Then another. Then, looking at the plate of food, his stomach lurched in protest. "I can't."

"Eat," Grant commanded.

Eric twirled spaghetti around his fork and shoved lukewarm pasta into his mouth. He took a few slow bites, waited for it to settle, then took a few more.

"Didn't the mob feed you?"

"They had food." Eric shrugged. "There were other things going on."

"Next time you're captured by a criminal syndicate, remember to eat." Grant attempted to keep it light, but Eric detected the warning in his tone. "How bad was it?"

He thought for a moment, his head clearer than a few minutes ago. "Could have been worse. Elise told her grandfather she didn't want anything to happen to me, so that helped."

Grant's eyebrows drew together. Eric had never known the man to mince words. He prepared himself for the inevitable. "How about telling me the truth?"

Eric looked away. Considering he'd been doing a convincing impersonation of a sloth, he might get away with playing dumb, but his misbehavior would surface eventually. He hesitated, wanting to choose the right words. "Elise is important to me."

The question came quick. Grant knew. Or at least

suspected. "How so?"

Eric set the fork on the plate and rubbed his hands up and down his thighs. "We have a connection."

Grant leaned forward, his lips stretched into a bitter smile. "What kind of connection?"

Eric grimaced and rubbed the back of his neck.

"Did you sleep with her?"

He didn't reply.

The other agent slammed his fist against the table. It shook, rattling the plate and fork, and making Eric jump. "For fuck's sake, Erickson. Are you kidding me?" He pursed his lips and stared off for a moment before meeting Eric's gaze with a glare. "Are we going to talk about the rules or is it too late for that conversation?"

Eric's stomach dropped. He'd fucked up. He hated disappointing anyone, especially Grant. "I didn't mean for it to happen."

A loose curl fell over Grant's forehead. He brushed it away and ran a hand through his hair. "I don't suppose you did."

After a few moments of deafening silence, Grant spoke again. "You care for her?"

Eric nodded.

"You want her out of the house?"

Eric exhaled hard. Maybe things would actually work out. "I've been studying the Koslov file, trying to find a weak spot. Someone or something I can leverage—"

Grant motioned for him to stop. "She stays there."

"But—"

"I understand wanting to rescue her, but she's safer there than anywhere else."

Grant might as well have reached inside Eric's chest

and crushed his heart.

"If she's a Koslov, they'll protect her. Outside, she's got a target on her back. Rocco and Vincenzo won't stop until they find her. Frankly, the threat analysis on Papi is much less serious than on the Alarios. He's no Boy Scout, but at least he doesn't use murder as a negotiation tactic." Grant lowered his voice. "I know you don't like it, but she needs to remain with her grandfather."

Eric slumped in his chair. Grant was right. He'd searched for something in the file to justify storming the compound but found nothing. "What about me?"

"I'm going to drive you home so you can sleep. Tomorrow, we talk about the insubordination." Grant jabbed his finger at him. "In the meantime, don't do anything stupid."

Eric nodded, but his brain had already bypassed Grant's admonishment.

Sergei said he'd reach out. Did he mean it? And if so, when?

Chapter Twenty-Six

Elise waited until almost midnight before tiptoeing out to meet Sergei. Wearing dark clothing as instructed, she zipped her sweatshirt and pulled the hood over her head. At the fence surrounding the tennis courts, she strayed off the path with its lights and their creepy shadows and diverted through the grass.

Sergei waited in the inky shade of a tree—right where he'd said he'd be. Part of her still didn't believe he was for real. "Ready to go?"

She gave a reluctant nod. Having gone through the pros and cons, she knew two things. One, she was a fool for trusting this man. Two, he might be her only chance to get away.

In the end, there was no real choice. Eric was worth the risk.

"Stay away from the lamps." Sergei motioned for her to follow. "Let's go."

She fell in step behind him. Guided by the dim illumination of the moon, they moved around an equipment shed to a gravel path where an SUV sat running. "Get in the back and stay down."

Elise climbed in and curled onto her side. Sergei covered her with a blanket. Once the back door closed, the SUV began to bump and roll. The brakes squealed. Conversation drifted toward her. Two voices. She couldn't make out any of the words.

They were moving again.

After several minutes, the vehicle slowed. She squeezed her eyes shut and held her breath. The door opened with a soft whirr and the blanket was yanked off her. "Come on." Sergei held out his hand. "We're past the guard gate. You can get in the front now."

She scrambled from the cargo area and into the passenger seat. She didn't speak as they traveled through back streets, finally entering a main road, and then merging onto the highway.

He retrieved a cell phone from his pocket and set it in a cup holder. "Once we're further down the road, we'll give your boyfriend a call."

"Where are we going?"

"Airstrip near the Pennsylvania border. My buddy runs the place. Said he'd open for us."

Another criminal, no doubt. "And from there?"

"Anywhere you want."

She drew her head back. It sounded too good to be true. She studied him with narrowed eyes. "What's in it for you?"

"You don't believe I'm doing this out of the goodness of my heart?"

"Not really, no."

After a long moment, he spoke. "Most people decide for themselves what to do with their lives. I didn't have that option. Others made those decisions for me."

"Who?"

"Grandfather. My dad. Right about the time your family left, they started bringing me in on family discussions, impressed upon me that as a member of this family I had responsibilities and obligations."

Elise stilled. Sergei had only been a kid when her

dad took them to Florida. "Is that what would have happened to Nate and Jack?"

"If they'd been here, the burden might have been spread out, but when my father died, I was the only one left."

"I'm sorry." What a completely inadequate thing to say. She'd never stopped to consider the ripple effect of her parents' decisions.

He shrugged. "You didn't grow up with the burden. It's not fair to thrust it upon you."

A sharp, unwanted pain invaded Elise's chest. She didn't want to feel sorry for Sergei, but revelations about his upbringing put her own into perspective. She wasn't the only one whose life had been hijacked. "What does this have to do with Eric?"

"I'm hoping he might help me out at some point."

Of course. A catch. "How? He won't do anything illegal."

"Not like that," he said, his tone impatient. "I might need help leaving the family. Especially after the stunt we're pulling tonight."

She sucked in a breath filled with self-recrimination. Sergei had risked everything to help her. The guard saw him leaving, and when Papi discovered her gone, it wouldn't be hard to figure out who orchestrated her escape. "Are you in danger?"

"No." His voice lacked conviction. "Not from Grandfather, but it doesn't hurt to have a Fed on my side."

God. Was she really that naive? The situation was so much more complicated than she'd imagined.

"Grandfather expects me to take over the business when he's gone, but I'm not interested. I've already given my entire life to this family. For once, I'd like to do something for myself. The organization is a huge machine. Dissolving it will be a complex process. Another reason I need all the goodwill I can get."

"That sounds dangerous."

Sergei nodded. His jaw tensed. "Hence my motivation for getting on Eric's good side."

Her heart accelerated. There was more to her cousin that she could have guessed. Never again would she doubt his sincerity. "What do you want to do with your life instead?"

He tapped a finger against the steering wheel and shifted in his seat. "Promise you won't laugh?"

"I'll do my best."

Passing streetlights revealed a flush creeping across his cheek and ear. "I sing and play guitar." The words came out in a rush. "My band plays at local bars and clubs."

"That's amazing." She tilted her head and grinned. "What kind of music?"

"Country."

"You seem embarrassed."

"I'm not, but I don't publicize it. Grandfather doesn't approve. Though he's tolerated it so far." His mouth turned down. "We've been approached about recording an album, but it'll never happen. It's not fair to the guys, but I don't see any way around it."

Consumed by her own problems, it never occurred to her Sergei had his own dreams. "I hope Eric can help."

He reached for his phone. "Speaking of—let's give him a call."

****

A familiar song cut through the haze. Eric blinked

and took in the dark room.

Phone.

He felt around the nightstand until his palm landed on the hard rectangle. The bright display stung his sleepy eyes. Unknown number.

"Hello." His dry throat made his voice crack. He rested the back of his hand on his forehead.

"Wake up, Zippy." *Sergei.* "Meet us at White Oaks in three hours." The line went dead.

Us. Meet *us.*

Now wide awake, Eric checked the time. Two a.m. Almost six hours of sleep—not enough to make up for what he'd lost, but enough to keep him going.

He popped out of bed, grabbed a towel, and opened to an internet map program. A quick search revealed one result for White Oaks. An airstrip near the Pennsylvania-New York border.

He zoomed in on the satellite photo, searching for spots Sergei might place men. He needed to prepare for everything, even an ambush. Located off a two-lane road, the surrounding landscape looked wide open—mostly farmland. A dirt road led to a small airfield with a single grass runway.

According to the app, it would be a three-hour drive. With some disregard for the speed limit, he could probably cut it down to two and a half. Still, he needed to hurry.

Should he call Grant? Yes, absolutely. But Grant would tell him to wait. He'd want to arrange backup, formulate a plan, organize a team. It would be the right thing to do, but it would take too long. He needed to get to Elise as soon as possible. He'd deal with the fallout once he knew she was safe.

After showering, Eric packed a small bag. In his inner ear, Grant's voice played on repeat. *Don't be stupid.* He ignored it, locked his apartment, and stepped into the elevator. Heart thudding, he strode toward his car. He'd devoted a big chunk of his adult life to the FBI. Choosing to ignore protocol should be a harder decision. But it wasn't. For one reason.

Years of training. Thousands of hours spent studying the Alario crime family. It all led to this moment. He wasn't about to let procedure keep him from getting her back.

Revving the engine of his Audi, he peeled out of his building's parking lot and sped north along the interstate, asking all three-hundred-and-fifty horses to give him everything they had. With few cars on the road, he made good time.

A mixture of worry and anticipation coated his stomach while thoughts of Elise flushed him with heat.

She'll be okay.

He couldn't let himself consider anything else.

His insides burned with the audacity of what he was doing, who he was meeting—putting his trust in a man who pointed a gun at him and threatened to shoot. *Please God, let this be the right decision.*

He turned off the interstate and onto a dark two-lane highway. The threat of wildlife and lack of road shoulder made him back off the speed, but the darkness gave him time to reflect.

Catching Alario still topped his list of concerns, but after more than twenty years, a few more days wouldn't hurt. Elise was his priority now. He could only hope she would forgive him for leaving. He'd do anything to make it up to her. Move to Florida? Sure. Quit the FBI to work as her first officer? If that's what it took. A Dungeons and Dragons themed wedding? If she was into that sort of thing, why not?

Thoughts of marriage—even ones made in jest—had never crossed his mind before, but he'd also not thought it possible to care this much for another person. Elise was special. He stroked the spot over his heart. The constant ache in his chest had started the moment he left Papi's compound. The further away he got, and the more time passed, the more it hurt.

Indulgently, he imagined embracing her, smelling her sweet scent, and tasting her soft lips.

Then imaginary Elise was snatched away. The image disintegrated. He grasped the steering wheel tighter. This might be a trap. But why let him go only to lure him back? He leaned forward and felt for the grip of the 1911 tucked into the holster on his waistband. His personal weapon. He relaxed and let out a huge breath.

She'd be waiting. If not, they'd tell him where she was. He'd make sure of it.

The sky to his right blushed pink with the first rays of the sun. He swung onto another deserted highway and checked the map on his phone. Only a few more miles.

****

Elise sat on a picnic table outside the small airport. The sun had only just started to peek through the trees. A dim streetlamp—the only illumination other than runway lights, flickered off and on. She zipped up her hoodie and stuffed her hands in the pockets.

"You look like the world's saddest ninja." Sergei leaned against an exterior wall of the only building on the property. Part office, part hangar, the structure served as base of operations for the tiny airport.

She pursed her lips and wished he'd stop talking.

What if Eric didn't show? Mild nausea fluttered through her stomach.

"Deputy Dawg should have been here by now."

"Stop calling him that. His name is Eric. Not FBI. Not Zippy. Not whatever other lame TV detectives you've thought of." Her muscles twitched. For Eric to go along with Sergei's scheme, he'd have to turn his back on the FBI.

She wrung her hands in her lap. *He's not coming.*

Sergei's mouth curled into a smile. "I'm just messing with him."

"Well stop."

Headlights flashed. A car rounded the corner at the airport's dirt entrance. Elise rubbed sweaty palms on her jeans and clasped her hands in an effort not to fidget. *Please be him.*

The car rolled to a stop. Head lights went out. She held her breath. For a moment, nothing happened. When the door finally opened, a tall form appeared. *Eric.*

Without realizing it, she'd gotten to her feet and started moving toward the figure.

Sergei cleared his throat. "I'll check with Buck to make sure everything's in order."

There was no mistaking the silhouette walking in her direction, a bag slung over his shoulder. Her knees went weak. *He came.* She raced toward him and flung herself into his arms.

Hugging him hard, she snaked her hands under his open jacket and smooshed her cheek against his hard chest. Being near him was like coming inside on a cold, winter day—warm, welcoming, safe. He felt like home. She inhaled the scent of leather and squeezed. In return, he wrapped her up like a blanket and rested his cheek on the top of her head. She hoped he'd never let go. But his hold loosened. He leaned back and pressed a finger under her chin, tilting her face toward his. "I didn't want to leave."

"I know." Her voice quaked and her heart pounded as she took in his gaze, bright with desire. He swallowed, then leaned forward. Time slowed. Everything melted away. Everything other than Eric. The brush of his lips, soft at first, then hard. He kissed her with an urgency that filled her insides and expanded into her heart and her soul. Not lust. Or desire. Something new. Something more wonderful than she'd ever thought possible.

His hands wound into her hair, but then he growled and disconnected. He rested his chin against her forehead. "We'll have time for this later."

Her chest loosened. She nodded.

He draped his arm over her shoulder. She squeezed him around the waist and tucked herself into him. Passing through the open gate, they headed toward the Cessna 172, where Sergei waited with the older, heavyset man.

The man extended a short, stubby hand as they approached. "Buck Montgomery. Pleased to meet you, Agent Erickson."

Eric shook it. "Likewise."

"The plane is on loan," Sergei said.

Eric's lips flattened. "Who does it belong to?"

"She's mine," Buck said. "Been around longer than you, but I've taken care of the old gal."

"You're okay giving her to a couple of strangers?"

Buck started to answer, but Sergei interrupted. "It's a favor for me."

"Uh huh." Eric looked skeptical. "You say you're not in a hurry to get it back?"

"Not really." Buck's ample belly shook with laughter. "I don't fit quite as well as I used to."

Elise squeezed Eric's arm. "Thank you, Mr. Montgomery. We appreciate your generosity."

The old guy's pale blue eyes sparkled when he smiled, drawing attention to his bushy white eyebrows. "My pleasure."

"I don't know how we'll repay you." Eric didn't miss a beat, and though he spoke to Buck, his gaze stayed locked on Elise. "We'll get her back to you as soon as possible."

The other man rolled on his heels and grinned. Eric inspected the outside of the plane. Elise followed as he circled the exterior.

She rested a hand on the fuselage. "Everything's ready to go. Buck and I did the pre-flight check before you got here."

He lowered his voice. "Are you sure about this? Trusting Sergei?"

She wet her lips. "He wants to help."

Eric gave a brisk nod and strode back to the other men. "If there's nothing else, we'll be going."

"Sounds good." Buck winked at Elise and ambled toward his office.

Sergei tousled Elise's hair. His voice broke. "We didn't have enough time to really get acquainted, but I hope to see you soon."

Elise leaned forward and hugged him. She'd never forgive herself if Papi retaliated. She kissed him on the cheek. "I appreciate your help more than I can say."

Sergei handed over the keys. "Call me when you

land."

Moving to Eric's side, she blinked back tears. Eric's terse nod communicated the appreciation he'd never put into words. He took off his jacket and clambered into the plane.

After one last hug, she climbed in and took her seat next to her man, who was already resetting the altimeters and checking the magnetic compass. The craft bore significant resemblance to the one her dad had used to teach her to fly. The simple cockpit made the model a flight instructor favorite. Warmth at its familiarity and having Eric at her side spread through her.

Shoulder to shoulder, with almost no room to move, Elise turned her head.

He gave her a sideways glance. "Where to?"

"Home, I hope." The comment sounded like a question.

He stared for a long, hard moment. Then his head began to shake. "Absolutely not. No way. Anywhere but—"

"Just for a couple of days. Then we can go wherever you want. Just the two of us." Would going home be reckless? Maybe. But she needed to see Nate and Jack, to close the gap widening between them.

"Do you think Vincenzo is going to just give up? Florida is the first place he'll look. Let's get where we're going, and then you can phone them, do a video call, something. But going home is a bad idea."

"Please." She clasped his hand and gave it a squeeze. "I have to see my brothers. I need to do this in person."

His jaw pulsed. His hands tightened around the yoke. His laser-beam gaze was almost enough to make her squirm. But then, his shoulders slumped and she knew he'd given in. "Next stop, paradise." He revved the engine.

"I hope you like mosquitos."

"We're short on sleep. Do we want to do this in one day or two?"

"One." The sooner she had it out with Nate and Jack, the better. "I figure seven hours, not counting stopping for fuel."

"Aye, aye, Captain."

She raised her eyebrows. "Why hasn't my first officer gotten this thing in the air?"

Eric smiled, the morning light streaming through the window as he turned onto the grass runway.

The soft glow enveloping the aircraft from the aft sun made her stomach flutter. A long-absent feeling of optimism filled her as they began their initial climb. She breathed deeply, inhaling freedom at last.

Chapter Twenty-Seven

The plane hit the runway with a pop and bounce. They taxied to the end of the airstrip, and Elise directed Eric to a hangar. "That's where we keep our planes."

Above the bifold doors, the words *Bahia Air* curved over a painted conch shell. He read it aloud and gave her a questioning look.

"Get used to it, buddy. You're in the Keys now. Ocean breezes, sunsets, and conch shells." She gave him a playful nudge with her shoulder. "That's how we roll."

He leaned into her and grinned. Coming here had been stupid, but now that they were on the ground, an unfamiliar lightness expanded his chest, almost as if his concerns had floated away.

A tall, rugged man rubbing his hands on a towel stepped through the open doors of the hangar. Elise's face lit up. "Jack!" She clasped her hands to her chest. She'd been separated from her brothers for months. It felt good to know he'd been the one to bring her home.

"Where do you want me to put her?" Eric pressed the toe brake, slowing the aircraft.

She pointed to a spot several yards from the hangar. "Tie her down over there for now. I'll see about moving her into the hangar later."

He parked, and as soon as the prop stopped spinning, Elise flung open her door and ran into her brother's arms.

Humidity seeped inside the plane, but it was nothing

compared to the Florida heat that awaited him. He stepped out of the small aircraft into air so wet and hot it could boil rice. Thickness oozed around him and soaked into his skin. He took his time tying down the Cessna, adding more knots than necessary to give Elise a moment alone with her brother. After a quick reunion, Jack threw his arm around her shoulder, and the pair walked toward the borrowed plane. Eric wiped sweaty palms on his jeans and came out from under the shadow of the wing.

Elise bounced on her heels and made the introductions.

Jack's rough palm gripped Eric's extended hand. They regarded each other suspiciously. "Pleased to meet you."

Her brother's mouth pinched tight. Like Elise, he had coppery brown eyes. His tan skin suggested significant time spent outdoors, and though younger than Eric, strands of gray streaked his dark hair. Eric pretended not to notice Jack's hands clenching and unclenching. Elise must have explained who he was. Any brother would be distrustful and protective. Earning her siblings' acceptance would take time.

"You need to shave." Elise ran her hand over Jack's dark stubble.

His expression softened. "You don't like it? I'm growing it out. When it gets long enough, you can braid it."

She gave Jack a playful punch. "Yuck."

He grinned and ruffled her hair. Scrunching her nose, she fixed her disheveled ponytail.

Eric shifted and pretended to study the airport, trying not to interrupt the homecoming. Sweat dripped down his back. He reached behind and pinched the wet shirt off his skin.

Jack noticed. "First time in Florida?"

Eric shook his head. He'd gone to the world's happiest place shortly after his dad's death. "Once. When I was a kid."

"Probably didn't faze you then. It's different when you're older." Jack wiped his brow. "I could use a cold drink. Let's go inside."

The siblings led the way across the apron to the terminal with Eric trailing behind. Elise didn't need him to keep hovering now that she was home. But after having her to himself, backing off wouldn't be easy. They entered the building through a side door that led down a long hallway into the lobby.

She spun backward but didn't stop walking. A huge smile spread across her face. "The airport used to be a single building about the size of a trailer." She whirled forward. They crossed the tile floor and passed a staircase. She pointed but kept moving. "Our business office is upstairs. We've also got space in the lobby."

In a booth adjacent to the car rental desk, a menacing-looking man leaned on the counter. Eric eyed the signage and groaned. Charter and Flight School. Something told him this brother was going to be difficult.

The man rested his chin on his hand, staring at nothing. As they approached, he turned. In a flash, his eyes went from dull to shining. His gaze locked on Elise. She gave a shy smile when he rushed around the counter and scooped her into his arms. "Peanut, it's good to see you." He kissed her on the cheek. "I'm sorry. For everything."

"Me too," she said, her voice husky with emotion. Her eyes shined brighter than Eric had ever seen. She worshiped her brothers. He could only hope they would accept him as the new man in her life.

This brother seemed like a giant. With his dark hair cropped short and his brows drawn together, he wore what appeared to be a perpetual grimace of displeasure.

"Eric, this is my brother, Nate." Elise lifted onto her toes and grasped her brother's arm. She tilted her head toward the large man with obvious affection.

Nate gave Eric a pointed look. "Who's he?"

Elise motioned to Eric. "He works for the FBI and was undercover on my flight." She shifted to Eric's side and grasped his hand.

Nate's scrutiny landed on their threaded fingers, then traveled to Eric's face. He could hardly blame the guy. "Is that so?" The flare of Nate's nostrils communicated more than words ever could.

Eric couldn't fault either brother for their suspicions. He deserved their scrutiny—and then some.

"Someone has some explaining to do." Nate's gaze bore into Eric.

Elise stepped between them. "You're right, Nate. You *do* have a lot to explain."

The eldest Hughes brother stared at her, but then his face relaxed. "Let's go upstairs."

Elise grasped Eric's hand. "Stay with me."

The office suite was snug, but comfortable. There was a small waiting area with a row of chairs and a water cooler in the corner. Down a short hallway were two small offices.

Nate and Jack each had their own space, but he didn't even see a desk plaque for Elise.

He bit his cheek to keep himself from saying something he'd regret. She'd been gone for months, and it wasn't his business.

The standoff between Elise and her brothers was about to begin. Eric wanted to be supportive, but she'd said she needed to handle it herself. He respected that. Besides, he had other things to worry about right now.

Unfortunately, that train of thought ran straight to Grant. He owed the man a phone call and an explanation—probably more than that.

Sure, he'd messed up from a procedural point of view, but he'd done a lot of good too. All that new intelligence on the Alarios came from him. He'd been the one to find the farm and alert the Nebraska division. Not to mention observing Koslov family operations from inside the compound.

He had a lot to offer. His career wasn't over. It couldn't be.

Elise stood in the middle of the room, hands on hips. "I want answers." She pointed at Nate. "I want to know what you knew about our real identities and when you knew it."

Neither man spoke.

"Now," she demanded.

The brothers shrank back from their hell-hath-no-fury baby sister. Eric almost chuckled.

"I was in eighth grade when mom left to visit a friend." Nate made air quotes with the words *visit a friend*. "We drove her to the airport, walked her to the gate and said goodbye."

The look in Elise's eyes was unfocused and far away. "I remember. Dad took us for ice cream on the way home."

Nate nodded. "Later that night at home—at Papi's house, I found Dad crying. He told me we were all in danger. Said we'd never see Mom again. That it was the only way to keep her safe." He glanced away. "Not long after, we moved and got new names. Dad said to forget about Papi, Sergei, and everything else I knew."

Eric couldn't imagine the stress this man had endured. Losing his mother. Leaving his home. Keeping secrets. All while barely a teenager. Who wouldn't be defensive after all that?

Elise paced. "I get that, but we're adults now. Why didn't you say something after Dad died?"

"What would be the point? This *is* our life. Our truth." He didn't even glance at her.

Eric's chest tightened. He understood the load Nate had carried, could almost feel the weight boring down on his own shoulders, but knew better than to butt in. It wasn't his place.

"It felt like the truth?" Elise's voice rose.

Eric offered Nate a small smile, this modest acknowledgement the best he could do without engaging directly.

Jack stepped forward, motioning with his hand for her to settle down. "It's not his fault. It's none of our faults."

She spun on Jack. "How long have you known?"

He didn't respond.

Elise clenched her fists and stomped her foot before turning her back on her brothers. "You should have trusted me with the truth. I would have understood. Instead, you put me at risk. It's your fault I was kidnapped."

Eric stepped to her side and grasped her shoulders. "Let's step outside and take a breath." He guided her into the hallway. "Your brothers think the world of you. Give them a chance to explain."

****

Elise resisted, shaking him off. Why was he taking their side?

She let him lead her away from the office door, out of hearing distance from her brothers. They stopped in front of the large window and the weird abstract airplane sculpture she'd never liked.

Eric put a steadying hand on her shoulder. "Cut your brother some slack."

"Are you kidding? He lied to me. For years."

He pinched his lips together as if trying to hold in his rebuke.

"Go ahead. Say it." She made an exaggerated upward motion with her hand. "Explain why he deserves a second chance."

He massaged his temples and blew out a gust of air. When he looked down at her, his face had softened. "He was given an impossible task. At thirteen, I could barely take care of myself, much less have someone else's life on my shoulders."

He hauled her into a hug, but she pushed back.

"You're an only child. You don't know anything about siblings."

His expression turned stony, his voice cold and flat. "I understand what it's like to want to protect someone. I know what it feels like to be a boy expected to act like a man."

Shit. Her shoulders sagged. Of course, Eric would understand. "I'm sorry. That was thoughtless."

"You don't need to apologize to me. But maybe give Nate a chance to explain?"

"Why bother? He's never going to tell me what I

want to know."

"Maybe he'll surprise you."

His soft words and calm tone crawled up her spine and left tension in its wake. "He won't. All those years, so many opportunities. He never said a word." She balled her hands into fists.

"This is why you wanted to come here." He blew out another frustrated breath and a wrinkle appeared at the top of his nose. "If you want to leave things as they are, that's your decision, but if you change your mind, we can go back in there. I'll stay while you and your brothers hash it out."

She took a deep breath. "No, you're right. But I need to do this on my own."

He smiled and pulled his phone from his back pocket. "I should call Grant. I'll be out here if you need me." He strode to the other end of the hall and scrolled through his phone.

With her hand on the doorknob, she looked at him one last time. Hunched against the wall, he stared at his phone. Her chest tightened. He'd risked everything for her. Even his career. She sighed and yanked the door open.

Her brothers stopped talking, their gazes wary. She avoided looking at them. "I'm ready to listen."

Nate motioned for her to follow into his office. He sat behind his desk, while she took a guest chair and Jack hovered near the door. "What do you want to know?"

"Where's Mom?"

"No idea. I don't think Dad even knew."

"He wasn't in touch with her?"

"Not that he told me."

"Did you know about his side business in Jamaica?"

"Of course not." He held her gaze. "I still can't believe it."

She sagged against the chairback. Geez, she'd been dumb. Sure, Nate had known their names were fake, but not much more than that. Eric was right. Her brother had been given an impossible task. Instead of being angry at him for concealing the truth, she should be thanking him for giving her a normal childhood.

"Thank you for looking out for me for all those years."

Nate blinked, whether surprised by her gratitude or trying to keep his emotions at bay, she didn't know. "I only ever wanted to keep everyone safe, but I didn't always go about it in the best way. I know I can be—"

"Domineering." Elise offered.

"Yes, domineering—"

"Opinionated."

Nate flinched. "Okay, sure. Sometimes I'm opinionated."

"Bullheaded."

"I'd probably say stubborn—"

"Bossy, overbearing, pushy—"

"Will you stop?" Nate gave his head an exasperated shake, but at the same time, a huge grin spread across his face. "Those words all mean the same thing."

Elise couldn't remember the last time she'd seen her brother smile. Or the last time they'd laughed together. "I love you both so much."

Nate tipped his chin. "The feeling is mutual."

Lightness swept into the room like an ocean breeze. She couldn't remember the last time they'd been so at ease with one another. It had to have been before their dad died.

She peered at Jack, then at Nate. "Can we agree to keep each other in the loop from now on? No more lies?"

"No more lies," Nate repeated.

Jack leaned against the wall. "Agreed."

Nate rested his elbows on the desk, his penetrating gaze making Elise squirm. "Since we're being honest, what's going on with this FBI agent you're dragging around?"

Elise's face flushed. Things with Eric were still new. She didn't think her brothers would understand. She certainly wasn't ready to tell them she'd fallen in love.

Chapter Twenty-Eight

Holding his breath, Eric dialed Grant's number. He prayed the man would answer but dreaded what he'd say.

"Eric? Where are you?"

Anger. Frustration. Eric expected to hear those things in Grant's voice, but there was something else. *Worry*? Of course, he'd be worried. As if being captured and released by Aleksander Koslov hadn't been enough, he'd disappeared again without a word.

Grant cleared his throat. "Hello? Are you still there?"

"I'm here."

"Are you all right? What happened?"

"I'm in Florida."

"Florida?" Relief crept into the voice on the other end of the line. "What are you doing there?"

How to explain it? "It started with a call from Sergei Koslov. Elise was with him. He'd freed her. We flew into Key Largo."

And he'd do it again.

A harsh laugh traveled through the phone. "You got a call from a known criminal, and you went to meet him on your own?"

"He said he wanted to help get her away from her grandfather."

"And you believed him? Jesus, Erickson. I've worried about your hotheadedness, but I never thought you had a death wish."

"I wanted her out of that house. He did it for me."

"You didn't tell anyone!" Grant yelled, his posh London accent now exaggerated by fury and disappointment. "You could have been killed."

A chance he had to take.

"I told you to focus on Vincenzo and Rocco. I told you to leave Elise with the Koslovs."

Eric ran a hand through his hair. Asking for forgiveness would be disingenuous. Better to have eyes on her, to know she was okay. "I don't regret it."

Grant cursed, then went silent. "How far are you from Miami?"

"Sixty or seventy miles."

"Get your ass to the Miami Field Office. You need to be debriefed." Grant paused. "Prepare for disciplinary action and a psychological review."

Eric pinched his nose and closed his eyes. He couldn't leave Elise. "Can it wait?"

"I'm going to pretend you didn't say that. I'll meet you in a few hours."

The phone went dead. Eric slumped against the wall. What now? Disobey another order and face certain termination or leave Elise in the protection of her brothers?

The harsh reality that his work at the FBI might be over slammed into him like a fist to the gut.

Hell, who was he kidding? The diligent agent he'd been a week ago disappeared the moment he met Elise. How could one person have such a fundamental impact on the things he valued most? No turning back now. He'd give it all up. For her.

A door latch clicked. He glanced to his left. Elise

emerged from the office, the tension gone from her face and body. At least one of them had been able to make things right.

She glided toward him. "How'd it go?"

He couldn't help but admire the sway of her hips, the gleam in her eyes. "I've been ordered to Miami."

"When?"

He'd promised to never leave her side again. If only that were true. "Now."

"You'll need a car."

She started toward the stairs. He grabbed her wrist. "I don't have to go."

Her gaze softened. "Yes, you do. I won't be the reason you lose your job."

"You can come with me. There's nowhere safer than the FBI field office." He offered his most disarming smile, hoping she'd be agreeable.

"No. I'll stay here. You should do this on your own." She stood on her toes and kissed him. "I'm not going anywhere."

"I can't protect you if we're not together. That's the only reason I agreed to come here."

"No matter where we were, you might have to go into an office, and I'd be alone. My brothers are here. I'll be safe."

Was he foolish to even consider this?

"I'd rather take you with me—" he stopped and gazed into wide, anxious eyes. Eventually, she'd have to talk to investigators. But she wasn't ready. Not yet. "Maybe it's okay if you stay here, but you need to be with one of your brothers at all times."

Wrapping his arms around her waist, he tugged her against him. Sweat, mingled with her now-familiar scent, filled his lungs. His cock strained against his pants. *Damn.* She drove him wild.

Not here. They'd have time for that later. Still, her soft, silky lips beckoned. He brushed his mouth against hers. A husky moan slipped from her throat and his breath hitched.

He broke their kiss and pulled her closer. "I've got plans for you when I get back." Once he started, he wouldn't want to stop. Duty called, and he was still an agent. At least for now.

Her heated glance sent shudders through his body. She nestled her head into the crook of his neck. Hopefully this sojourn to Miami wouldn't take long. "Promise me you'll stay with your brothers. I should be back this evening."

She squeezed his arm. "I'll be fine."

Leaning his forehead against hers, he closed his eyes. He was doing the one thing he swore he wouldn't do. He kissed her a final time, then strode to the office, threw open the door and jabbed his finger at her siblings. "I have to go to Miami. Can you provide protection while I'm away?"

Nate's head popped up. "I think we can handle it."

"Don't let her out of your sight."

****

Restlessness clawed at Elise. She'd never been good at having nothing to do. Leaning on the counter of the company stall, she watched Nate pore over the monthly expenses. "How can I help?"

His gaze flicked to the ceiling. She'd seen that exasperated expression many times, reserved specifically for the pesky little sister. For the first time in a long time, it didn't bother her. Just Nate being Nate.

"It's a slow day," he said. "Why don't you catch up on your email?"

He offered no other suggestions, and she couldn't think of anything better. Her dad's old computer sat on the small desk in the business office behind the counter. With a shake of the mouse, the screen came to life.

After a few minutes, Nate stepped into the room and shuffled his feet. "I just want to make sure you're okay. Jack and I are here if you need to talk. But if you'd rather see a professional, we understand."

Elise's mouth fell open. *What in the world?* Heart to hearts were not in her brother's repertoire. The anguish on his face made her pulse race. She held up her hand. Best to put him out of his misery. "The only thing I need is a shower."

He turned pensive. "Jack's with a student. I've got an appointment with a new customer, but when I'm done, I'll take you over to my place."

Elise rubbed her hands on her legs. She hated being at someone else's mercy. "I have my own home." She couldn't wait to get back to her small, one-story home on the water. "Have you been keeping an eye on it?"

"One of us tries to go by once a week. Jack put up the hurricane shutters a while back."

"I didn't hear about a storm."

He gave a dismissive wave. "Cat 2. Looked like it might head this way. It turned."

She liked knowing her brothers were still looking out for her. "Thanks for taking care of that."

"You'll be ready for the next one. We didn't take them down."

She jerked her head. "When did you put them up?"

"Three or four weeks ago."

She drew a deep breath, then exhaled. "A month?" Perpetual shutters were the universal sign for no one's home. "Were you hoping I'd get robbed?"

"We never heard from you and didn't know when you'd be back." Nate crossed his arms with an exaggerated sigh. "Between worrying about you and keeping the business going, it wasn't a priority."

She really couldn't blame Nate and Jack. She shouldn't have left the house for them to deal with. Her voice cracked. "I'm sorry."

"Don't sweat it."

The chirp of a bell sounded. Nate peered into the front. "Someone's at the desk." He disappeared without shutting the door.

She shook her head. It was only a house.

Her brother's voice drifted into the small office. "I'll show you the planes."

After he left with the client, she opened a web browser and typed in her email credentials.

She perused the inbox. Advertisements and not much else. An ache shot through her chest. The lack of emails from concerned friends and acquaintances reminded her how empty her life had been. Not anymore. Now she had Eric.

She jotted out a quick email telling Peter she was safe but wouldn't be returning to Rocky Mountain Charters. She logged out and ran an internet query for "Koslov crime family." Thousands of search results appeared. *Ugh.* Maybe later. Diving into her family's sordid history required more energy than she could spare at the moment.

A yawn came out of nowhere, cracking her mouth wide open. It had been days since she'd had a good night's sleep, but a little sleep deprivation would be worth it if it meant more nights with Eric. Heat swirled between her legs, bringing back memories of the feel of him inside her.

"Hey, Elly?"

She bolted upright, cheeks burning.

Nate stuck his head through the door and motioned over his shoulder with his thumb. "I need to go upstairs for my meeting. I'll close the counter. Do you want to stay here or come with me?"

Yes, she was home, but that didn't mean she was ready to jump back into the family business. "I'll wait for Jack."

"You might have to hang tight for a while. Jack just finished a lesson. He's headed to your place to take down the shutters."

"He didn't have to do that."

"Guess you shouldn't have made a fuss then." Nate gave a practiced oh-well shrug, his not-so-subtle way of saying the shutters could have waited. "I think he already left."

She crossed her arms and leaned back in the old wooden desk chair.

"So, you're staying here?"

"Do I have anywhere else to go?"

"Let me know if you need anything."

There was no telling how long Jack would be gone. *God*. She hated waiting. What did Dad used to say? *Boredom makes smart people do stupid things.* She tapped her fingers against the desk. First order of business for returning to a normal life? Make a grocery list.

She tugged open a drawer and the mess immediately

reminded her of her father. He never threw anything away, yet always knew where to find whatever he needed. She took a shaky breath. He had his reasons. She understood now. She forgave him—mostly—but didn't think she'd ever be able to excuse the smuggling.

She patted the junk in the drawer, her fingers touching nearly every item. No pen or paper. Dumping the contents on the floor was tempting, but not practical. About to slam the drawer shut, she stopped when her hand landed on a small plastic container. She pulled it forward and popped it open. Keys.

The familiar metal airplane charm on one of the key rings made her heart sing. The tightness in her chest disappeared. *Home*. Gripping the key ring in a fist, she lifted it to her chest, then set it on the desk to pick through the rest of the box.

Another key with a large square head caught her eye.

Dad's truck.

The last time she was here, the ancient pickup had been parked in a spot behind the office. She opened the back door and peered outside. Still there, its chrome bumper and red body covered in dust. Had it been moved in the months she'd been gone? It certainly hadn't been washed.

What she wouldn't give for the freedom to climb into that truck and drive herself home.

But that wasn't going to happen. Not now, anyway. She'd promised Eric she'd stay put.

The old, rotary phone trilled, the tinny sound reminding her of afternoons spent doing homework at her dad's desk. She let go of the door and twisted toward the sound, surprised the old thing still worked. *Weird.*

Dad had insisted on keeping the number, but no one used that line anymore.

Probably a telemarketer. Might as well let it ring. And it did. For several minutes. Was the darned thing broken? Finally, after what seemed an eternity, the warble of the ringer stopped. Thank goodness—

Brrrng. Brrrng.

Her heart slowed to a heavy thud. Why was this getting to her? It must be a wrong number. She took a slow step forward and reached a trembling hand toward the receiver.

Brrrng.

She snatched the handset off the cradle and lifted it to her ear. "Hello?" Her voice came out small and raspy.

"Hello, Elisa. I was beginning to think you might not take my call."

Vincenzo. Ice shot through her veins. "What do you want?"

"Is that any way to treat a house guest?" He tsk-tsked. "I'll be honest, I was expecting a lot more hospitality. Don't worry. I let myself in."

Her vision blurred. She braced a hand on the desk. "Excuse me?"

"I was glad to hear you were back in town." The voice on the line was cold. "We have business to discuss."

"Get out of my house." Her heart thrashed against her breastbone with enough force she thought it might knock her off her feet. "I'm calling the police."

"No. You're not." His flinty tone bore an eerie calmness. "And you're not going to tell anyone where you're going either."

"Why's that?"

"Because if you do, your brother dies."

The line went dead.

Jack. She choked back a sob. *Breathe.* Loosening her grip on the handset, she dropped it onto the phone. Her brother was in danger, and it was her fault. Why had she made an issue of the stupid shutters?

She kicked the desk. *God dammit!* Chewing on her bottom lip, she paced the length of the room. Jack was in trouble. She couldn't let him get hurt. Vincenzo said not to tell anyone, but Nate knew things about their family, their history. She rushed from the office and up the stairs, her breaths shallow. Squeezing her eyes shut, she inhaled before yanking open the office door.

The strain and tension poured from her at the sound of Nate's voice. *He'll know what to do.* His calm, authoritative tone settled her nerves like a warm bubble bath. "Minimum requirements are fifteen hours with an instructor and five solo, but we always recommend additional training, as well as ground instruction."

She stepped into the short hallway and rapped on the open door to get her brother's attention. He glanced up and smiled. "Speak of the devil."

The middle-aged man sitting opposite Nate looked at Elise.

"Mr. Jones is considering getting his pilot's certificate. I was telling him you're the best instructor out there." He looked from Elise to the customer. "You'll be in good hands."

"Call me, Tony." The man stood and extended his palm. "I understand you've just come back home from out west."

"That's correct." She gripped the man's hand and nodded, but barely made eye contact before turning to

Nate. "Could we talk for a moment?"

"Can it wait?" Impatience threaded her brother's voice. He raised his eyebrows and tilted his head toward the customer. Elise returned his stare with one of her own.

Tony's gruff voice cut through their silent discussion. "It's hard being separated from family. Wondering if they're okay, worrying they might get hurt."

A cold chill swept through Elise. She gawked at the stranger standing before her, noticing for the first time his wide forehead and broad, stocky physique. His mouth curved into a sneer.

She took a reflexive step back. This man wasn't a customer. He was Vincenzo's insurance policy.

The man pulled a phone from his pocket. "If you two need to talk, I'll step outside. I need to check in with my employer anyway."

Holding up her hands, Elise backed out of the room. "Stay. Please. Finish the meeting. I'm sorry for the interruption." She turned to leave, her body on autopilot. Vincenzo had a man watching Nate. He might have Jack. too. She closed her eyes and took a deep breath. When she opened them, she stood in the downstairs office, but had no recollection how she got here. Her gaze fell to the keys on the desk. *It's the only way.*

Tucking her phone in her pocket, she headed out back. Behind her, the office door slammed with a thud. The old engine of Dad's truck sprang to life without so much as a sputter. Gripping the steering wheel at ten and two, she leaned her forehead against the hard plastic. Should she call Eric? *No.* She'd never forgive herself if he alerted the FBI and one of her brothers got hurt.

She clutched the gear shift in her sweaty palm and maneuvered it into reverse. With her arm on the back of the bench seat, she eased the old gal from her spot. At the stop sign, she glanced back at the airport. This was going to end badly. But what choice did she have? She waited for an opening and turned into traffic.

****

Not even thirty minutes after leaving Elise at the small airport, Eric found himself in standstill traffic. *Figures*. He flipped through the radio stations looking for a news program—anything to distract him from thoughts of Elise and the danger that threatened her. No such luck.

He switched off the stereo and glanced at his phone. He had cell service, but no data. Didn't really matter since the car didn't have Bluetooth. *Damn it.* The last thing he needed was to be left in traffic with nothing but worry swirling through his head.

Up ahead, a van inched forward. One by one, the vehicles behind it moved. The car trailing Eric inched ahead until it was nearly on his bumper. He stared at the driver in the rental's rearview mirror, then glanced at the time. A nudge sent the rental car forward. Eric pushed his foot into the brake to prevent a chain reaction and glared into the mirror. Was the guy an idiot or was something else going on?

The red taillights on the Toyota in front of him blinked out. The car started moving. *Finally.*

Twenty miles per hour. Thirty miles per hour. Forty. Brake lights ahead. He growled. Not again. He slammed the steering wheel and slowed. All he wanted was to make his penance at the Miami office and get back to Elise.

A small glimmer of hope flickered deep within. Maybe it would go better than expected. He'd always been skilled at reading people, able to talk his way out of almost anything.

He shook his head. This was different. The higher ups at the Bureau wouldn't be swayed by emotional appeals. Confidence and a calm demeanor were key. He needed rational explanations for his behavior.

Southbound traffic moved unencumbered. Cars sped past on the opposite side of the road, and he wished he was over there, already heading back to Elise. His Black Sabbath ringtone screamed from the cup holder. He lifted his phone and checked the display. *Grant*. He sucked in a deep breath. "Are you there already? I'm stuck on South Dixie Highway. Gridlock." He rolled forward several feet and braked.

"Not why I'm calling." Tension knitted through Grant's voice. "I just got word. Vincenzo was spotted in Miami. Yesterday."

Eric tightened his grip on the steering wheel. Acid worked its way up his chest. There was only one reason for Vincenzo to be in Miami.

"Where is he now?"

"Don't know for sure."

Eric's heartbeat quickened. "He's here for Elise."

"That's my thought. Where is she?"

"With her brothers."

"Safe?"

Eric clenched his jaw. For days now, Elise's safety had been his one and only thought. "What do you think?"

Grant allowed a tight chuckle. "Okay, I get it. Give them a call. Tell them to be vigilant."

Eric hung up and dialed Elise's number. No answer.

Traffic started to move. He pulled the car onto the shoulder to do a quick internet search for the family airline.

"Hello?" The voice sounded strained.

A chill ran up Eric's spine. *You're overreacting.* "Is this Nate…or Jack?"

"Nate. Who's this?"

"It's Eric. I need to talk to Elise."

Silence.

Eric's mouth went dry. "Where is she?"

"Best guess? Home. She'd been complaining about needing a shower."

Eric punched the steering wheel, wishing it was the other man's face. "You were supposed to watch her."

Nate gave a humorless laugh. "I can see you don't know our Elly too well yet. She interrupted my meeting, said she needed to talk, but then changed her mind. The client wrapped things up not long after, but she'd already left by the time I got downstairs."

Eric wet his lips and took a deep breath. He needed to calm down, think. "What did the client look like?"

"Regular guy. Late forties. Dark hair. Short and squat. Said he was from Jersey."

Damn it. "Name?"

"Jones."

Obviously fake. *Fuck.* "Are you sure she left of her own volition?"

"Dad's truck is gone. I figure she found the keys and decided to check on her house." Nate paused. "I'm heading there now."

"Stay where you are. In case she comes back." Eric pinched the bridge of his nose. "And call me immediately if you see her."

"How much trouble is she in?" A slight tremble in Nate's voice betrayed his worry.

"Give me the address." Eric jabbed the location into his GPS. "Let's hope it's not too late."

Chapter Twenty-Nine

Elise's stomach heaved as she pulled into the driveway of her still-shuttered home. No sign of Jack or his car. Did Vincenzo have him stashed away somewhere? Was he hurt?

She parked in the carport beneath the elevated structure. Humidity assaulted her the moment she exited the truck. On a typical day, she might stop to savor the thick sea air. Not today. She ran a jerky hand through her ponytail. What was she walking into? Vincenzo had every advantage, whereas she couldn't even protect herself.

What she needed was a weapon. Her gaze flicked to the cinder block storage closet. *My old compound bow.* If memory served, she'd stored it in there. The keys jangled and her fingers twitched as she fumbled with the lock. When she finally wrenched open the door, a crescent-shaped plastic case lay on the floor. Thank God.

She lifted the lid, unfastened the straps holding the bow in place and inspected its condition. A frayed bowstring and a possible cracked limb. Not ideal, but better than nothing. She plucked an arrow from the plastic holder in the lid. It wouldn't compare to the firearm Vincenzo carried, but it might buy some time. She doubted a blow from a target arrow would be fatal, but the pain of a close-range shot would be excruciating.

Her hand hovered over the remaining arrows. *No.*

She needed to be fast and agile. Chances were, she'd only get one shot anyway.

Striding across the front yard, she climbed the steps to the door and inserted the key. Stale, stagnant air hit her the moment she pushed it open. Darkness. She flicked the light switch. Nothing.

"Hello?" Her voice echoed through the empty home. A prickle of unease worked its way up her back. "Jack? Mr. Alario?"

He was trying to unnerve her. It was working.

She wasn't going to let the old asshole scare her or hurt her brothers. And she wasn't going down without a fight.

There was a flashlight app on her phone. She nocked the arrow on the bowstring and engaged the rest, freeing her right hand to reach for her phone and turn on the flashlight. Holding the phone in the air, she pushed through the door and stepped into the dark entryway. The light bobbed in front of her as she made her way through the foyer. When she entered the family room, she stumbled over something. *Damn it.* She shook a rug off her foot and kicked it to the side. As she emerged into the large room, something moved. Goosebumps danced up her arms and the back of her neck.

She froze.

"Hello. Elisa. Wonderful to see you again."

****

A concrete partition separated northbound from southbound traffic. Eric backed off the gas to peer around the car in front of him. *Fuck.* The damned road cut straight through the Everglades. It could be miles before he came upon a cross street. He steered from left to right across the lane while tailgating the car in front of him.

It hurt to breathe. He white-knuckled the steering wheel. He'd told her to stay put. She'd agreed. Something must have happened.

Vincenzo.

His mouth went dry.

"Damn it!" He forced his way into the left lane between a van and a little sports car. Somewhere there was an opening. Had to be. Emergency vehicles needed a place to turn around. And this *was* an emergency.

Finally. There it was.

Veering onto the inside shoulder, he pressed the brake and hit the hazards, ignoring the concrete barrier only inches away. The little car straddled the white line.

Tires squealed. The guy behind him laid on the horn.

Southbound traffic zipped by in a never-ending stream. At last. An opening. He stomped on the gas. The car lurched forward, back tires skidding, but he managed the one-hundred-eighty-degree turn, swerving onto the swale beside the road. Horns blared.

He didn't care. He had to get back to Elise.

The car rattled and vibrated as he drove over the rumble strip and merged back into traffic. The garbage sedan hit its max at seventy-eight miles per hour. *Go faster!* He hit the steering wheel with the heel of his hand. *Piece of shit.*

How could he have been so stupid? He never should have left her. Gripping the steering wheel, he took deep breaths. A bead of sweat slid down the side of his face. He swallowed through a tight throat.

Please be okay. He'd never forgive himself if something happened to her. Remembering the feel of her kiss, he touched his fingers to his lips. He had to get to her before Vincenzo. The mobster was a dead man if he so much as laid a finger on her. His veins strained against the collar of his shirt. His vision blurred. He shook it off.

Coming up on the bend where South Dixie became Overseas Highway, he slowed and checked his GPS. The light turned red. He beat out an anxious rhythm on the dashboard. He needed to keep his head. Remember his training.

Green. He forced the pedal to the floor.

Six more blocks.

She was going to be okay. He couldn't believe otherwise.

****

Elise froze. Vincenzo's bulky shadow rose, indistinct and menacing. Her body stiffened, muscles coiling like a snake ready to strike. This was her home. He didn't belong here. "Where's Jack?" She gripped the bow and aimed the light at the intruder. She wanted to see every movement, every facial expression.

He raised a brow, his gaze falling to the bow. "A friendly chat. That's all I ask." A cough drop rattled against his teeth. "Why don't you put on a kettle and make us a cup of tea?"

He took another step. Her legs shook. *Don't let him see your fear.* She stood firm, forcing herself to stand her ground. "I want to see Jack."

He advanced another step. "We all want something. I want my daughter to be alive."

"I did what you asked. Call off your man at the airport. I need proof that Jack and Nate are safe."

He started to laugh but began to cough. Bent at the waist, his body shook.

She hooked two fingers around the bowstring and

started to lift the bow. This was her chance.

He withdrew a handkerchief, wiped blood from his mouth, and straightened. "Not so fast."

Think. "I can't help you. I don't know anything."

"I know. It's unfortunate." He moved with quick, quiet steps. "Now put that toy weapon down."

Her muscles twitched, ready to draw. "No."

With a lightning-fast motion, he plucked a gun from behind his back. "Maybe you can't help me find your mother, but there is something you can give me. Satisfaction."

Instinctively, she retreated, with him matching her step for step until she'd nearly backed herself into a corner. "Don't come any closer." With her left hand, she pushed into the grip of the bow and raised the arrow until it was even with the old man's chest. *Aim high.* She lifted the arrow again.

Vincenzo adjusted his hold on the weapon. "Really? You brought a bow to a gunfight?"

Her fingers trembled on the bowstring. Her breath froze in her lungs. What if she killed him? Could she live with that? *Draw, dammit.* Her arm wouldn't obey.

Vincenzo closed his left eye and sighted. "I think I'll start with your hand. Or maybe your leg." He adjusted his aim, angling the gun toward her thigh.

She was going to die. Her legs weakened and black spots floated in her vision. She couldn't move. Or look away. The faces of those she loved rotated through her mind. Nate. Jack. She shoved down a sob. *Eric.* If only she could tell him she was sorry. If only she could say goodbye.

Vincenzo pulled the trigger.

Nothing happened.

For a moment, it was as if her brain had stopped working.

The gangster narrowed his eyes and frowned. Laying a hand over the top of the gun, he jerked backward on the slide.

She needed to end this.

Everything she'd been through in the last five days came rushing back. This man had started it all. He'd ruined her life. Invaded her home. Possibly hurt her brothers.

Now it was her turn.

Her back and shoulder muscles finally complied. She pulled the bowstring to the corner of her mouth, a motion she'd done thousands of times. Looking through the peep, she lined up the arrow and let it go.

Chapter Thirty

The house was set back from the road, obscured by a row of tightly planted palms. Eric swerved onto the lawn and rammed the gearshift into Park. The car lurched forward into an abrupt stop. A red pickup sat parked in the carport. *Thank God.* Now he needed to find Elise and get her to safety. He slid his gun from its holster and raced to the front door.

Movement to his left. He stopped. A shadow slid behind the house.

Fuck. Vincenzo hadn't come alone.

Eric edged through the carport, then peered around the back of the open structure. Slinking along the exterior wall was a man. A man with a gun. A man about to step onto Elise's back deck.

Eric slid around the corner and crept forward. The guy stopped and tilted his head. Eric froze. The prowler started forward again, and Eric gave up stealth. He pressed the barrel of his gun into the back of the intruder's head. "Keep your mouth shut. Hand me your weapon and turn around."

The thug placed a handgun into Eric's palm. His mouth curved into a sneer. "You're too late."

Eric grabbed the collar of the man's shirt and twisted. He thrust his gun into the man's chest. "Shut up."

Patting the flunky down, he felt his torso and pant

legs for additional weapons. An ankle holster revealed a second firearm with a barrel not much bigger than his pinky.

His peripheral vision blurred and his body shook. There was only one reason a mobster carried a .22. His fist flew at the side of the man's head. Endorphins flooded his body the instant his knuckles slammed into the guy's temple. The gangster dropped to the ground like a bag of cement.

Hand throbbing, Eric nudged the slumped body with his foot. Out cold. He ripped a string of twinkle lights from the deck railing and bound the man's hands behind his back. Adrenalin surged as he pulled the knot tight and kicked the firearms under the deck.

Now to find Elise.

****

The arrow hit Vincenzo in the fleshy area between his left shoulder and collarbone. Mouth slack, he stared at the projectile sticking out of his chest. Then, leveling a fevered stare at Elise, he grasped the arrow shaft in one fist. Red-faced, he let loose an animal-like growl and yanked it free. "You bitch!"

She stared at the blood soaking his shirt, the spot growing larger by the second. *Holy shit.* She'd shot him. A laugh burbled up her throat. "I think you were supposed to leave it in."

"You're going to regret that." Still clutching his gun, he staggered toward her, eyes wide and unblinking.

This man had made her life a living hell. It was his turn to suffer. Gripping the bow like a baseball bat, she lifted it over her right shoulder and planted her feet.

He lurched toward her, arm dangling, one heavy step at a time.

She rotated her entire body into her swing, letting the bow crack against his skull. Vincenzo clutched his head and stumbled back, dazed. A flush of warmth swelled in her chest. Finally, one for the good guys. Her fingers itched to hit him again. But she needed to know about her brothers. She bounced on her toes, wielding the bow like a club over the old man. "Where's Jack?"

Vincenzo rubbed a hand against his head and squeezed his eyes shut. Despite obvious pain, he laughed. "If you recall, I never actually said I had your brother."

"Then where is he? He told Nate he was coming to take down the shutters." Had she come here for nothing? No, Vincenzo was lying. Nate was still in danger. "Call off your guy at the airport." She prowled forward and arced the bow into the gangster's gut.

He doubled over again, laughing and wheezing. "Do you know how easy it was to learn you were back? Didn't your father teach you anything about survival?"

Her breaths came louder and heavier. She'd never wanted to hurt another person so much. Never thought she had it in her. She readjusted her grip on the bow.

The gangster took three steps back. "Your brothers are unharmed. My man left right after you did. He'll be here soon." He tipped his gun to the side, shaking the unfired bullet to the floor, then released the slide and pointed the weapon at her. "But I plan to have some fun before he finishes you off."

****

Eric readjusted the hold on his pistol and twisted the doorknob. His hands shook. A thin sliver of light revealed a short hallway. With his hip, he nudged the door further and stepped inside. Voices. Straight ahead and to the right. Moving along the wall, he crossed one light step behind the other. At the corner, he stopped and peered into a living area.

Two shadows.

"Enough already." Elise's tone shook. She stepped forward, then stopped, her stance wide. Over her shoulder, she held a compound bow by the riser.

A sinister laugh came in reply. "*You've* had enough? I've lived with this for years. Your family has a debt to pay."

"Revenge won't ease your pain." Her voice held a soft warning. "It won't bring Sophia back."

"Don't say her name!" Vincenzo roared. "I bided my time, thinking your mother couldn't stay hidden forever. I'm done waiting. An eye for an eye, a child for a child. If I can't take Irina from her father, I'll take her daughter instead."

Eric glanced around the corner. He had a clear line to Vincenzo, but what if Elise stepped into his shot? No way would he risk hitting her.

For years, he'd fantasized about what he would do to Vincenzo if he got the chance. One good shot. Avenge his father, rid the earth of this piece-of-crap who'd forced Elise's family into hiding for years. He gripped his gun tighter. A justified kill in anybody's book. He leaned around the corner again, looking for a way to take him down without risking Elise's safety.

Vincenzo's head jerked in his direction. "Well, well. If it isn't the sneaky pilot with the hots for this little rat. You're too late." With obvious effort, Vincenzo raised his gun and pointed it at Elise.

There was only one thing to do. Eric charged into the room, positioning himself between Elise and the mobster. "FBI. Drop the weapon."

****

Eric.

Elise slowly lowered the bow.

His broad, backlit figure stood in front of her, his gun pointed at Vincenzo. Although she couldn't make out his shadowed features, she knew how he must look. The set of his jaw. The way his lips pressed into a hard line. He'd moved with authority, calm and deliberate.

Fear slammed into her. He was going to get killed. And it would be her fault. She took a ragged breath. All the things she wanted to say rushed to her lips, but only one thing came out. "I thought he had Jack. I'm sorry."

Eric motioned with a flick of his hand. "Me too. Now leave."

"Not so fast." The old man's weapon pointed straight at Eric's chest. He glared at Elise. "You leave, he dies."

"Do you know who I am?" Eric asked.

Vincenzo sneered. "A guy about to get himself killed."

"Not quite." Eric kept his gun trained on the crime boss.

"One more step and she's dead." The old gangster stepped to the side and readjusted his aim—the gun pointed straight at her heart.

Eric maneuvered himself between them again.

She clutched the bow in both hands.

"I've been watching you," Eric said. "For a long time."

Vincenzo gave a bored sigh. "And?"

"And now I'm going to arrest you."

The old man's condescending laugh grated on

Elise's ears. "Not likely. Only one person leaves this room alive. I'm betting it's me."

Eric inched closer to Vincenzo. The crime boss appeared not to notice.

"You're awfully serious. I sense more is going on here than some cliched FBI versus mob standoff." Vincenzo flicked his weapon toward Elise. "Is it her?"

She tightened her grasp on the bow.

Eric's response came from his throat, low and guttural. "You shoot her, I kill you."

"Ah. So, she does mean something to you." A smile crossed the gangster's lips. "But I don't think that's all of it. Not the way you're gripping that gun."

Eric set his jaw and leaned forward. His shoulders tensed. "My father was Arthur Erickson."

"Doesn't ring a bell."

"Twenty-three years ago, at the Pump Room in Queens. You might remember the bloodbath you left."

Vincenzo's brows lifted. "The bar owned by my enemy." He spat on the floor and gestured the gun toward Elise. "Her grandfather. Bastardo. If your father was at that bar, he deserved what he got."

Elise's heart pounded so hard she thought it might explode.

Eric shook his head and crept forward another inch.

She wanted to tell him to stop. If she could distract Vincenzo, she might get one more swing of the bow and knock his gun away. She took a step to the side.

"Elise." The firmness of Eric's voice froze her in place. "Stay where you are."

She stilled. His gaze never left the intruder, yet he knew her every move.

"My dad was doing his job."

The old man snorted. "Anyone working for Papi"—he spit the name—"deserved what he got."

"He didn't work for Kozlov." Eric's voice rose, the tightness in his body impossible to ignore. "He was a police officer responding to a call."

"Oh. Him." Vincenzo shrugged again. "It's been so long, I hardly remember. Wrong place, wrong time."

Eric's face twisted in fury. "Is that all you have to say?"

Vincenzo sighted his gun. *No.* She couldn't let him shoot Eric. Adjusting her grip, Elise jumped forward and swung, slamming the bow onto the mobster's forearms. At the same time, Eric's hand shot out and shoved hard against her.

Crack!

A thunderous boom reverberated against the walls. Ears ringing, she crashed to the floor. The smell of gunpowder hung in the air.

Scuffling sounds and then the thud of something slamming against the wall. She opened her eyes. Vincenzo sat hunched against the sliding glass door, face contorted in pain. His hand grasped his shoulder—the side she hadn't hit with the arrow. Blood seeped between his fingers. Eric's foot pressed into the old man's hand. Vincenzo's gun lay a few feet away.

Sirens wailed, growing louder by the second.

"Why did you do that?" Eric's voice was hard.

"I…I thought he was going to shoot," she stammered.

His jaw pulsed. "I had it under control."

Vincenzo's eyes rolled back. He slumped over. Eric kept his gun on the unconscious man. Then his gaze met hers, and his expression softened.

The house rumbled as if a herd of elephants arrived on her porch. "Police!"

Eric yanked his badge from his pocket and held it in the air. "Special Agent Erickson, FBI. Subject is down."

Heavy footsteps shook the floorboards. Officers in helmets and Kevlar stormed into the tiny space. The noise and the chaos faded into the background. There was only one person in this room she gave a damn about, and she couldn't stay away from him for another second.

With two quick strides, she jumped into Eric's arms, laced her hands around his neck and took his mouth in a hard, desperate kiss. She pulled back and peered into his eyes. For a moment, they inhaled and exhaled together, breathing the same air.

"I was so worried I'd lost you." His voice cracked. He cupped her cheek. "I can't do this without you."

Her heart settled into a slow rhythm, pumping heat through her body. "You don't have to."

Chapter Thirty-One

Eric slid burgers onto the open buns on Grant's plate.

The case agent took a swig of beer and slapped him on the back. "I thought for sure you were out of a job. Kinda surprised you're not, all things considered."

Elise's grill sizzled as Eric eased four more patties onto its hot surface. They'd already discussed Eric's omissions about his past. Grant likely wouldn't forget what he'd done but seemed willing to forgive. Eric was grateful, but just couldn't find it in him to regret the choices he'd made. Those choices led him to Elise. He rubbed the back of his neck. "I should have told you."

Grant's gaze swept over the inlet, stopping at the entrance to the channel. "I'm glad you're still part of the team."

"Me too." He meant it. After he learned he'd be allowed to stay with the Bureau, he assumed it meant a transfer to another department. Never did he think he'd get to stay with organized crime. Of course, Vincenzo Alario had eluded law enforcement for nearly thirty years, and being the agent who apprehended him came with a certain notoriety, both within the Bureau and the press. Eric's undercover days were over, and that was fine with him.

The theme song from a popular police show sang from Grant's pocket. He pulled out his phone, looked at the screen. "I need to get this."

Grant stepped away. Eric watched as Elise and her brothers played an insane game that involved the high-speed tossing and slapping of cards while shouting and calling each other names. It looked fun. And exhausting.

Jack sat to her right. Since learning he'd been the reason Elise went to meet Vincenzo, he'd been her shadow, never wanting to leave her side. Turned out he'd not gone to take down the shutters because he'd been pulled into a last-minute lesson with one of his regulars.

Breathless, Elise leaned back in her chair and flashed a grin that filled Eric with an overwhelming sense of gratitude. He had to be the luckiest man alive. He tipped his beer and winked.

A week had passed since Vincenzo had accosted Elise in her home, but it felt like a year. He couldn't believe the speed with which his life had changed. He flipped the burgers and closed the grill lid. Grant returned, looking unhurried and relaxed. Eric raised an eyebrow.

"The Alario guy shot at the farm in Nebraska wants to make a deal." Grant leaned against the porch railing and let out a deep, satisfied sigh. "Now that Vincenzo is in custody, his subordinates can't seem to roll over on one another fast enough."

Eric clapped him on the back. Good news. That meant more charges. More arrests. The Alario organization was toppling one goon at a time.

"Rocco?" Eric lifted the grill hood and poked at the charred discs. He'd overcooked these, but it didn't matter. Thinking of the younger Alario still at large had robbed him of his appetite.

Grant shook his head. "No one knows. There are

indications he's in contact with associates, but his whereabouts are still unknown."

So, it's not over. Eric pried the burgers from the grill and transferred them to a plate.

"We'll find him." Grant stuffed the last of his burger in his mouth and set his plate on the grill's shelf.

Eric nodded, his gaze wandering to Elise as it always did when she was near. Happy and carefree, she wore a huge smile. The sunlight in her hair illuminated reddish highlights. She was so beautiful. Every time he looked at her, he was struck by wonder. This woman loved him.

Grant cleared his throat. "I should be going."

"Spare a minute? Elise will want to say goodbye." Eric crossed the deck to tell her Grant needed to leave. She popped up. Her brothers did as well.

The siblings approached to say their goodbyes. Elise gave Grant a hug. Despite having just met the man, she'd taken to him immediately.

"Are you headed back to the Northeast?" Jack asked.

Grant shook his head. "I'm staying in Marathon tonight and then I'm heading down to Key West. I've never been there. I hear there's a festival of some sort."

"Fantasy Fest." Elise grinned. "It's like Mardi Gras and Halloween rolled into one."

The conversation moved from the back deck to the front door. Everyone waved as Grant backed out of the driveway.

Arms crossed, Elise leaned against the doorframe and smiled. She'd not wanted to stay in the house that first night. Not after the tangle with Vincenzo, but once the blood was scrubbed clean and the agents gone, they'd been here every night since.

Nate finished his beer and tossed it in the recycling bin. "We should get going too."

Jack wrinkled his nose. "The sun's still out."

Nate pushed his brother into the family room. "Get your stuff. Let's go."

The brothers stopped to give Elise a hug and shake Eric's hand, then got into their vehicles—a pickup for Nate and a little sports car for Jack.

Draping his arm over Elise's shoulder, Eric walked her to the back deck to clean up before the sun began its descent. Sunset had become his favorite part of the evening. Scratch that. Second favorite. Nothing could compare to the pleasure of holding Elise, kissing her, and falling asleep with her in his arms.

And to think, he'd almost lost her.

Seeing Vincenzo locked up had brought a measure of closure, but it hadn't made him whole. Elise did that.

****

Later, they sat in silence watching the sun's nightly performance. It didn't disappoint. With bold, brilliant strokes, the glowing orb painted shiny, metallic hues as it began its descent to the horizon. The moist air tasted of salt and the slight lapping of the waves lulled Eric into a contemplative mood. Inside, a serene, hopeful warmth filled him. He'd seen countless sunsets, but before Elise, he'd never taken the time to appreciate them. With her, it meant something, the symbolic ending of one chapter and the beginning of another.

He laughed to himself. Clearly, love had made him sappy.

She squeezed his hand. He didn't need to see her face to know she shared his relaxed state of mind.

No longer would he dwell on the past. The time had come to put the bitterness he'd carried since his father's death behind him. Nothing could bring back the lost years, but at least he'd seen justice served.

He rubbed his thumb across the back of Elise's hand and hoped one day she would accept that sometimes good people made bad decisions. Coming to terms with her father's misdeeds was a constant struggle, but she tried to remember the man she knew him to be.

Forgiving her mother would be a bigger task. One she'd said she wasn't quite ready to tackle.

Somehow, they'd both faced down demons and come out ahead.

But he and Elise couldn't let their guard down. Rocco Alario was still out there. As long as he was alive, he'd want revenge. Both of them were lucky to have escaped Vincenzo, but luck could be fickle. No telling which of the Hughes siblings might be in the mobster's crosshairs next.

Eric took a swig of his beer. "The Bureau approved my time off."

"That's great."

"I thought I might like to see what this 'island time' is all about."

She laughed. "I don't think you're cut out for it."

He'd always been too regimented to fully embrace a lifestyle that treated the hands on the clock as mere suggestions. "Doesn't mean I can't try." A lightness filled his chest. "For two weeks, my schedule is packed with nothing to do."

She chuckled and took a sip of beer. "You have no idea how to relax. The hurricane shutters are down, the rotted deck boards replaced, and I even have a new garbage disposal."

He pointed his thumb at his chest. "It's nothing but shorts, T-shirts, and sandals for this guy."

"Sandals? You know, there's a saying in the Keys, 'If you're not barefoot, you're overdressed.'"

"Is that so?" He stood, took her hand, and tugged her to her feet. "Sounds like if I really want the island experience, we need to get rid of some of this clothing."

Her eyes lit with a mischievous twinkle. He grasped the waistband of her shorts and dragged her against him with a possessive tug. With a low growl, he wrapped his arms around her, the tropical night air no comparison to the warmth of her body.

God, he loved this woman.

"Are you going to kiss me or just stare?"

He raised an eyebrow and twitched up one side of his mouth.

"Oh, good grief." She grasped his face and pulled his mouth to hers.

Something near his heart shifted. He needed her like he needed air. "I love you."

"I know. I love you. too."

In one smooth motion, he lifted her off the ground. She wrapped her legs around his waist, and he carried her to the bedroom.

Elise Hughes owned his body and his heart. There was no going back. And he didn't want to. Turned out the FBI didn't have anything on real life. Loving Elise was far more exciting.

A word about the author…

Evie Jacobs loves words. As a child, she read constantly. And when she wasn't reading, she was writing. Not much has changed. By day she works in a library surrounded by books, and by night she writes steamy action/adventure romance.

https://www.eviejacobsauthor.com/

Acknowledgments

I think a lot of new writers expect to sit down, spit out a story, and move on to the next. To my knowledge, this is never the case, and it certainly wasn't for me. There is so much more that goes into writing a novel, and so many people who contribute along the way. I have many people to thank, and if I've missed anyone, I apologize.

First and foremost, Dan. You have been nothing but supportive, even when you're tired of talking about writing. You are smart and funny and your encouragement keeps me going.

Along the same lines, Sean and Rebecca, you have been endlessly patient as I've prattled on about this story or that while picking your brains for ideas and insights. An additional thank you to Sean for being one of my first readers, as well as an early and enthusiastic cheerleader.

Alice, you probably don't remember this, but that hike we did at Brainard changed everything. We talked about how much we enjoyed writing, and it was that conversation that prompted me to pull out an old manuscript and get back to work.

I am so very fortunate to have a wonderful online writing community filled with many talented writers whom I am lucky enough to call friends. C.S. Smith, Nancy Sartor and Mia Kay, my Killer Writers. Your feedback on my work has been invaluable. My RAMP Mentor, Christina Hovland, was one of the first to see the potential in this manuscript. C.P. Rider, I appreciate your weekly check-ins and sprints. To the RAMP kissing books group: Kate Happ, Lille Moore, Caragh Leon, Maggie Eliot, and Maureen Ewing. I couldn't ask for a more supportive group of writers. You always make me feel like maybe I'm better than I think I am. To everyone who read a draft of this story and offered feedback, I appreciate you.

Thank you to The Romance Writers of the Rockies. I've learned so much from all of you. The retreats are a godsend.

Finally, thank you to my editor Kaycee John for believing in this story and The Wild Rose Press for publishing it.

Thank you for purchasing
this publication of The Wild Rose Press, Inc.

For questions or more information
contact us at
info@thewildrosepress.com.

The Wild Rose Press, Inc.
www.thewildrosepress.com

Milton Keynes UK
Ingram Content Group UK Ltd.
UKHW021927010924
447661UK00011B/510

9 781509 256990